IN THIS BOOK LIES THE ANSWER TO ONE OF
THE GREATEST MYSTERIES OF ALL TIME:

IS TIME TRAVEL POSSIBLE?
(Obviously. See title.)

Praise for
The Book That Proves Time Travel Happens

"This is such **a terrifically fun, mind-bending book,**
I want to go back in time so I can start reading it again!"
—Chris Grabenstein, author of *Escape from Mr. Lemoncello's
Library* and coauthor of the I Funny and Treasure Hunters series

"**Zany, clever, endlessly inventive,**
and genuinely one of a kind."
—Trenton Lee Stewart, author of *The Mysterious Benedict Society*

★ "Any reader who loves an adventure or time travel will
enjoy this book....The characters are **well-crafted** and
charming....Clark, a **masterful** storyteller, manages to write
about these thoughtful topics and yet moves the plot along at
a **page-turning** pace. School librarians and teachers will
definitely want to add this to their collections."
—*School Library Connection*, starred review

"Where **time travel, historical fiction and nonfiction,
ancient Chinese design and Morse code collide**—keep up,
or risk being left in the past...or the future....
[This book] will **extend readers' knowledge** of history
and expand their concept of '**diversity.**'"
—*Kirkus Reviews*

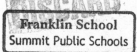

The Book That Proves Time Travel Happens

Henry Clark

illustrated by Terry Fan and Eric Fan

Little, Brown and Company

New York Boston

Little, Brown and Company

Hachette Book Group
1290 Avenue of the Americas, New York, NY 10104
Visit us at lb-kids.com

Little, Brown and Company is a division of Hachette Book Group, Inc.
The Little, Brown name and logo are trademarks of Hachette Book Group, Inc.

First Paperback Edition: April 2016
First published in hardcover in April 2015 by Little, Brown and Company

The Library of Congress has cataloged the hardcover edition as follows:

Clark, Henry, 1952–
  The book that proves time travel happens : a novel / by Henry Clark ; interior illustrations by Terry Fan and Eric Fan — First edition.
    pages cm
  Summary: Twelve-year-olds Ambrose, Tom, and Frankie are transported to the boys' hometown of Freedom Falls, Ohio, in 1852 when Frankie blows her Romani family's magical trombone, and to return home they will have to use both Morse code and the ancient form of divination known as the I-Ching.
  ISBN 978-0-316-40617-8 (hardcover) — ISBN 978-0-316-40615-4 (ebook) — ISBN 978-0-316-40614-7 (library edition ebook) [1. Time travel—Fiction. 2. Ciphers—Fiction. 3. Divination—Fiction. 4. African Americans—Fiction. 5. Chinese Americans—Fiction. 6. Romanies—Fiction. 7. Ohio—History—19th century—Fiction. 8. Humorous stories.] I. Fan, Terry, illustrator. II. Fan, Eric, illustrator. III. Title.
  PZ7.C5458Boo 2015
  [Fic]—dc23

                                                                                   2014015130

Paperback ISBN 978-0-316-40616-1

10 9 8 7 6 5 4 3 2 1

RRD-C

Printed in the United States of America

Dedicated to Samuel Finley Breese Morse

—

••••

•—

—•

—•—

•••

•••

•—

——!

A •—	**H** ••••	**O** ———	**V** •••—
B —•••	**I** ••	**P** •——•	**W** •——
C —•—•	**J** •———	**Q** ——•—	**X** —••—
D —••	**K** —•—	**R** •—•	**Y** —•——
E •	**L** •—••	**S** •••	**Z** ——••
F ••—•	**M** ——	**T** —	
G ——•	**N** —•	**U** ••—	

The ancient Chinese designs in this book—the "hexagrams" of the *I-Ching*—are real and have existed for over three thousand years.

Contents

CHAPTER 1
The E=Mc Squad

I lost my best friend, Tom Xui, twice. The first time, I simply wasn't paying attention. Everything had been going wrong that afternoon.

First, my locker wouldn't lock. Then the crossing guard turned out to be Cautious Carl, who doesn't let you cross if there are leaves blowing down the street. And then Tom vanished. It was like a conspiracy to keep me from getting to the carnival.

Tom had been running next to me only moments before. I looked down—remembering that he'd once, during the summer, fallen into an open road-repair ditch—and then I looked back. There was Tom, hiding behind a mailbox.

"What?" I asked, not getting it.

"My mom!" he whispered fiercely, pointing at the street.

We were on Hartnell Road, which starts at the Freedom Falls fire station, runs the length of the town, and ends down near the river at the fairgrounds. A blue Ford Focus was passing us, and although the woman driving it had black hair and Tom's mother's determined look, she wasn't Chinese.

"Relax," I said. "It's not her."

Tom eased out from behind the mailbox and tracked the Focus until it turned at Mordred's clothing store and disappeared down Troughton Avenue. Tom's mother thought he was at an after-school meeting of the E=Mc Squad, the school science club. She never would have given him permission to go to the carnival.

I grabbed him by the sleeve and pulled him along.

"We really should get our story straight," he said. "If she asks, what was today's meeting of the squad about?"

We raced past the new Burger King, and then past the old hot dog stand that had recently changed its name to Wienie President.

"Pattern recognition," I said, impressed with my own

quick thinking. We had talked about pattern recognition in science class that morning. Our teacher said it led to discoveries like DNA, computer language, and planets beyond the solar system. He also said there was such a thing as false pattern recognition, which led to people seeing the man in the moon and clouds in the shape of Mickey Mouse. "And the other thing," I added, "where people see the face of Elvis on a piece of toast—"

"Apophenia!" cried Tom, remembering the weird word for it, because that's the way he is. "Perfect! My mom won't know what that is, and it sounds very scientific!" He turned to face me and slapped the pattern on the front of his sweatshirt. "You'd be surprised how many kids asked me today why I have a huge computer bar code on my shirt! That shows you apophenia happens all the time!"

Tom's shirt had a series of lines on the front. They looked like this:

I had no idea that those lines were about to change our lives. Like the other kids, I had just assumed they formed a giant computer bar code. Or maybe an *H*, for Harvard, the college Tom's mother wanted him to go to.

I steered Tom into the street, crossing diagonally to save steps.

"BRO!" he shouted, pulling me back just as a delivery truck sped by inches away from me.

"HEY!" I shouted at the driver, even though I knew it wasn't his fault. I looked both ways and resumed my diagonal. Tom kept pace, but he wasn't happy.

"You should be more like Cautious Carl," he said.

"What?" I said. "And wear a belt *and* suspenders? My dad is picking us up at five. That gives us ninety minutes. What if there are people ahead of us?"

"Nobody's going where we're going. They'll all be heading for the rides or the games."

"The kids will. It's the grown-ups I'm worried about."

Camlo's Traveling Wonder Show had opened on the Freedom Falls fairgrounds the day before, on Tuesday, and would be there through Sunday. It came every year in mid-October, and the kids from Ambrose Bierce Middle School always flocked there the minute last period ended. I had gotten one of the kids who had been there on opening day to draw me a map, so I knew exactly where Tom and I had to go once we got in.

It was the first year my parents were letting me go on my own. They said I was showing more responsibility—I took out the trash a couple of times without being asked, and I found a new way of jamming stuff under my bed so my room looked clean—and it didn't hurt that my dad worked at the school, so I could touch base with him before I left and he could pick me up at the fairgrounds once he finished his after-school stuff.

We sprinted past Gaiman's Funeral Home and cut behind the sign that, from the opposite direction, declared:

Welcome to Freedom Falls, Ohio
Population 16,429
A Pleasant Place to Live

I don't know how many people actually live in our town, but I agree it's pleasant enough. I liked the way the sunlight streamed through the buckshot holes scattered all over the sign.

Admission to the carnival is five dollars, but once you

pay, you can go back as often as you want. We found the ticket booth with the shortest line, paid, and got our hands stamped. Tom pulled his sleeve up and got his stamp halfway to his elbow. If his mother saw the bright blue star, she'd know where he'd been, and she'd tack on at least another hour of study to the four hours he was expected to do each day.

We headed down the midway. At a funnel-cake booth we made a right, then a left at a ride that turned you upside down (and, according to the kid who drew me the map, shook money out of your pockets), then, finally, out of breath, we arrived in Fortune's Way.

It was a narrow alley lined with the tents of palm readers and psychics. Tom and I were going to get our fortunes told. He wanted to know if his mother was ever going to undo the parental lock she had recently used to block every channel on their TV.

I had a much more urgent question to ask.

In all, Fortune's Way was home to seven tents and seven different ways of seeing the future. The dullest was one where somebody looked at tea leaves in a cup. The weirdest was the one with the banner saying Mess-o-Mancy, where a guy smashed a jelly doughnut with a mallet, then predicted your future by studying the splatter. The cool thing about that one was, after it was over, you got to eat the doughnut.

"We don't truly believe this stuff, do we?" I asked Tom, hoping he'd give me an argument. I needed at least some of it to be real. Maybe not the doughnut guy. But somebody. I desperately wanted an answer to my question.

"No, we don't believe any of it," he replied, disappointing me. But then he shrugged. "Then again, maybe some people really are psychic. Did I ever tell you *I* almost always know when a phone is about to ring?"

"You have two sisters. The phone rings every thirty seconds."

"You're telling me! Hey, that must be Dr. Lao!"

He nodded at a tent at the end of the alley. It was covered with Chinese writing. A sign in English declared: WISDOM OF THE ANCIENTS. CONSULT DR. LAO. Another said: SEEK GUIDANCE FROM THE *I-CHING*. A thin Chinese man was standing next to the tent flap. Posters on either side of him were covered with horizontal lines similar to the ones on Tom's shirt.

"Okay," said Tom, standing straighter. "Here I go!"

He walked up to the doctor, who nodded when Tom bowed. Tom disappeared into the tent.

I looked around. The only tent other than Dr. Lao's that didn't have a line belonged to Madam Janus.

SEIZE ALL

NOSE ALL

said the sign above the entrance. A poster showed a single head with two faces looking in opposite directions.

When I got closer, I discovered the entrance flap tied shut and a small sign pinned to it: SESSIONS 6:00 TO 8:00.

It was 3:30. This stopped me for maybe twenty seconds. I couldn't wait. I scooted under the flap.

I guess I expected Madam Janus to be living in the tent, and that I'd find her sitting on her sofa. But the tent, as far as I could see, was empty.

It was big, about the size of my bedroom, only without any underwear on the floor. A rug stretched from the entrance all the way to the back, with a small table and two chairs in the middle. In the center of the table, on a hokey coiled-dragon pedestal, sat a crystal ball.

"Hello?" I called. Then louder, when nobody answered: "Anybody?"

Fortune-teller things filled glass cases along the walls of

the tent. Bottles of potions, dream catchers, smaller crystal balls—all of them with price tags.

The ball on the table winked at me, catching my reflection as I moved. I slid into one of the chairs, leaned forward, and gazed into the sphere.

I had thought a crystal ball would be crystal clear. It wasn't. It was full of murky blotches and tiny bubbles and fissures. It looked like a giant round ice cube. My eyes followed one of the fissures to a cloud in the ball's center, where misty shadows seemed to move.

"I assume you don't like jelly doughnuts." At the sound of the brittle voice behind me, I jumped up, knocking into the table and causing the ball to rock. I grabbed it with both hands to steady it.

"Or are you allergic to tea leaves?" the voice continued. "Are you afraid of getting a paper cut from a tarot card? There must be some reason you came in here, rather than to one of the open tents!"

A girl about my height stepped out from between two display cases. She had long black hair and olive skin almost as dark as mine. Dressed in blue jeans and a white shirt with peacocks on it, she clutched a spray bottle of Windex.

"I'm looking for Madam Janus," I said, trying not to sound guilty.

"I'm her daughter, Shofranka," said the girl, taking a step toward me.

"Show—?"

"—franka. Most people drop the 'Sho' and the 'uh' and call me—"

"Fran?"

"Frank. I also answer to Frankie."

"I'm Ambrose."

"Didn't you see the sign?"

"It said 'sessions six to eight.'" When she just stared, I added, "It didn't say 'do not enter.' There was another sign that said 'sees all, knows all.' I need somebody like that."

"'Seize All, Nose All' is my family's motto," she said, folding her arms across her chest, like she was daring me to argue. "In the original language of my people, it means more like, 'Grab the Day; Check Out Everything.' Or maybe, 'Be Nosy.' I try to live by it, but every time I do, I get grounded. Why do you want to see my mother?"

"That's . . . personal." I didn't see any reason to trust this girl with my family problems.

She pulled a notebook from a shelf and flipped it open.

"I make her appointments," she said, turning to a page near the back. "I can probably get you a spot on October fifteenth...of next year. She's pretty much booked up otherwise."

She looked at me expectantly. I knew what she wanted, and I decided, reluctantly, to give it to her.

"I want to know if my parents are going to stay together," I said.

Her defiant expression softened a little.

"Well," she said. "At least, that's something *I* never have to worry about."

"Oh," I said, annoyed. "Your parents are pretty solid, huh?"

"I've never seen them argue." She gave me a hard squint, and then her hand shot out, grabbed my chin, and twisted my head toward the light.

"What instrument do you play?" she asked.

"Trumpet. How can you tell?"

"The center of your upper lip. A mouthpiece always makes a callus. You must practice a lot."

"I like playing."

It was one of the things I enjoyed most.

"Ambrose what?"

"Brody."

"Ambrose Brody? Do they ever call you Bro Bro?"

"Only if they stutter."

Tom Xui had once introduced me to one of his friends as "my bro, Bro Bro," but I'd asked him never to do that again.

"What about Rose?" Frankie asked. "Does anybody ever call you Rose?"

"Never!"

"You've made a mess of my mother's crystal, *Rose*. And I just finished polishing it!"

She picked up the ball in one hand, and three of her fingers disappeared into the bottom.

"Crystal balls have finger holes?" I asked.

"This one does. My mother bowls. See the mess you made?"

She tilted the crystal closer to my face. The murky cloud in its center parted and I jumped back.

"Who was that?" I demanded.

Frankie glanced around the tent. "Where?"

"In the ball. I saw a face."

"In the ball?" She sounded like she didn't believe me. "Describe it."

"It was a guy with messy black hair and an eye patch. Like a pirate."

Frankie clutched the crystal to her chest, throwing an arm

around it protectively, as if my seeing something in it might damage it. She eyed me suspiciously.

"Do you often see strange things in shiny surfaces?" she asked.

"Sometimes," I admitted. "I once saw my uncle Leon in the bathroom mirror."

"Was that, by any chance, on the day he died?"

"It was the day he fell asleep in the bathtub."

She plunked the ball back on its dragon, sprayed it vigorously with Windex, then aimed the spray nozzle at me. I put my hands up.

"There are seven fortune-telling tents here," she told me, "all within twenty feet of one another. Why did you choose this one?"

"It was the only one without a line."

"That's all? You didn't feel yourself drawn here by some strange unearthly power?"

"Not that I noticed. I just wanted to ask somebody about my parents. My dad, mainly."

"What about him?"

"He showed up at dinner two nights ago wearing the uniform of a World War One soldier."

"What? Something he found in the attic?"

"No, something he bought. A sergeant's uniform, with a helmet. At least he took off the gas mask when he sat down to eat. My mother said it was the last straw and told him she was going to visit my aunt Maya. Usually when that happens, she's only away overnight. This time it's been two days." She'd called me each morning to check on me, but she wouldn't answer when I asked her when she'd be back. "I thought maybe a fortune-teller could tell me what was going to happen. I don't want this to be serious."

"I don't quite see what your mother's so upset about."

"She doesn't like my father dressing up. At least, not at dinner. Last week, he was a Native American chief, with a full headdress. There were feathers in our soup."

"He dresses in clothes from other time periods."

"Yes." I was surprised by how quickly she understood. "And he's been doing it at work and out in public for way too long now, and . . . it can be very embarrassing. My mom and I have both told him it's really not a good idea."

Frankie nodded, as if nothing I said surprised her. She stared into space for a moment, then snapped her attention back to me.

"What are you doing tonight?" she asked.

"Homework?"

"No, I'm sure that can wait. I want you to meet me at the main gate when the carnival closes at nine."

"What?"

"There's a Camlo family treasure hidden somewhere in your town, and I need somebody who knows his way around to help me find it. I think you may be the one. In fact, from what you've just told me, I'm positive."

"What kind of treasure?"

"I'm a Camlo," she said, ignoring me. "My father's the *Rom baro*; he owns the carnival—so the treasure's as much mine as it is anyone's. Someday I'll be its official Keeper."

"Frankie?" came a voice from behind the tent's rear wall. "Where are the Twizzlers?"

"My mother!" Frankie whispered, and pushed me toward the tent's front.

"Madam Janus?" I resisted her push. "Maybe she'll see me. Is she any good?"

"She's the best. Even if, sometimes, she can't find the Twizzlers. But I'm telling the truth—she's booked for today. If you help me with my quest, I can try to get you an appointment with her later in the week."

"Maybe if I just went back and said hello—"

"No! She's very self-conscious about her appearance. She'd probably want to change. You don't want to annoy her!"

Frankie forced me out the way I had come, and followed me into the dusty lane in front of the tent.

"Do you own a flashlight?" she asked, smoothing my shirt where she had grabbed it.

"A flashlight? Uh, yeah—"

"Bring it tonight. And wear dark clothing. Don't fail me! This is important!"

"SHOFRANKA!" came Madam Janus's voice from inside.

"Nine o'clock! Treasure!" Frankie reminded me, and dived back into the tent.

CHAPTER 2
An Ancient Roman English Teacher

I was dazed as I fell into step with passing carnival-goers. I couldn't believe I'd agreed to go on a treasure hunt with some strange girl after dark. How could I get away with it?

"There you are!" said Tom, grabbing me by the elbow. "Look what I got!"

He steered me between two tents and then out onto the midway, where there was more space and less chance of our getting trampled. He waved a book in my face.

"Dr. Lao gave it to me. He taught me how to read the *I-Ching*!" He pronounced it "ee-Ching." The book was a thin paperback with a picture on the cover very similar to the one on Tom's shirt. The picture looked like this:

Above this odd symbol it said *If You Have an I-Ching, Scratch!*, and below the symbol it said *A Modern Guide to an Ancient Form of Divination, by Richard K. Philips.*

"Uh, cool?" I said, not certain how he expected me to react. "He gave you this?"

"Well, after I paid him twenty bucks to have my fortune told. He had a stack of them."

"Did you find out if your mother is ever going to take the lock off your TV?"

"Yes! She will! But not until after I'm married. That's not important. I want to show you how this works."

He dug in his pocket and pulled out a quarter.

"We have to flip a coin a few times—"

"Listen!" I said, clutching his hand before he could toss. "Something really strange just happened to me in the crystal ball tent—"

"AMBROSE!"

A familiar voice interrupted me from the direction of a cotton candy booth. Sheila Gurwitz, a girl in most of my classes at school, broke away from two of her friends and came running over. She had a furry pink mustache from the cotton candy she was eating. "I'm so sorry about your dad!" she blurted.

I froze. "What about my dad?"

Her hand flew to her furry mouth, and her eyes went wide. "You don't know?" Her two friends came up on either side of her and looked at me sadly. "They let him go!" she announced, and her friends nodded like the bobblehead dolls on our math teacher's desk. "McNamara called him into his office at the end of the day and fired him! Everybody was talking about it on the way here! I'm so sorry! Your dad's a good teacher... except for that one... weird... thing...."

I shoved past her. Sheila's mom worked in the office, and I could only assume she was the reason everybody knew about what happened. Over my shoulder I said to Tom, "I gotta get home!"

"Right!" he agreed, snapping his book shut and keeping pace as I sprinted down the midway toward the entrance.

There was a commotion up ahead, and my heart sank as I recognized one of the voices.

I broke through the crowd and there was my father. He was surrounded by a ring of some of the tougher high school kids.

"Hey, Mr. Brody!" one of them jeered. "Nice skirt!"

"It's not a skirt," my father explained. "It's an apron." There was a burst of laughter from the high schoolers, but my father kept talking. "The technical term is *pteruges*. The dangling strips of leather are weighted at the bottom and hang down in front, over the tunic, to protect the groin during a sword fight."

They all laughed again when Dad said "groin." Part of me wanted to run to him, but another part of me was too embarrassed. I hovered at the edge of the crowd, unsure what to do.

My father was wearing his Roman legionnaire costume. He had a crested helmet on his head, light armor around his torso, and sandals on his feet. A red tunic under the armor and *pteruges* ended an inch or two above his bare knees.

"Nice legs," said a kid with ANTHRAX on his T-shirt.

"Thank you," said my father, who never notices sarcasm. "Now, if you'll excuse me, I have to find my son."

Anthrax stepped in front of him and placed his hand on my father's armored chest.

"Take your hand off my cuirass," said my father.

"Apron" and "groin" had gotten laughs from the high schoolers, but "cuirass" gave them hysterics. Anthrax yanked his hand back as though he had burned himself. "Your queer *what*?" he asked.

"Cuirass," my father enunciated more clearly. He tapped his chest with his fist, causing the metal to ring. "Let me pass."

Anthrax stood his ground. "You failed me four years ago, Mr. Brody. I had to take summer-school English because of you!"

"And I was right there through that hot summer teaching it to you again, Mr. Killbreath," my dad reminded him. "You finally passed it, with a D, as I recall."

"If everybody had known back then that you were a nut job, you wouldn't have been teaching!"

"Then somebody else would have flunked you and been forced to tutor you. My being a nut job wouldn't have made you any brighter, Leonard."

"It's about time they canned you! Look at you! I wouldn't want you teaching me! You shouldn't be around kids!"

I launched myself at Lenny Killbreath. I was going to knock him down and beat the anthrax out of him. But a man in black stepped out of the crowd and caught me by the shoulders, holding me at arm's length.

"Whoa there, young fry! No donnybrooks at my show, if you please!"

I looked up at him. He was wearing a black coat, a fancy green vest, and a tie like a huge floppy shoelace. He had messy black hair and an eye patch.

It was the guy I had seen in Madam Janus's crystal ball.

"My name's not Donny!" I said, and tried to get past him again.

"Manner of speaking," he said, gently pushing me back. "A donnybrook is a contretemps." As if that explained it.

He let go of me, took my father's hand, and shook it. "Orlando Tiresias Camlo," he said, "proprietor of Camlo's Traveling Wonder Show, at your service. And you"—Camlo twisted my father's hand sideways, to show the crowd the blue star on its back—"have had your hand stamped, so *you* paid to get in. This makes *you* an honored guest."

Camlo bowed, let go of my dad's hand, and turned, sweeping his gaze across Lenny Killbreath and his buddies.

"I notice others here have *not* had their hands stamped. This makes *you* fence-jumpers—and unwelcome!"

Lenny and his boys melted into the crowd.

" 'The earth hath bubbles, as the water has, and these are of them. Whither are they vanished?' " said Camlo, and I had no idea what he was talking about. Possibly he was calling Lenny a bubblehead. He certainly talked the way I imagined someone who owned a treasure might.

"*Macbeth*," said my father.

"Pleased to meet you, Mr. Macbeth." Camlo beamed. "It's quite a coincidence, you being named Macbeth. I just quoted from a play of the same name."

"I was identifying the play," explained my father.

"Why would you do that? Did you think I didn't know what I was quoting?"

"My name is Hannibal Brody," said my father, sounding the tiniest bit annoyed.

"Pleased to meet you, Mr. Brody!" Camlo looked my father up and down. "Are you, perhaps, in search of the rest of your marching band?"

"I am in search of my son," said my father, straightening and nodding in my direction.

"Who I presume is this feisty lad," Camlo decided. "So you have found him, and I see that he, too, paid to get in—honest families are the axle grease of commerce—meaning my work here is done. Enjoy your visit! The briefness of our encounter has made it all the sweeter!" He turned on his heel and bubbled away.

"They fired you!" I yelled at my dad. And on top of that, I couldn't believe he had shown up at the carnival after I had been there only half an hour. I hadn't expected to see him before five. His Roman legionnaire outfit made him look like the bad guy in a gladiator movie.

He winced and put a finger to his lips. I realized I had shouted. The crowd surrounding my father had pretty much dispersed when the high schoolers left, but a few people lingered, as if they thought my dad might suddenly start juggling.

"I was hoping to find you before you heard it from some-body else," my dad said, so quietly I had to get closer to hear him. "And I'm not exactly fired. It's more of a suspension."

"*Kids* get suspended!" I snapped. "Teachers don't!"

"Sometimes they do," said my father apologetically. "I'm not fully fired. Not yet. They've called a special session of the school board for tomorrow night to review the case. Mr.

Garlock will be teaching my classes until things get worked out."

"I *told* you!" I sputtered. "You didn't listen to me! You didn't listen to Mom!"

"This isn't really the place to discuss it. Maybe we should go home? You can always come back here later."

"Sure! Fine! Whatever!"

I turned and headed for the exit. I knew he was right behind me from the squeaky sound of his armor, but I was so mad, I couldn't look at him.

When we got to the car, I realized Tom was still with us. "You said you'd drop me off," he reminded me.

"Hop in," my dad said to both of us, and I think he was relieved to have Tom along. He slid into the driver's seat, I got in beside him, and Tom squirmed into the back. The car's sunroof was open, and the crest of my dad's helmet stuck out and rippled in the breeze.

"You don't have to do this!" I declared once we were on our way. "You could dress like a normal person!"

"I am a normal person," my father assured me. "I just happen to be a trans-temp."

"Mom says there's no such thing!"

"Trans-temporals are a small but growing minority," my

father assured me. "As of this morning, we even have our own newsletter." He reached between the seats and fished out a tablet, thumbed it to life, and handed it to me. The screen glowed with something called *Out of Time: A Journal for the Trans-Temporal Community*. The lead story was illustrated with a pattern showing how to make Napoleon's underwear.

I scrolled to the credits. It was just as I expected.

"You're the editor!"

"And currently the entire staff," my dad acknowledged. "But it has fourteen subscribers, and it's only been online for eight hours. Trans-temporals, or trans-temps," he said over his shoulder for Tom's benefit, not knowing I had already explained it to Tom way too many times, "are people who are not comfortable wearing the clothing of the twenty-first century and prefer to dress in the attire of other time periods. When they do this in public, they usually offer some lame excuse—'I'm on my way to a Renaissance fair!' or 'I'm a Civil War reenactor!' But then, sadly, when they *don't* explain themselves in some silly way such as this, they are frequently persecuted. This persecution must stop! I am striking a blow for freedom of expression by publicly dressing in the manner in which I am most comfortable!"

I was reading the *Out of Time*'s editorial, which welcomed

everybody to the first issue and went on to say, "Trans-temps will almost never come out of the closet, since they're too busy trying on the older stuff in the back."

"You could have stuck with the Mark Twain suit," I said. "That *has* to have been more comfortable than something that clanks." I punched my dad's shoulder. The armor made a noise like the Tin Woodman.

During the weeks my father had taught *The Adventures of Tom Sawyer*, he had worn the plain white suit Mark Twain wore in old photographs. His students had loved it, and the other teachers had said it was a good trick to hold the kids' attention. My father had offered extra credit to any of his students who came in dressed as one of the characters from the book, and a few of them had. One had gotten beaten up by bullies. He had been dressed as Becky Thatcher.

"I'm sure I'll wear Twain's suit again someday—white is great for summer—but I feel the need to experiment with other time periods."

"NO, YOU DON'T!"

"A copy of Shoeless Joe Jackson's 1915 White Sox uniform arrived in the mail just today. It's perfect, even though they forgot the shoes."

"This was okay when you were only doing it around the

house," I said bitterly. "You don't have to do it outside! You don't have to dress weird at school! It's my school, too, you know!"

"Most of the kids like it," said Tom from the backseat. I whirled and glared at him. "We all look forward to seeing how you'll dress next. I thought the fur trapper was cool."

"I do believe most of the students are good with it," agreed my father. "You're still at an age when you're open to new things. Most of you." He gave me a look. "It's the adults who are having trouble with it."

"Like Mom?" I snapped.

My dad's hands tightened on the steering wheel. "Your mother," he said, "will come around eventually. I sent her roses this morning. She responds well to roses."

"She's not happy," I said.

"She needs time."

"The *time* she needs is the present, and she needs you to stay in it! Or at least dress for it!" I pretended to be interested in a passing lamppost. I would get too upset if we kept talking about my mom. And it was obviously not the time to ask if I could go out at nine to meet somebody from the carnival.

"Are you going to this emergency meeting of the school board tomorrow?" I asked.

"Of course."

"And what are you planning to wear?"

"I was thinking samurai. Only not with the sword. That might be seen as threatening."

"You think a samurai sword might be seen as threatening? Really?" My voice cracked. "OKAY! OKAY! I'M GETTING OUT *HERE*!" I fumbled with my seat belt as we rolled up in front of Tom's house. I had to get out; otherwise, I knew I'd start hitting my dad.

I popped the door and jumped. "I'm sleeping over," I informed my father. "Tom says it's fine. Right? It's fine?" I shot the question at my friend as he struggled out of the backseat.

He froze, saw my expression, then nodded emphatically. "Yeah, yeah, it's fine—it was my idea. We study well together. My mom's okay with it."

I told my dad, "If you wear a samurai suit to the board meeting tomorrow, I swear I'll move in with Tom permanently!"

"Whoa!" yelped Tom, and I jabbed him with my elbow. "I mean, *woe*! Woe to you, Mr. Brody, if you do the samurai thing! That doesn't sound like a good idea to me!"

"I'd like to talk to you more about this, Ambrose, once you calm down," my father said. "Do you have your cell?"

I shifted my book bag on my back so he could see it. "Yes."

"Then call me when you're ready to talk."

"No!" I said furiously. "You call *me* when you've made up your mind to wear a jacket and tie to the board meeting. A *normal* jacket and tie! So you're dressed the same as the board members! That would help!"

I slammed the door and stalked away from the car. Tom chased after me.

As I stomped through the open gate at the side of his house, out of the corner of my eye I saw my father slowly pulling away. He kept looking in my direction.

I felt awful. When I got to the backyard, I threw myself into a lawn chair.

"Your father is just being who he is, Bro," Tom assured me.

"A lot of people hide who they are, if it helps them keep their job," I said. "My mom can get really mad, but you never see it when she's selling houses."

Two years earlier, my mother had sold the Xui family their house. Tom and I had hit it off immediately. I especially liked the way he substituted some of our longer vocabulary words for curse words—he once called our gym teacher a *figment* and the school bully a *pedestrian*, and if he was angry, he might exclaim *fiduciary!* or *paramecium!* and then get all red in the face because he had used profanity, which, according to Tom, included words like *cacophony* and *defibrillate* and *glabrous*.

"I can't believe he let them fire him instead of just wearing normal clothes," I muttered.

"It's certainly *crepuscular*," Tom agreed, trying out his latest curse. "But maybe you shouldn't think about it for a while. You said something strange happened to you in the crystal-ball tent?"

Tom's mother popped her head out the back door and bellowed, "Tom Xui! Why aren't you practicing piano? March yourself right in here this instant! Hello, Ambrose. DID YOU HEAR ME? THIS INSTANT!"

We both jumped up.

It would be a while before I told Tom anything about hidden treasure.

CHAPTER 3
If You Have an I-Ching—Scratch!

Tom practiced piano for an hour. I sat next to him on the piano bench and turned the pages of his sheet music. It looked a little more complicated than trumpet music. I was glad I played an instrument that couldn't hit two notes simultaneously.

"Of course Ambrose can stay over," Mrs. Xui agreed when Tom asked her. "He is always welcome here. You can help each other study for next week's math test. Ambrose is a good boy." She patted me on the head and veered off into the kitchen.

I like Mrs. Xui, but she says odd things sometimes. I

once heard her call me "Tom's nice African friend," which I thought was pretty funny. My mom is black, but she's from Canada, and she can speak French because that's the only way she could talk to her grandparents. My dad is Irish, and he says he's the palest man in Ohio, which anybody who's seen him in a toga would definitely agree with. *Irish* doesn't describe me, and neither does *African*, although I do look more like my mom than my dad.

Tom stopped playing Chopin's eleventh polonaise, held up a finger, and said, "Now!"

A moment later, a phone rang. Tom's twin sisters, Dorcas and Yvette, catapulted across the living room and dived into the sofa. Yvette emerged with a phone from somewhere deep in the cushions.

"What did I tell you?" Tom asked, tapping the side of his head. "Psychic!"

I sat next to Tom's great-grandfather at dinner, which was tacos and fajitas, in keeping with Mrs. Xui's vow to always eat American, and Tom spoke with him in Chinese.

"Is that Mandarin?" I asked when they had finished. I had recently learned that the Chinese language had a bunch of subdivisions, and Mandarin was the most common.

"No," said Tom. "It's this dialect that practically nobody

speaks anymore, from the province my Gee Gee Pa came from originally. My Mandarin is much better."

"Gee Gee Pa" was Tom's nickname for his great-grandfather. He and his sisters also had a nickname for their very strict mother—"Tiger Mom"—until Mrs. Xui sat them down and told them they must never, ever call her Tiger Mom, because tigers aren't native to North America. They could, however, call her "Puma Ma." That would be perfectly all right. So they called her Puma Ma, and Mrs. Xui seemed very happy with it.

Gee Gee Pa turned to me, smiled, and said, "We are the only Xuis in America."

They were, as far as we knew, the only Xuis anywhere. Most Chinese people spell the name *Xiu*, but an immigration official had messed up the spelling when Gee Gee Pa had first come to America, and no one had ever bothered to fix it. Whether you spelled it *Xiu* or *Xui*, it was pronounced "Shewy," to rhyme with "chewy."

"And as the oldest Xui at this table, I will tell you that you must always show respect to your ancestors," Gee Gee Pa said to Tom.

"That means he wants the last taco," Tom explained, passing the platter.

After dinner Tom and I made a great show of sitting at the dining room table and quizzing each other with math questions. Mrs. Xui hummed happily to herself in the kitchen. It wasn't until Tom was off what his mom called the "Study Clock," and we were both in his room together, that I was finally able to tell him I was meeting a girl when the carnival closed.

"*Protoplasmic!*" he exclaimed. "She works at the carny?"

"Her mother is Madam Janus, the fortune-teller." I told him everything, including how I'd seen Orlando Camlo in the crystal ball before I met him in person.

"So it's just as well I'm not sleeping at home tonight," I said. "This makes things easier. Which window do you normally sneak out of?"

I raised the window above Tom's desk. He had a reputation for slipping out of his house after hours, especially when his mother's Study Clock got to be too much for him. She constantly pushed math and science and music on him, ignoring the one subject he really liked, which was history. ("History?" I once heard her say. "There's no future in it!") And the things he liked to do to relax—video games, old movies, and graphic novels—she refused to have in the house. He came over to my place as often as he could, and we binged on all three.

"Not that one!" Tom said, stopping me as I fumbled with the window screen. "The one with the tree outside." He nodded at the room's other window. "Unless you want to land on your head! It's only eight o'clock. It takes twenty minutes to get to the fairgrounds. We have time to plan this out."

"We?" I asked.

"Of course. I have to go with you. This may be a trap. You need someone to watch your back! We should be dressed all in black."

He tossed me a black sweatshirt. I shrugged into it, checked myself in the mirror, and discovered I had put it on inside out.

"Leave it that way, Bro! Everybody knows that's good luck. And the inside's not as faded!"

He found a sweatshirt for himself, which I vetoed—it had a picture of my favorite hip-hop artist, Kan Sa$s, on the front, which was way too attention-grabbing—so he tossed it aside and dug out a plain dark navy one. Then he rummaged around and came up with a flashlight. "The trick is to convince my mom we've gone to bed, and she won't buy that any time before eight thirty. But I've got something that will help us plan our strategy. We'd be crazy not to try it before we left." He pulled out the book he had gotten at the carnival. "Have you ever heard of the *I-Ching*?" he asked.

"No," I admitted.

"It's a real thing. You can look it up. It was invented in China over three thousand years ago. A lot of people think it's a way of seeing the future. But Dr. Lao told me it's more like a compass that points you in the right direction, as long as you read it right. I'll show you how it works."

I was more interested in getting out the window and tracking down treasure, but Tom was so enthusiastic, I didn't want to bum him out. I did my best to pay attention.

He grabbed a notepad and a pencil stub from his desk and snatched a quarter from a jar of loose change, and we both sat with the book at the foot of his bed.

"Think of a question," he said.

"That's easy. 'What will happen if we meet Frankie Camlo at the carnival tonight?'"

"Good! We both concentrate on that, and one of us flips the quarter. It's your question, so you should flip."

I did and—

"Tails!" declared Tom. "That means we draw this."

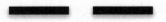

"A line with a break in the middle is called a *yin* line," he explained. "Any time you flip tails, you draw a *yin*. Toss again."

I tossed, and it was tails again.

"The second line is always drawn above the first. So now we have something that looks like this."

"We're making something like what's on your shirt," I said, seeing the connection. Tom nodded.

I flipped the coin again. This time it was heads.

"Heads means we draw a *yang* line!" he said excitedly, as if he had just discovered a gold nugget in his aquarium gravel. "They're unbroken lines. It goes on top of the first two. We're halfway there."

"We need a total of six lines?"

"We're making a *hexagram*. *Hex* means 'six.'"

"Like...a *hex*agon is a six-sided figure," I said, pleased

with myself. The meetings of the E=Mc Squad hadn't been a total waste.

I flipped the quarter three more times.

Tails, heads, tails.

Yin, yang, yin.

Tom drew them in the order I flipped them, one above the other over the first three, until we had this:

"Now what?" I asked.

"Now we look it up and find out the answer to our question." Tom opened the book to the back, where there was an index. "There are only sixty-four possible hexagrams," he said, running his finger down a series of the six-lined figures printed along the side of the page. "Each one has a name, along with some advice that goes with it. Here we go! This is hexagram thirty-nine. Page one twenty-four."

He flipped to the center of the book.

"The answer to our question, 'What will happen if we meet up with whatshername,' is—"

He blinked and his head shot back. He turned the book in my direction so I could see.

"—TROUBLE!"

I snatched the book from him. At the top of the page was a hexagram identical to the one we had drawn, except that the book's artist had owned a ruler. Beneath it were these words:

HEXAGRAM 39

TROUBLE.

OBSTRUCTIONS AND DIFFICULTIES.
A CHALLENGE TO BE OVERCOME.
WATCH YOUR BACK; YOU MAY HAVE
TO RETREAT IN THAT DIRECTION.
THAT WHICH DOES NOT KILL YOU
WILL PROBABLY TRY HARDER NEXT
TIME.

"Who wrote this stuff?" I asked.

"An unknown sage during the Zhou dynasty, three thousand years ago," said Tom, reading the information off the back of the book. "I think *sage* means 'wise person.' This 'modernized, reader-friendly' version is by Richard

K. Philips, who, it says, spent two weeks on vacation in Beijing in 2013."

"So he's an expert?"

"I guess."

"Do we take it seriously?"

Tom shrugged. "You think we should bring nunchuks?" he asked.

"You *have* nunchuks?"

"That pair I showed you."

"What? The ones you made when you were six?" He had made them from a couple of cardboard paper-towel tubes. They *did* make a cool *ponk!* noise when you hit something with them. "You really think we'll need them?"

"It says *Trouble!*" Tom tapped the hexagram. "Maybe she's going to kidnap you and take you away with the carnival. Or maybe the treasure is guarded by anacondas!"

"It's just a bunch of lines," I reminded him.

"Yeah," he agreed. "And what's cool about them is they're either broken or unbroken. The *I-Ching* is binary code, like computers use."

"Yeah?" I said, unimpressed. "It looks more like Morse code to me. You know, the dashes and dots?"

In social studies, we had learned about Samuel Morse and his telegraph. The teacher had shown us Morse code on the Smart Board and given us printouts with a coded message to solve for homework.

"What?" said Tom. "Oh. Yeah. A little. If you pretend each unbroken line is a *dash*, and each *half* of a broken line is a *dot*..."

He trailed off, scowling at the hexagram. I glanced at the clock. It was almost eight thirty. We would have to leave soon. Heading for something that might be *Trouble*, with a capital *T.* I opened the window with the tree on the outside and removed the screen. I was happy to see a hefty branch within a foot of the sill. I rattled the screen impatiently, to get Tom's attention.

"*Fiduciary!*" he sputtered.

"What?"

"The *Trouble* hexagram. Look at it!"

He shoved it under my nose. It hadn't changed since the last time I saw it.

"What about it?"

"What you said. Morse code. Morse would be read from the top, left to right, like written English. Let's say that top line is two dots."

"Okay. So?"

"A single dot is Morse code for the letter *E*."

"So two dots would be two *E*s," I said. "What word begins with two *E*s? *Eek*? *Eel*? As in, 'Eek! I stepped on an eel'?"

"Maybe only one letter is an *E*. The first letter. Then that's followed by a dot, a dash, and another dot. Dot-dash-dot is Morse for the letter *R*."

"Wait a minute. Are you trying to tell me you've *memorized* the Morse code?"

He looked sheepish.

"Well, yeah. A little. Puma Ma made me. She makes me memorize a lot of stuff. I'm hoping she never finds out about the periodic table of the elements. And I probably don't know Morse *perfectly*; I should cross-check, just to be sure."

He got up and rummaged in his schoolbag, pulling out the social studies homework with the complete Morse code on it. He flattened out the page next to his drawing of the thirty-ninth hexagram.

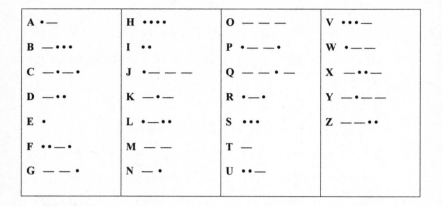

A •—	H ••••	O — — —	V •••—
B —•••	I ••	P •——•	W •——
C —•—•	J •———	Q ——•—	X —••—
D —••	K —•—	R •—•	Y —•——
E •	L •—••	S •••	Z ——••
F ••—•	M ——	T —	
G ——•	N —•	U ••—	

Next to the *Trouble* hexagram, he wrote:

$$• = E$$

$$• — • = R$$

"Right after the Morse for the letter *R*," he said, "there's half of a *yin* line and a full *yang*, which you could think of as a dot and a dash, Morse code for the letter *A*. Then there's two broken lines—two *yins*—which, I think it's obvious, should be read as three dots—making the letter *S*—and a final dot, which would be a final *E*."

He finished writing. I looked over his shoulder.

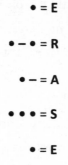

• = E

• — • = R

• — = A

• • • = S

• = E

"That's really weird," Tom said, shaking his head like he couldn't believe it. "The *I-Ching* hexagram for *Trouble* contains a hidden message in Morse code—the word *erase*! What do you do with trouble? You try to erase it! That is one *ubiquitous* coincidence!"

"You just told me this *I-Ching* thing is three thousand years old," I said. "Morse code was invented"—I searched my memory for the date we learned in social studies, and I was amazed when I found it—"in the 1830s. That's less than two hundred years ago. There can't be Morse code in the *I-Ching*; Morse hadn't been invented yet!"

"That's what's so weird about it. And you're the one who discovered it!"

"Me?"

"You're the one who said it looked like Morse." He flipped through the pages of *If You Have an I-Ching—Scratch!* and got a worried look on his face. "I wonder if any of the other hexagrams…"

"Lights out, boys!" Mrs. Xui called from the hall as she walked past. It was eight thirty. Tom had a ridiculously early bedtime, but then, the whole family got up at five every morning.

Tom tucked the Morse code page and his pencil into the *I-Ching* book, folded the thin book in half, and jammed it in his back pocket. He stepped into the hall and said his good-nights, and five minutes later we were on our way to the fairgrounds.

• • •

By ten to nine we were at the entrance to Camlo's Traveling Wonder Show. The carnival was emptying out, but everything, including the parking area, was still brightly lit. We found a bale of straw where we had a good view of the main gate and sat down to wait.

"You really think Frankie Camlo can't be trusted?" I asked Tom.

He shrugged. "Most people looking for treasure are pirates."

"But she said it was some sort of *family* treasure."

"So? Pirates can have families."

A bunch of noisy older kids clustered around a battered green convertible noticed us, and one of them started walking over. As he got closer, I realized it was Lenny Killbreath, the kid who had been messing with my dad.

I remembered the *I-Ching*'s prediction of trouble.

"Well," I said quietly to myself, "that didn't take long."

CHAPTER 4
The Camlo Shagbolt

Y ou're Crazy Brody's kid, aren't you?"

Lenny towered over me, even though I had jumped to my feet at his approach.

"*You are,*" he sneered, answering his own question. "I seen you around. Why aren't you dressed like a Pilgrim?"

"Why should I be dressed like a Pilgrim?" I asked. "Just because you're a turkey?"

Lenny grabbed me by the collar and hauled me into the air, until we were eye to eye. Tom jumped up, shouting "You let him go, you stupid *cacophony!*" Then he pulled something from his pocket and whacked Lenny across the leg with it.

There was a hollow *ponk!* and Tom's cardboard nunchuks promptly fell apart. Lenny ignored him.

"You tell that crazy father of yours," Lenny hissed, lowering me to my feet without letting go of my collar, "this town doesn't need any loony weirdos living here! Tell him he should move his sorry jerk family someplace else!"

He twisted my collar so tightly I couldn't breathe.

"Lenny! C'mon!" shouted one of his cronies from across the lot. "Beer's gettin' warm!"

He turned me loose.

"You just deliver that message to your dad for me!"

He started to walk away, and I lunged after him. Tom grabbed me around the waist and pulled me back.

"He's twice your size!" he whispered. "We need better nunchuks!"

Lenny joined his buddies and they piled into the car. One of them must have won a large pink poodle and had to hold it overhead before they could all fit. The car backed up, the tires squealed, and they sped away.

"*Bilious!*" Tom cursed, and sat back down. He tugged on my pant leg until I joined him. "You're not going to let that *astrolabe* get to you, are you? We have better things to think about."

I nodded, but I was still seething inside. Tom started

flipping his quarter and drawing *I-Ching* lines in the dirt with a stick.

I pulled my cell out of my pocket and stared at it. I wanted to call my father and apologize for yelling at him. He didn't deserve that from his own son, especially when there were strangers saying such stupid things about him. But then I started thinking about how he had brought it on himself, and I started getting angry all over again.

He had begun dressing up around the house a few years ago; one night he came to the dinner table wearing cowboy clothes. They were the sort of clothes cowboys were still wearing, so my mother and I just assumed he was about to tell us we were going on a vacation to a dude ranch (in which case I would've been happier if he had been wearing Mickey Mouse ears). But dessert came and went without any vacation announcements, and the next day he mowed the front lawn dressed as a court jester. Whenever he stopped to empty the grass catcher, the bells on his hat jingled. From then on, he wore the clothing of other times as often as he did his own. More frequently, in fact.

I wasn't ready to speak to my dad. I tucked the phone back in my pocket.

"I don't believe this!" Tom muttered.

"What?"

"Look!"

Tom had drawn a new hexagram in the dirt.

"I wanted to know how I'm going to do on next week's math test—whether I'll do well enough to make Puma Ma happy. I flipped the coin six times and got the fifty-fifth hexagram, which is called *Abundance!*"

He seemed distressed, and I couldn't figure out why.

"So, that's good," I assured him. "*Abundance* means 'a lot.' It's saying you'll ace the test. Maybe ace-plus it!"

"That's not the point. Once I got the hexagram, I checked to see if there was a Morse code message hidden in it."

"And?"

He scribbled in the dirt with his stick. "Three dots, that's an *S*; a dot and two dashes, that's a *W*; a single dot is an *E*; another single dot is another *E*; and a single dash, that's a *T*!"

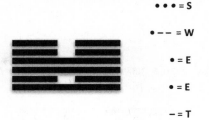

"The fifty-fifth hexagram, which for thousands of years has meant 'abundance,' contains the Morse code for *sweet*!" Tom sounded like he might explode.

"Well," I said reasonably. "If you've got an abundance—a whole lot of stuff—that's sweet, isn't it?"

"Yes! Of course it is! That's the problem! Not only is there a Morse code message, but the message relates directly to what the hexagram is about! The odds against that are astronomical! It's impossible! There's something supernatural going on here! Let's do another one and see what happens!"

Carnival lights started dimming, and the Ferris wheel came to a halt. Music from most of the rides stopped, leaving a lone song playing from the midway. I recognized "Hello Goodbye" by the Beatles.

"We're both going to concentrate on the same question," Tom informed me. "You flip the coin this time."

"Is this really all that important to you?" I said, jumping to my feet. "I think maybe we should stop sitting here and go into the carnival. Frankie's not here. What if something happened to her? Maybe somebody else is after the treasure, and they've got her tied up or something."

"Or maybe she went to the bathroom," Tom replied. "It's only two minutes past nine. She said she'd meet you at the entrance. Let's do this. If she's not here by the time we're done, we'll go looking for her."

I grudgingly sat back down. Tom pressed the quarter into my hand.

"We'll both concentrate on the same question," he said.

"What?"

" 'What's going to happen to us next?' "

"Didn't we ask something like that already?"

"I want a second opinion!"

I flipped the coin six times, and Tom drew a broken line for each tail and an unbroken line for each head.

"All right, now we look it up—" Tom turned to the book's index and quickly found a match. "Hexagram fifty-six, page one seventy-seven...here it is! The hexagram is called—*Travel*!" He showed me the page, as if I wouldn't have believed him otherwise.

HEXAGRAM 56

TRAVEL.

STRANGE LANDS AND CUSTOMS. AN
UNEXPECTED JOURNEY. THE ROAD
WILL RISE TO MEET YOU, AND HIT
YOU IN THE FACE. IT IS BETTER TO
TRAVEL HOPEFULLY THAN IT IS TO
ARRIVE: YOUR LUGGAGE PROBABLY
WENT TO THE WRONG PLACE
ANYWAY.

"This can't be a good translation," I decided.

"Now we see if there's a hidden Morse code message!"

Tom began looking back and forth between his printed Morse alphabet and the hexagram, as if he no longer trusted his memory. "The unbroken line at the top is a dash—that could be a *T*, then two dots is an *I*—"

I stabbed my finger at the middle of the code key and said, "Two unbroken lines could be two dashes—two dashes is Morse for *M*! Maybe we're going to travel with some guy named Tim!"

"We're not finished yet!" Tom snapped, waving his hand at the remaining lines. "There's a broken line—"

The parking lot lights went out, plunging us into darkness. We could no longer see what was printed in the book, and Tom's hexagram vanished in the gloom.

"*Filibuster!*" Tom muttered, using one of his most powerful swear words.

I was carrying our flashlight, but before I could get it out of my pocket, the hum of a motor came from our left, and then the shadowy form of a golf cart slid to a halt in front of us. The silhouette driving it leaned toward us.

"Is your name Tim?" Tom asked.

"Do I look like a Tim?" Frankie Camlo hopped out of the cart and put her fists defiantly on her hips. She had changed into a sweatshirt and added a charm bracelet to her left wrist. A small zippered backpack hung from one shoulder.

"Uh, no!" Tom was flustered. "Definitely not!"

"My name is Frank!"

Tom became even more flustered.

"You don't look like a Frank, either!"

"Well, I am! Frankie, if you must." She glared at me. Even in dim lighting, it was obvious. "I should have known you wouldn't show up by yourself," she said. "What is it with boys that they always have to travel in packs?"

"There's only the two of us," I said defensively. "This is my best friend, Tom Xui. Tom, this is Frankie Camlo."

Tom held out his hand. Frankie looked at it warily. Then she took it, shook it twice, and snapped her hand back. "I'm possibly pleased to meet you. We'll see. Now, both of you, in the cart!" She slid into the driver's seat. "The sooner we get this over with, the better."

I hopped aboard. If it would get me a meeting with Madam Janus, I was willing to drive off with Frankie Camlo, no questions asked. Tom wasn't so willing. He stood in front of the cart, his arms folded, and said, "Where are we going? What are we looking for?"

Now Frankie glared at him.

"WE are going to run you over," she growled, "and WE are looking forward to seeing you in the rearview mirror, except this thing doesn't have a rearview mirror. Dr. Lao said I might run into someone like you, but I didn't think he meant literally."

"Come on," I said. "Your *I-Ching* thing said *Travel*."

Tom blinked. "It did, didn't it?"

He squeezed in beside me. Frankie stomped on the gas, and the cart shot out of the lot and into the middle of Hartnell Road, then veered onto the shoulder and churned gravel.

"You're too young to have a license!" I said.

"You don't need a license for a golf cart," she said. "They're toys. They can't go over fifteen miles per hour, have no headlights, windshields, or, as I said, rearview mirrors"—she twisted around in her seat and looked behind her—"which makes it hard to see if you're being followed."

Tom and I swiveled to the rear and peered into the receding darkness.

"You think somebody might be following us?" I asked.

"It's possible, if my father got wind of this."

"He doesn't like you out late?"

"He doesn't like me messing with things he's forbidden."

"Like the golf cart?"

"Like the family treasure. One of you should watch behind us. Let me know if you see anything that looks like a giant gorilla."

"A giant gorilla?" Tom squawked. He twisted around on the seat, staring anxiously in the direction we had come.

"I said 'looks like.' It wouldn't be an actual gorilla. The Wonder Show isn't a circus. Did you bring a flashlight?"

I yanked the one Tom had given me out of my pocket.

"Aim it ahead," she said. "If your friend sees anything behind us, turn it off!"

I did as I was told, giving the cart a pool of light to chase.

"I'm assuming you two know how to get around your town," said Frankie. "I need to know how to get to Pertwee Avenue without taking any of the main roads. The police might stop three kids in a golf cart."

"There's a dirt road up ahead," I said. "Try that."

She made the turn. The road was one lane with a grassy ridge running down the middle. Trees closed in above, blocking out the half-moon's light. I wondered what we were getting into. The *I-Ching* had said *Travel*. Possibly with some guy named Tim. Then I remembered we hadn't finished decoding the Morse.

"You could have looked at a map," said Tom. "You didn't need us for this."

"I did look at a map. Maps don't tell you which streets are busy and which streets you can drive down without being noticed. And this cow path we're on wasn't on the map. Only someone from around here would have known about it. So, obviously, I need you. Or, at least, *one* of you." She gave Tom a look. He pretended not to notice.

"What's this treasure we're looking for?" I asked.

"The Camlo Shagbolt. I believe it's hidden in your town."

"The Camlo what?"

"Shagbolt."

"Is that like . . . some kind of . . . old-time race car?" It was a lame guess, but it was the best I could do. I didn't have a clue what a shagbolt might be.

"It's the most valuable thing in my family's possession," said Frankie, swerving around a rock. "We argue about it constantly. Half of us feel the Shagbolt should be kept with the carnival; the other half feels the Shagbolt is dangerous and should be hidden away where only a special few can get to it."

"What's a shagbolt?" Tom demanded.

Frankie hesitated. "Do you know what a chatelaine is? Or a diadem? Or a tiara?"

"Uh, different types of jewelry?" Tom guessed.

"That's right!" Frankie sounded delighted. That should have made me suspicious. "There are probably lots of different types of jewelry you've never heard of. Let's just say the Shagbolt is the Camlo family's crown jewel."

"And it's dangerous," I said, imagining an ax covered in rubies.

"In the wrong hands, yes, it could be. But right now, I *need* the Shagbolt, so I'm on the side that wants to keep it handy." Low branches whipped across the cart's front, like bony fingers lunging from the darkness. Frankie didn't flinch. "My father heads the faction that wants it hidden; my mother is on the side that thinks it shouldn't be. No one voted when my father decided to hide it; he should have called a meeting. But it doesn't matter now because I think I've figured out where he's hidden it."

Frankie slammed on the brakes and we all lurched forward. The scariest of all Ohio's wild animals blocked our path. Its eyes gleamed a devilish red in the beam of my light. The three of us clutched one another in terror.

"Don't move," I whispered. "It can smell our fear!"

"No," Frankie corrected me. "*We* can smell *its* fear—so don't spook it!"

The skunk finished the berries it had been eating, looked up at Frankie, nodded as though some message had passed between them, then ambled off into the bushes.

I sniffed. The night still smelled of honeysuckle. Far behind us, a tree branch snapped.

"What the—?" said Tom, and he and I swiveled to look.

"Hang on!" Frankie shouted, stomping on the gas. The cart sped forward. Behind us, the shadow of something huge and troll-like separated itself from the surrounding darkness and began running after us. "Put it out!" Frankie slapped my hand and I snapped off the light.

We couldn't see anything. Frankie was only able to keep the cart on the road because the wheel ruts on either side acted as a track; if there was anything in the road's middle, like a log or a stray cow, we were going to hit it.

The thing chasing us was hard to see, but occasional breaks in the overhead branches dappled it with moonlight. It looked twice the size of a man, with gangly arms and a head like a prizewinning pumpkin. It seemed to be wearing a Hawaiian shirt and plaid shorts. We weren't losing it. In fact, it was gaining.

"What *is* that thing?" I asked, clutching one of the metal pipes that supported the cart's plastic roof.

"It's not a *thing*," Frankie informed me. "It's Mr. Ganto. He works for my father."

"Is he part of the freak show?"

"He's not a freak, and I'll thank you not to call him one! We don't have a freak show. We Camlos hate the idea of freak shows. There are no freaks. Mr. Ganto is a roustabout. He helps set up and take down the carnival. He stays out of sight during the day."

There was a loud *klonk!* as a rock hit the underside of the cart. The wheels on the right tangled in a vine, the cart lurched, then the vine tore free and we continued on.

"He's gaining!" Tom reported.

I turned to look. Mr. Ganto was maybe a hundred yards behind us, and coming up fast.

"What's that ahead of us?" Frankie demanded.

Through the trees, lights were visible in the distance.

"That's Baker Lane, at the edge of the industrial park," I said. It had been my idea to get to Pertwee Avenue through the factory district along the river. I figured the streets there would be deserted and nobody would notice three kids in a golf cart.

"If we can get to a place with streetlights," said Frankie, "that will slow Mr. Ganto down. He prefers to hide in shadows."

"Still gaining!" hissed Tom, a panicky edge to his voice.

The cart hit something again, this time big enough to stop us. The three of us tumbled forward into the branches of a tree limb that lay in the road, blocking our path. I switched on my light. The limb was big, but if we lifted together, I was pretty sure we could move it.

It took only seconds for us to wrestle it off the path, but they were seconds we didn't have. As we turned back to the cart, Mr. Ganto was standing ten feet behind it. Two of his strides would put him on top of us.

"Shofranka," he said, in the deepest voice I had ever heard. He sounded sad.

I shined my light at him. He threw hands the size of catcher's mitts in front of his eyes, but not before we all saw his hairy bearded face with its shelf-like brow and bulbous nose.

"Bigfoot!" exclaimed Tom.

"*Gigantopithecus*," Frankie corrected him.

"No way!" said Tom, as though *Gigantopithecus* was part of his everyday vocabulary. It had too many syllables to be one of his swear words.

"Give this up," Mr. Ganto rumbled. "It can only make trouble." He stepped forward.

His foot came down on a skunk.

Musk exploded upward into Mr. Ganto's face. He reeled back, as though he had stepped on a land mine. He clutched his eyes and began a series of tree-shaking snorts and sneezes. We got only a whiff, but it was enough.

Whether it was the same skunk that had blocked our path a few minutes earlier or its farther-down-the-road cousin, it was impossible to tell. The critter skedaddled, and so did we. Frankie, Tom, and I threw ourselves into the cart, Frankie floored the gas, and we spun off down the road. I kept my flashlight switched on and aimed ahead of us.

"He's doubled up, like he's in pain," said Tom, staring over his shoulder.

"He has a very sensitive sense of smell," Frankie explained as the trees thinned out and Baker Lane became increasingly visible at the top of the approaching hill. I was never so grateful to see the Dingleman Hole-Punch factory in my life. "He can track people by their smell; that's probably how he found me. For him, that skunk must have been like a bomb going off. I hope he's all right!"

"All right?" I said. "That monster almost had us!"

"That 'monster' helped raise me," Frankie said indignantly. "Sometimes my mother isn't around; sometimes my father isn't around; but Gantsy is always there for me. He's like my nanny."

The golf cart topped the rise, fishtailed on pebbles, and took off down the cracked pavement of Baker's desolate, factory-lined street.

"*Gigantopithecus*," said Tom.

"Yes," confirmed Frankie.

"The Chinese *Gigantopithecus*?" Tom continued. "From the Sichuan province?"

"Most of the fossil record for *Gigantopithecus* comes from Sichuan, if that's what you mean. And Mr. Ganto *is* very fond of hot, spicy food. So I guess, yes, the Chinese *Gigantopithecus*, although in their heyday they could be found as far south as the Malay Peninsula, where many of them had vacation homes."

"*Gigantopithecus* has been extinct for over a hundred thousand years," said Tom.

"Tell that to Mr. Ganto."

We passed a parked green convertible with a pink stuffed poodle impaled on its antenna. Four boys sitting in the car gaped at us through a cloud of cigarette smoke. I heard Lenny Killbreath shout, "Hey!"

"Well, that's unfortunate," said Tom.

The convertible's engine gunned to life.

"They're going to chase us," I informed Frankie, feeling even more panic than I had when Mr. Ganto was after us.

"Why?"

"It's what they do."

They didn't have to chase us. We could only go fifteen miles per hour. They rolled up next to us and Lenny leaned out the window.

"Hey, jerks!" he shouted. "The golf course is back that way!"

Then he caught a glimpse of me, scowled, and in a much less friendly voice added, "It's that stinking wacko's kid! What are you doing out past your bedtime? Don't you know it's dangerous?"

The car cut in front of us and Frankie slammed on the brakes. Lenny leaned over us from the car door and demanded, "What are you three hemorrhoids doing here?"

"These are not the hemorrhoids you're looking for," Tom said in his best Obi-Wan voice.

Frankie hit reverse, and we sped backward away from them.

"GET 'EM!" Lenny hollered at his driver.

The convertible made a U-turn and headed straight for us.

CHAPTER 5
A Field Trip Every Day of Your Life

Frankie backed the cart over the curb and onto the sidewalk, flipping it out of reverse and driving away from our pursuers, who started to pass us to cut off our escape. But the cart blocked the driver's view of a fire hydrant. Frankie veered unexpectedly and scooted around it, but the convertible hit it with a loud *kabang!* The car lurched to a halt, and water fountained up around it.

I leaned out the back of our cart and did a victory dance with my hands. A moment later something heavy hit the roof, and the soaking-wet, semi-severed head of a pink poodle dangled down in front of Frankie. She batted it away.

"If you stay on this," I said, "there'll be an entrance to Gust-imuck Park. We cut across the park and come out on Pertwee."

Frankie took my directions, and in a few minutes we were in the park, following one of the bike trails.

"*Paramecium!*" Tom announced. "That was the most fun I've had in a *long* time."

"You have an odd definition of fun," said Frankie.

"I mean it," said Tom. "Usually, Puma Ma has me studying all the time."

"Poo Mama?" asked Frankie.

"Puma Ma," Tom corrected her.

"I don't hear the difference."

"Then you could never speak Chinese. The Chinese lan-guages all depend a lot on the tone of voice. Puma Ma—my mom—wants me to go to Harvard. She expects me to become a surgeon. Or a concert pianist. Or maybe both."

"Are those things you want to be?" Frankie asked as we passed Nellie's Erratic, the huge graffiti-covered boulder that marked the entrance to the park's best picnic area.

"No," Tom admitted. "I'd rather be an archaeologist. I love finding out things about the past. I went to archaeology camp last summer—you had to dig to find your bunk! So cool. I'm so glad math camp was full."

"Gypsy parents can be difficult, too," said Frankie.

"Cut through the picnic tables there," I told her. "Then past the snack bar and that's Pertwee. You're a Gypsy?"

"I shouldn't have used that word," said Frankie, maneuvering the cart between a row of barbecue grills. "*Gypsy* is a name outsiders have for us. Some of my relatives find it offensive, but I don't. More correctly, we're Romani. We're travelers; we never stay in one place too long."

"So you're homeschooled," I decided. She came across as pretty smart.

"No, Rose," she said, ignoring my wince. "I'm carnival-schooled. That's so much better."

"Really?" said Tom. "What's it like?"

"It's like being on a field trip every day of your life."

The cart passed through a gate and we were on Pertwee. Frankie leaned forward and surveyed the street. "We're looking for a building that was called the Armory on an old map. It probably isn't called that any longer, but it should be a big, squat, forbidding-looking dungeon of a place with too few windows and possibly a moat."

Tom and I looked at each other.

"That would be our school," I said. "But there's no moat, except on the south side after a lot of rain. Make a right."

Two minutes later we were in front of Ambrose Bierce Middle School. As far as I knew, it was the only other Ambrose in Freedom Falls.

"This is where you go to school?" Frankie sounded like she couldn't believe it.

"I know," Tom agreed. "It doesn't have a Ferris wheel. But it's not all that bad, once you get used to it."

The central part of the building looked like a Greek temple dedicated to one of the shorter, chunkier Greek gods, while two modern wings stuck out on either side like a fake arrow through the head of a birthday party clown. I had never really appreciated how awful it looked.

"How do we get in?" asked Frankie.

"In?" I responded, dumbfounded. "You think your father hid the Shampoo in our school?"

"Shagbolt," Frankie muttered, restarting the cart and slowly cruising the parking lot. "My father had the Armory circled on a map, which he foolishly left lying around in his safe. Look at the place. It's built like a fortress. It's not going to burn down, a tornado would bounce right off it, lightning is probably scared of it. What better vault to hide the Shagbolt in? The carnival passes through Freedom Falls every year; it's on our loop. He can't keep it with the carnival; he would be afraid one of us might be tempted to use it."

"Use it?" asked Tom. "Just what kind of jewelry is it?"

"Is it a bomb?" I asked.

"What would a carnival need with a bomb?" Frankie snorted. "We get along very well with the other carnivals, even Cooger and Dark's, and they're our main competitors. I assume the doors are locked?"

Much to my surprise, I heard myself saying, "One of the science-lab windows is only held shut with duct tape."

CHAPTER 6
Caught in the Banned Room

Isn't this breaking and entering?" Tom asked a few minutes later as he played the beam of his flashlight across the science lab's tables. We had resealed the window after wiggling in. "If we get caught, Puma Ma will ground me for life."

"You don't have to be here," Frankie reminded him. He made a face but stopped complaining.

"We're students," I said quietly, opening the door a crack and looking down the hall. "We're allowed. We're just here later than usual."

The hall was empty. I opened the door fully and stepped

out, Frankie and Tom close behind. Most of the overhead lights were off, giving the place a spooky feel, as if at any moment the coffin-like lockers lining the walls might open and release thirsty vampires. Some of the locker vents smelled of the undead.

"So where do you think this Shagbolt thing might be?" I asked Frankie.

"Do you have a band room?" she replied.

"What? A room where we're forbidden to go?" asked Tom.

Frankie gave him a look. "Not *banned* room. *Band* room. If you can't hear the difference, you could never speak Romani. The Romani languages depend a lot on the tone of voice. Where does the orchestra practice?"

"In the band room," I answered. "Behind the auditorium. This way."

I took the lead and tiptoed to the end of the hall, passing a cheerful poster for the Drama Club's upcoming play, *The Crucible*, which showed a bunch of terrified people cowering in a corner. We made a left, and then slowed when we heard voices.

"Is this the only way to get there?" whispered Frankie.

I nodded. The voices were coming from the principal's office.

"You should have fired Brody outright," I heard a man's voice say. "Never mind this suspension nonsense. I don't want to come back here tomorrow for the emergency board meeting. I work late; it was hard enough getting here tonight."

"I appreciate your being here," said another voice. It sounded like Clyde McNamara, our principal. "It was the input from you four that led to my decision. If there's a vote tomorrow, you'll all pretty much *have* to be here. I lean with the majority."

I poked my head in the doorway and looked across the secretary's office to McNamara's inner office, where the door was ajar. No one was looking out; no one would notice if we scurried by. I started past the door, then altered course and slipped inside.

Tom sputtered, but I felt him and Frankie come in behind me. We all crouched behind the secretary's desk just outside McNamara's door. I had to hear what was going on.

"The man's a menace," said a woman's voice, and I recognized Cynthia Moon, president of the PTA. "The other day I caught my Tommy trying on a buckskin jacket with ridiculous fringe—whose fault could *that* possibly be? I yanked it off him and told him no son of mine was going to dress like it was the eighteen sixties, and he said I was *so* ignorant, he was dressing like it was the *nineteen* sixties, peace, love, don't-trust-anyone-over-thirty, and he looked directly at me as he said it. *Eighteen* sixty, *nineteen* sixty; what difference does it make? He was dressing *outside* his own time period. Couldn't he see how wrong that is?"

"My boy got beat up because he showed up in school dressed like a *Tom Sawyer* character," said the man I had first heard speak. Meaning he was Billy Osborn's father.

"Your son got beat up," said McNamara, "because he showed up in school wearing a dress."

"A nineteenth-century dress."

"What's this play the school is putting on?" asked a whiny new voice. "*The Crucible*? What's that about?"

"The Salem witch trials," explained McNamara.

"So you'll be encouraging our children to put on *more* nineteenth-century outfits."

"Seventeenth century," said McNamara. "The witch trials took place in 1692."

"You should find a newer play," said Whiny. "This is where it starts, in theater and the arts. Brody was probably in school plays when he was growing up. Find a play that takes place *now*, or have the kids perform this *Crucible* thing in modern clothing. We have a wide selection of contemporary tees at reasonable prices over at Mordred's." So Whiny was Millicent Mordred, owner of the town's largest clothing store.

"*The Crucible* in T-shirts and tennis shoes?" McNamara said thoughtfully. "Possibly."

"The important thing here is that Brody is gone as of tomorrow. He's a bad influence. He gives the kids the impression they can dress however they want. We can't let him encourage unnatural behavior." This was a new voice, but one I recognized immediately. It was Quentin Garlock, the substitute teacher who would be taking over my dad's classes. He had been a sub for as long as anyone could remember. He always said that the thing he wanted most was to become a full-time teacher.

McNamara sniffed. "Does anybody here smell skunk?"

I wanted to jump up and shout, "YES, and its name is Garlock!" Instead, I inhaled deeply. McNamara was right; there was the tiniest scent of polecat in the air.

Tom shifted position and the top of his head grazed the underside of a clipboard that was jutting out over the edge of the desk. The clipboard fell, hitting the floor with a resounding clatter.

"What was that?" demanded Mordred, her voice shooting up an octave. "Is it a skunk? I'm wearing Donna Karan; don't let it near me!"

Garlock was first out the door, followed closely by McNamara. They were just in time to see us scramble to our feet and make a run for it. We hit the hall, veered to the left, and raced toward the auditorium.

I hit Nooby Wilson's locker hard as I passed it, and Nooby's locker, which was notorious for springing open because of the incredible amount of junk in it, burst open and debris flew out, blocking the way. Garlock's foot came down on a poorly resealed blister pack of salami slices and he skidded, going down on one knee. McNamara tripped on him. They went sprawling as we dived through the open doors of the auditorium.

"Stop this instant!" McNamara bellowed from the hall as we pelted down the aisle and jumped on the stage. "You have no business being here after hours! Stop, or I'll call the police!"

The only lighting in the auditorium was the four red EXIT signs above the doors, and by the time McNamara and Garlock followed us in, we were hidden in *The Crucible* set. From behind a seventeenth-century judge's bench, we watched the two men begin searching for us between the room's many rows of seats.

"You can't escape!" McNamara shouted. "Come out now, and it will only be a month's detention! Otherwise, I'll suspend all three of you!"

He had only seen us from the back. I was pretty sure he didn't know who we were; he just assumed we were three students from his school.

"Whoa!" Garlock slipped sideways and then caught himself by grabbing McNamara's necktie.

"What is *wrong* with you?" McNamara bellowed in a strangled voice.

"Sorry! There's salami on my shoe!"

I nudged my friends, and we moved to the back of the stage, dodged behind a curtain, and slipped quietly through a door. Tom turned on his flashlight, and we could see rows of chairs and music stands.

"This is the band room!" Frankie whispered excitedly. "Where do they store the instruments?"

"Shouldn't we be getting out of here?" asked Tom. "Once McNamara sees we're not hiding behind the seats, this is the next place he'll look!"

"There!" I said, pointing to a huge metal cage at the end of the room. It was a cube made from chain-link fencing. Frankie dragged Tom by the flashlight until they were both standing in front of the cage's padlocked door.

Frankie positioned Tom's arm so he was aiming the light

at the padlock. Then she grabbed the lock with one hand and shook her charm bracelet into the palm of the other. She fiddled with one of the charms, stretched it out like a telescoping radio antenna, and inserted it into the lock.

"I hope you two don't believe all the things you may have heard about Gypsies," she said as she fished around in the depths of the lock.

I had heard nothing about Gypsies, other than that they traveled a lot.

"Like what?" asked Tom.

"Like some of us are experts at getting into places we're not supposed to. I'm guessing you're both too smart to believe such nasty ethnic stereotypes." The lock sprang open. "Am I right?"

Tom and I stared disbelievingly at how easily she had picked the lock.

"Am I right?"

"Oh, yes!" I chirped.

"Absolutely!" agreed Tom.

She dropped the lock and opened the door, and we followed her in.

Two rows of metal shelving ran parallel down the length

of the cage, ending in more shelving along the back. Musical instruments—some in cases, some not—filled the shelves from top to bottom. Violin cases were everywhere. A bass drum loomed above us in an overhead rack, like the boulder that had chased Indiana Jones.

"You think the Shagbolt is hidden in here?" I asked incredulously. It didn't look like the kind of place you'd find treasure, unless maybe you were John Philip Sousa.

"If you were going to hide a tree," said Frankie, walking slowly down the aisle, glancing at every shelf, "would you hide it in a desert, or in a forest?"

"Uh...forest?" answered Tom, like he thought it might be a trick question.

"Yes," Frankie said approvingly. "Always hide things with other things that look like it."

"The big drum is broken on one side," I said, looking up. "Maybe inside it?"

"Too small," replied Frankie. "But if it's broken, it hasn't been used in a while. There's a lot of dust on it. I wonder..."

She reached up and pulled a wooden wedge out from behind the drum. The drum rolled along parallel rails toward the rear of the cage, where it

A. struck the neck of a violin that stuck out in its path from a high shelf, which

B. spun the violin around,

C. knocking a cup full of brass mouthpieces off the shelf into the bell of a tuba on the floor below, causing the tuba to

D. tip over and

E. hit the first of three saxophones on stands so that the saxophones went down like dominoes, the last one

F. hooking the strap of a guitar case that dangled down from a higher shelf,

G. pulling the guitar to the shelf's edge, which

H. pushed a triangle off the shelf to

I. swing on a string,

J. hit one of the shelf supports,

K. and go *ting!*

"There!" said Frankie, sounding pleased.

"Your family treasure is a *triangle*?" Tom squawked.

"Some people might see a triangle," Frankie conceded. "I see an arrow pointing to the back of that shelf."

She strode to the rear of the cage and brushed the triangle aside. Tacked to the wall at the back of the shelf was a dusty banner declaring REGIONAL CHAMPIONS 1974. Frankie lifted the banner and exposed a niche in the brick wall. From the niche she pulled a long wooden box with brass locks and latches and a leather suitcase handle. She turned to me and jammed the box against my chest. I crooked my arms to support it.

"Is this it?" I whispered.

"Yes!"

"That was amazing!" declared Tom.

"What?" asked Frankie. "Oh, the thing with the drum and the saxophones? I'm sure that was just a coincidence. We would have looked behind the banner eventually."

She used a small key on her charm bracelet to unlock the latches and raised the lid.

I don't know what I expected to see. A king's scepter covered in diamonds? A knight's sword encrusted with emeralds? A solid gold toilet plunger?

"It's a trombone," said Tom.

"Yes," conceded Frankie. "But it's not just *any* trombone. This is the Camlo Shagbolt. *Shagbolt* is an old-time word for trombone."

"You said it was jewelry," Tom said accusingly.

"No. I talked about jewelry, and you assumed it was. If I had said it was a trombone, you would have thought I was crazy."

"If it makes you feel any better," I said, "I'm thinking you're crazy now."

She lifted the instrument carefully out of the velvet lining of its case. It didn't look like a modern trombone. The metal was so tarnished, it was almost black, and its tubing had extra twists and turns, along with two awkwardly positioned piston valves, as though it had started out to be a trumpet and then changed its mind.

"Is it valuable?" I asked.

Frankie shrugged. "How much is your freedom worth?"

"GOTCHA!" announced Quentin Garlock, and his shout was followed by the sound of a padlock snapping shut.

Tom blinded him with a light beam, and Garlock threw a hand in front of his face.

"So you've got a flashlight and I don't," he jeered. "We'll have the lights on in a jiffy and then we'll see who we've got. GET THAT OUT OF MY EYES!"

Tom aimed his beam elsewhere. Garlock sang out, "Clyde, I've got them! They're in the band room!" McNamara stumbled through the backstage door.

"Good work! Who are they?"

"Too dark to tell. I snuck up on them. Locked 'em in!"

"Why aren't the lights on?"

"I'm not sure where the switches are. They weren't by the stage entrance."

"They're by the hall door," muttered McNamara, and headed that way. Frankie nudged Tom and me with the Shagbolt and got us to squat behind an upright piano. I didn't see the point. We were caught.

The lights came on and McNamara came over.

"Where's the key?" he asked Garlock.

"What key?"

"The key to the lock!"

The silence said Garlock had no idea where the key was. My guess was it was with Ms. Jampole, the orchestra teacher.

McNamara sighed. "Go back to my office. There's a key ring in the middle drawer of my desk. Bring it. One of those keys should fit."

Garlock took off. McNamara walked from one side of the

cage to the other, trying to get a look at us. The piano, plus the two kettle drums next to it, pretty well blocked his view.

"Who are you?"

I opened my mouth to tell him, since he was going to find out anyway, but Frankie squeezed my elbow. "Shh!" she hissed.

"You have no business being in this school after hours," McNamara informed us. "We're going to get this thing open, find out who you are, call your parents and, possibly, the police. It's silly of you to hide behind that piano. Step into the light so I can see you."

I started to rise, but Frankie hauled me back, shaking her head.

"This is trespassing," McNamara continued. "I can accuse you of vandalism. I can accuse you of theft. But I won't do any of those things if you agree to tell no one what you overheard in my office. Private meetings are my right, but there are those who would object. I don't need that headache."

My heart sank. My father was already in trouble. Now his son had broken into the school. It would make him look even worse and make it so much easier for the school board to fire him. I wasn't happy with the way he dressed, but he was my dad.

I really didn't want him losing his job because of *me*.

Frankie put the trombone's mouthpiece to her lips, slid the slide out three inches, and blew.

An elephant farted.

"Now, that's just rude," said McNamara.

In rapid succession Frankie played five more notes, all of them sounding like various animals experiencing gastric distress. Possibly a moose, followed by two cows and a bull, then the elephant again. The notes were nothing you would ever hum, unless you had a job tuning whoopee cushions.

"Stop this insolence at once!" barked McNamara.

Frankie played a final note—a hippo after eating refried beans—and everything around me blurred. I couldn't focus, and colors whirled around me like a tornado hitting a paint store.

I felt my body turn to powder, blow away, and reassemble itself somewhere else. My supper came halfway up, made a left turn, then dropped back into my stomach.

And I fell on my butt in bright green grass beneath a noonday sun.

McNamara, the band room, and all of Ambrose Bierce Middle School had vanished and been replaced by a tree-lined meadow on a warm summer's day.

CHAPTER 7
Bold as Brass

I was still clutching the trombone case. The lid fell shut on my fingers, and I didn't even notice. Tom was sitting in the grass next to me, holding his flashlight over his head like he was about to hit somebody with it.

"The trick to staying upright is to plant your feet well apart, with the rear foot at a ninety-degree angle to the front. It takes practice." Frankie was standing, legs positioned like she was riding a surfboard. She shook herself like a dog after a bath, then looked at me and my friend.

"Both of you, huh?" she said quizzically. "I was expecting

Rose. Tom is a surprise. I was pretty sure he was going to be left behind."

"What. Just. Happened?" I sputtered.

"We escaped from those horrible people. I can't believe you go to school in that place. It's like a prison."

"How did we escape?" I felt myself relaxing the tiniest bit. I eased my fingers out from under the lid, put the case aside, and got shakily to my feet.

"We traveled back in time. And, if my eyes aren't playing tricks, about a half mile to the east. This isn't where I wanted us to be." Frankie frowned. "You'll notice it's daylight, so don't argue with me about the time-travel part. And I know we're half a mile to the east because of that." She pointed behind us.

I turned, cautiously, to discover Nellie's Erratic looming over us. There was no mistaking Gustimuck Park's signature boulder: It was twelve feet tall and looked like one of the frozen trolls from *The Hobbit*. A gentle breeze rippled the grass around it.

"Where's the graffiti?" asked Tom, slowly getting to his feet. Nellie's Erratic appeared untouched by human hands.

"Most of it's waiting for the invention of spray paint," Frankie said, still frowning. "If you look closely, though, there are a few things scratched into the base."

I took a step closer and made out the words:

JAKE SMITH

LEAVING FOR CALIFORNY

JUNE 10, 1849

"Is that the date? You've brought us to 1849?" Tom squeaked.

"I was aiming for March 1852," Frankie admitted. "But that inscription is weathered; it might be about three years old. This *could* be fifty-two."

"But it doesn't feel like March," I said, looking up at the blazing sun.

"No," agreed Frankie. "It feels more like July or August. And I was hoping we'd be on Fourteenth Street in New York City."

"The Camlo Shagbolt did this," I said.

"Mostly. But each of us played a part."

"It's a time trombone."

"Oh, some people call it *the* Time Trombone, but I hate that. It makes it sound like something from a kids' book. I much prefer 'Shagbolt.' *Trombone*, in French, means 'paper clip.' It's obviously not a paper clip. Whoever heard of a time-traveling paper clip?"

"Whoever heard of a time-traveling trombone?" I shot back.

"I grew up with one. It's been in my family for generations. It's how we escape from people who don't like us. And I'd like to thank you two for helping me find it. Where would you prefer to be dropped off? Outside the school or near the carnival?"

She raised the trombone to her lips.

"You're taking us *back*?" Tom whirled with his fists clenched.

"No choice, really—it's going to *have* to be the school," Frankie said, giving the slide a wiggle. "We left the golf cart there, and I have to get it back to the carnival. All three of us should concentrate on the place where we parked it. And try to imagine a time about an hour after we first found the Shagbolt. That should be safe. I'll play the area code and we'll pop right back. Are we ready?"

Tom grabbed the slide and wouldn't let her move it.

"No!" he said. "Are you kidding? All my life I've wanted something like this to happen! I've always wanted to travel back in time! And now that I've done it, you're saying all I'm going to see is this stupid rock? That's, that's—*bicameral*!"

"Let go!" Frankie demanded.

"Wait," I said. "You're going to *play the area code*? Is that how it works? You play the *1812 Overture* and you go to 1812?"

"Area codes are five to ten notes long," Frankie explained impatiently. "And they have to be notes that no composer in his right mind would ever put together. The *1812 Overture* is too long, and it's too musical, except for maybe the cannon-firing part. A good area code should sound terrible when you play it."

"The one you played sounded awful."

"Thank you. The area code takes you to the decade you want. For the actual date and place, the time travelers have to put some thought into it."

"So," said Tom, letting go of the horn, "if we *don't* think of the same time and place as you, we might go to the wrong place?"

Frankie sighed. "Yes. In fact, I'm pretty sure that's what just happened. I was thinking of March 20, 1852, New York City. But one of you must have been thinking of this place."

"That was me," Tom confessed. "I wanted to be anywhere except inside that locked cage. I was thinking how nice it would be to be back in the park."

"That explains the wrong location." Frankie nodded. "But

it doesn't explain why it's summer when I was aiming for spring."

"You can't take us back," Tom said defiantly. "If you try, I'll concentrate with all my might on some other date and some other place, and screw it up!"

"It's obviously past somebody's bedtime," Frankie snapped.

"*Condescension!*" Tom growled.

"What?"

"He likes to use long words as curses," I explained.

A flock of blackbirds took flight from a tree not too far from us. I should have wondered what spooked them, but I didn't. I was new to the nineteenth century.

"So what is it you want?" Frankie asked.

"I want to see the town," said Tom. "I want to see what Freedom Falls looked like in 1852. That would be cool, right?" He looked to me, and I nodded. It wasn't past *my* bedtime.

"And after you see it, you'll cooperate, and let me take you back?"

"Yes! Of course. We both have school tomorrow."

Tom picked up the trombone case, opened the lid, and held it invitingly in front of her.

"You have no idea how dangerous this is," she said,

nestling the trombone into its formfitting velvet. "I've done this before; I know what I'm doing. Neither of you is a Camlo; you're not even Romani; you're outsiders. Outsiders always mess things up. If we do this, you talk to nobody—*nobody*—and if I tell you to hide, you jump behind the nearest tree. Got that?"

We nodded as she snapped the latches on the case and handed it to me. "You dropped your book," Frankie said crossly to Tom, pointing at his feet. The *I-Ching* was there in the grass. "That's exactly the sort of stupid thing we can't do! We can't leave stuff from the future behind! Somebody could find it, and it could change the course of history!"

Tom snatched up his book and started to jam it in his pocket, but then got a funny look on his face and opened the book instead.

"*Fiduciary!*" he exclaimed. "Holy cow!"

"What?" I asked.

"The fifty-sixth hexagram—the one we were working on when the lights at the carnival went out?"

"The one called Travel?"

"Yeah. Remember, we had only gotten halfway through the Morse?"

He shook out his code sheet and pulled out his pencil.

His hand flew as he finished decoding the message. Then he stood trembling as he looked at it. He turned the book so I could see.

"The hexagram called *Travel* contains the Morse code for *times*, and we've just traveled to different times! You can't tell me that's a coincidence! The *I-Ching* is sending us messages. Us! Specifically! You and me! And maybe her!"

"What is this?" said Frankie, craning her neck to see, and sounding seriously concerned. Tom explained it, and she looked thoughtful.

"And you say there are other hexagrams that contain Morse?"

Tom showed her. She shook her head.

"I'm not going to argue with the *I-Ching*. Maybe you two *are* meant to be with me. I wonder..." She trailed off, with a look on her face that said she didn't like what she was thinking.

In the woods to our right, an owl hooted. It seemed to me to be an awfully sunny, hot time of day for an owl to hoot.

"We'll take a really quick peek at your town and be on our way," Frankie said. "Since I can't convince the two of you to behave sensibly."

We found a pair of parallel ruts, each about the width of a wagon wheel, with a Mohawk haircut of weeds growing between them, and we decided it was a road. We took it in the direction of Freedom Falls.

"Great example of a snake fence!" Tom exclaimed, pointing to a jumble of logs to our right.

"That's supposed to stop snakes?" I said.

"No—it's called *snake* because of the way it zigzags. That is *so* nineteenth century! This is so cool!"

Tom was acting like he had died and gone to archaeology camp.

"So," I said, catching up with Frankie, "anybody who hears the Shagbolt travels through time?"

"Obviously not," she snorted. "That McNamara man isn't deaf, is he? The Shagbolt filters out what we Camlos call oppressor types. OTs always lack the necessary mental component. Most people lack it; oppressors *always* do. Your Mr. McNamara is definitely an OT."

"Why were you surprised that I wasn't left behind?" asked Tom, whiffling through the weeds behind us.

"Because so few people have a psychic talent. That's the component that oppressor types never have, and very few other people have, either. I know Rose has one, because he saw my father's face in my mother's crystal, but I thought the chances of his best friend also having a talent were pretty slim."

"You were ready to leave me behind? Locked in a cage?"

"It's not like I invited you along! I'm sure you would have talked your way out of the situation. That man McNamara didn't seem all that sharp to me. May I ask what your talent is?"

"My talent?" said Tom, proving he was keeping up with the conversation no better than I was.

"My aunt is clairvoyant," Frankie informed us. "That's French for 'clear vision.' She can sometimes see what people are doing many miles away. My cousin is clairgustant—he can taste what other people are eating."

"Yes!" said Tom. "That's me! I do that! Or I try, but I usually get my hand slapped."

"My cousin can experience the taste without being anywhere near the person who is eating. He sits quietly by himself and smiles whenever there's a big banquet at the White House."

"Oh, no." Tom changed his mind. "That's not me."

"I have another cousin who can cause toothpaste to burst into flame just by looking at it."

"What good is that?" I asked.

"It's absolutely no good at all. In fact, it's kept her from brushing her teeth for years. Nobody makes a fireproof tooth-brush. But it *is* a psychic ability. It's her *talent*. And my father is a master of glammering."

"Glammering?" said Tom, as though sizing up the word for curse potential.

"It's related to the word 'glamour,' although I'm sure no one who uses the word 'glamour' knows it once meant 'magic.'"

"Your father is a magician? He sort of dresses like one," I admitted.

"My father always wears jeans and a T-shirt. And I mean *always*. But people see him in the black suit, or the sword swallower's costume, or the security guard's uniform, or—or however he wants them to see him. That's what glammering is. It tricks the minds of others into seeing you the way you want to be seen."

"*Monosyllabic!*" said Tom, possibly contradicting himself. "That must be really useful!"

"It certainly saves money on wardrobe," Frankie agreed. "You, Rose, saw my dad in a crystal ball, so either you're clairvoyant—if what you saw was the present—or you're *precognitive*—if what you saw was the future."

"When I saw him in the ball, all he was doing was smiling and waving a cigar around."

"A cigar? Really?" She seemed perplexed. "My father doesn't smoke."

"Maybe someday he will."

"Oh. If that's true"—she didn't sound like she believed it—"then what you saw was the future. You have precognition. We may have a harder time figuring out Tom's talent. Sometimes it isn't obvious."

"Ack!" Tom stopped, squeezed his eyes shut, and held up his hands like somebody trying hard not to sneeze. Then he blurted, "Phone!"

"Excuse me?" said Frankie.

"Phone!" Tom repeated, relaxing a little. "A phone's about to ring!"

"That's impossible," said Frankie. "The phone hasn't been invented yet."

A phone rang.

I jumped. It was mine, in the pocket of my jeans. It rang again, and I fumbled it out of my pocket. I stared at it in disbelief.

"Who is it?" asked Tom.

"It's me!"

The number on the caller ID was my number, the number of the phone I was holding.

"You butt-dialed yourself," Tom suggested.

"This can't be my butt calling! I don't have myself on speed dial. I can usually get in touch with myself pretty quick."

The phone had rung twice more as we spoke. It sounded urgent.

"Answer it!" ordered Frankie.

I thumbed the button and brought the phone to my ear. "Hello?"

"Listen to me," said a voice I found vaguely familiar. For all I knew, it *was* my butt calling. "Whatever you do, don't let Dwina drown! You got that?"

"What?"

"Don't let Dwina drown! Repeat it!"

"Who is this?"

"Repeat what I just said!"

"Uh, don't . . ."

"Let Dwina drown!"

"Let Dwina dwown. I mean, drown."

"Good. Now duck!"

"What?"

"DUCK!"

I dropped. Something whistled through the air above my head. It was a rope lasso, which struck Tom's shoulder, fell to the grass, and was immediately yanked back by whoever had thrown it. A second lasso flew in from the opposite direction, and this one dropped around Tom like a perfect throw in a game of ringtoss. The rope tightened and pinned Tom's arms to his sides.

Three men were running at us from three different directions, two of the men with ropes and one waving a club. All three started whooping and shouting "Git! Git! Git!" and making yodeling sounds like they were cheerleaders at a rodeo. The one who had lassoed Tom pulled hard on the rope, and Tom crashed to the ground. Frankie dodged another incoming rope and sprinted for the trees. I ran in the opposite direction, jamming the phone in my pants.

The man with the club changed course to cut me off,

swinging the club as if he wouldn't hesitate to knock in my skull. I tried to run around him, but in the moment I took to change my path, a rope snaked around me. Suddenly I was lassoed as tightly as Tom. The rope yanked me hard and I fell into the weeds. Then I was dragged ten feet.

I struggled to lift my head and saw that Frankie had almost made it to the woods—until a man on a horse emerged from the trees in front of her. He bent down, caught her by the arm, and threw her across the saddle in front of him, leaning back so her kicking legs missed his face. She screamed things that might have been in Romani, but their meanings couldn't be misunderstood.

My face was shoved in the dirt, and my hands were pulled behind me and tied together. I had been shouting the word *STOP* over and over, but since no one was stopping, I tried screaming, "WHAT ARE YOU DOING?" That only got me hit in the head with somebody's fist, and I shut up so I could hear my ears ring. A burlap bag that smelled of rotten potatoes was thrown over my head, and I was pulled to my feet. Somebody, somewhere, was sobbing. It might have been me.

I heard the horse gallop to a halt and its rider say, "Tie this 'un up, too, and gag her! I had my doubts, but that must be some African lingo she's spoutin'."

"That's a girl?" asked a different voice. "Wearin' trousers?"

"Awful, ain't it?" replied the horseman. "A sure sign she don't come from no place civilized!"

The commotion next to me was loud and quickly over; I was pretty sure it was Frankie being bound, gagged, and bagged. I staggered as she was thrown against me, and I would have fallen if Tom hadn't been thrown against me at the same time from the opposite direction. I felt a rope tighten around my waist and realized the three of us were being tied together. Once this was accomplished, a new voice, gruffer than the horseman's, barked, "March!"

I was prodded forward and I started walking, my friends strung out behind me like the charms on Frankie's bracelet. I heard the horse do a slow *clip-clop* beside me, and its rider said, "Bold as brass, you walkin' down the road in broad daylight. Stupider 'n most, are ya?"

"Who do you think we are?" I asked. It was clear to me it was a case of mistaken identity.

"Who do I think ya are?" I could tell he was grinning from the shape of his words. "I think yer the king an' queen o' England, and the king o' France, to boot! Who do I think ya are? Yer escaped slaves! Make no mistake 'bout that! An' me 'an my boys are gonna make sure ya get back to wherever it was you escaped from. Ain't that right, boys?"

There was a ragged chorus of agreement. I knew enough from movies and TV not to argue with anybody who used expressions like "Ain't that right, boys?" but I argued anyway.

"We're not slaves! Why would you think we're slaves?"

Something clobbered me on the side of the head with enough force to knock me to my knees. Then somebody grabbed me by the shoulder and hauled me to my feet.

"There'll be no more talkin' 'til we get to where we're goin'," our captor cheerfully announced. To his men he said, "Chester, you head up town way, see if you can get a lead on them other runners. Bert, you an' Zack take these three to the Hole. I'll meet ya there in half an hour!"

The horse galloped off, the sound of its hooves fading in the distance. Our captors shoved us forward.

We had been captured by slave catchers.

And we no longer had the Time Trombone.

CHAPTER 8
The Ghost Candle and the Real Smart Pencil

L et's jus' say I'm a naturally curious cuss, so I would like to know whose house it was you broke into, an' why, of all the swag you coulda taken, you stole a slide horn and some gutta-percha pitcher frames."

It was about ninety minutes later. Frankie, Tom, and I were sitting on the threshing floor of what appeared to be an abandoned barn. Each of us had our back to a post, our arms pulled behind us, and our hands bound on the post's far side. The posts supported a hayloft from which dust occasionally drifted, as if small, frightened creatures might be hiding in the hay above us.

The man who had been on the horse sat on a rickety-looking chair a few feet from us, his booted feet crossed on the bench in front of him. Next to his feet was the Time Trombone's case, with the trombone half out of it, along with two cell phones, Tom's flashlight, the *I-Ching* book, Frankie's charm bracelet, and her backpack. The backpack, looking flat and empty, had not been opened; no one had guessed how the zipper worked.

"Gutta-percha?" asked Tom.

"Is that a Chinese word? Sounds kinda Chinese to me. Gutta-percha pitcher frames"—he nudged the cell phones with his heel, then grabbed the flashlight and mimed hitting someone over the head with it—"gutta-percha cudgel. Cudgel's jus' a guess; I don't quite *get* the li'l glass window in the end."

Gutta-percha, I decided, was some sort of early plastic. It could have been a lyric from one of Kan Sa$s's hip-hop songs.

He turned the flashlight toward himself and squinted at the bulb. His hand inadvertently slid the switch and he blinded himself, tossing the flashlight away and falling backward off his chair. He scrambled to his feet, snatched a pistol from a holster on his hip, and fired a frantic, unaimed shot that splintered wood an inch above my head. He fired again, this time more accurately, hitting the flashlight as it rolled across the floor and sending it flying against the wall, where it flickered and went out. He stayed in a crouched position with his gun aimed at it until he was certain it was dead.

"This is not going well," murmured Frankie.

A door at the opposite end of the barn flew open, and the man who had lassoed Tom ran in, gun drawn, ready to fire if he needed to. "You okay, Kill?" he asked the guy who had murdered the flashlight.

Kill straightened up and holstered his gun. "I'm fine, Bert. Better 'n fine. Jus' showin' these runners why it's no good to run. Bullets fly faster 'n they can. Chester back yet?"

"Not yet."

They were both dressed like shabby Abe Lincolns, in long coats, black vests, and stringy neckties, Bert in a derby-type hat and Kill bareheaded with his blond hair parted in the middle. There was something familiar about Kill.

"Lemme know the minute he shows up," Kill told Bert. "We ain't lingerin' here any longer than we need ta."

"Right," said Bert. "You decided what to do with the China boy yet?"

"Gonna sell 'im down the river with the other two." Kill picked up his fallen chair and set it upright. He settled back into it.

"They ain't using Chinese down there, boss."

"They should be. Why shouldn't they? Chinese ain't *us*; that makes 'em fair game in my book."

Bert nodded and left. Kill turned his attention back to us.

"Your name is Kill?" I asked.

"An' don't you furget it!" he snapped. "Short for Killbreath. Born an' raised in Cincinnati!"

And I knew why he looked familiar. There was a family resemblance. Kill had to be Lenny Killbreath's great-great-grandfather. Or maybe great-great-great. I wasn't sure how many greats into the past we had gone.

"We're not runaway slaves," said Frankie.

"Don't matter if you is or not." Kill shook his head. "Fugitive Slave Law says I can take you back and collect my fee for findin' ya. Slave catcher is a honorable trade. Didn't always think so, but then I saw the light."

"Did you shoot it out when you saw it?" I asked.

"This ain't no minstrel show," Kill said, drawing his gun and waving it casually in the air. "Don't need no jokes. I got papers in my pocket say you property of certain owners. All

I gotta do is fill your names inta the blanks. Owners ain't gonna argue if they don't zackly recollect you. Happens all the time. Or, if I wanna take the trouble, I kin take you farther down the river and sell you myself in Louisville. They's always somebody willin' to buy in Louisville. So now"—he cocked the gun and aimed it in Frankie's direction—"what names do I put on my papers?"

Frankie looked at him steadily and, after only a moment's hesitation, said, "Dorothy Gale."

"Uh-huh." Kill nodded approvingly. He pointed the gun at Tom.

"Atticus Finch," said Tom.

"Good." He aimed the muzzle at me.

"Marty McFly."

"Fine. See how nice we gettin' along? Like ol' friends." He put his gun away and pulled papers from the inside of his coat. He fished in both pockets of his vest and when he didn't find what he was looking for, he pulled Tom's pencil stub out from between the pages of the *I-Ching* book. He held the pencil in front of his face and frowned.

"Now, just what in tarnation is this little pink thing? Looks like a itty-bitty piece o' hog's tongue!"

"It's an eraser," volunteered Tom.

"Stuck on the pencil? That there's an idea gonna make somebody a whole pot o' money!" He drew a line on one of his papers and promptly erased it. "Hoo-wee!" He did it again, to see if the experiment was repeatable. Somewhere in his tiny mind, there was a scientist trying to get out. "Dang! Works! So, again I gotta ask—where'dja all steal this stuff from?"

"It's ours," I said defiantly.

"You can't have possessions. You *is* possessions." He pulled his gun out once again. "Where'dja get it all? The fancy slide horn an' the ghost candle and the real smart pencil? You break inta the house of some crazy inventor fella? I got a friend in the patent office; all I need's some big brain who invents. Where's the house you got this stuff from?"

He leveled the pistol at me for the third time.

"*Ubiquitous!*" Tom cursed.

"Whadya jus' call me?" Kill went red in the face. "You call me a *bickwidus*? NOBODY calls me a bickwidus!"

He swung the gun in Tom's direction. But before he could pull the trigger, the barn door flew open and Bert bustled back in.

"Chester's back! He says those runners that slipped by us yesterday are heading for the cooper's. We gotta move if we're gonna catch 'em!"

"Man alive!" said Kill, holstering his weapon. "Nothin' I like better 'n derailin' the beneath-the-ground railroad! Busybody conductors should all be lynched!" To us he said, "Looks like you three's gonna have some company! Make the trip worth it!" To Tom he added, "We'll see who's a bickwidus!"

He started for the door, then turned and came back. He poked the Time Trombone into its case, dropped the lid, and tucked the case under his arm. "There's a guy I know 'tween here and the cooper's that'll pay good money fer somethin' like this!" he said, throwing us a wolfish grin. "You three jus' sit tight 'til we get back!"

And he was gone, the door banging shut behind him.

"This is, possibly," said Frankie, "why my father is so against unauthorized use of the Shagbolt."

"Really?" I said. "You think? We're stuck here over a century in the past, we've just lost our only way to get back, and we're about to be sold into slavery because some idiot doesn't like the color of our skin! I'm on your father's side!"

"Oh, I'm sure he'd appreciate that," Frankie replied icily. "And I'm on *your* father's side, so there!"

"What's that supposed to mean?"

"I would have no problem whatsoever with a parent who

dresses for other time periods. That's downright *dull* compared to—"

"Compared to what?"

She turned her face away and didn't answer.

"Anybody's ropes the least little bit loose?" Tom asked.

"Mine are so tight, my hands are all pins and needles," said Frankie.

"Same here," I agreed grudgingly. "There's no way we're getting untied."

"One of the charms on my bracelet is a glass cutter," Frankie informed us.

We all looked at the bracelet. It was on the bench ten feet away from us. It might as well have been a mile.

"What?" I asked. "You've got Batman's charm bracelet?"

"It actually belonged to my grandmother. She had some unusual hobbies. If I had the bracelet, I could probably cut through my ropes."

I stretched my legs as far as I could toward the bench. I wasn't even close.

"Where is Harriet Tubman when you really need her?" I muttered.

"We should try standing up," Tom suggested. "There

might be a nail or something sticking out of the back of one of these posts that we could saw through the ropes with!"

We struggled to our feet. The posts turned out to be annoyingly smooth.

"Any other ideas?" I asked.

"What if we whistled the area code?" said Tom.

"What?"

"You know. The area code you would have played on the Shagbolt to return us to our own time. What if we whistled it? Or sang it, or something?"

"It would help if one of us was a musical instrument made from an alloy containing meteoric iron," said Frankie. "There's no way the notes are going to work by themselves."

"Time travel only works for people who have a psychic talent, right?" I said. "Maybe one of us has a talent for time travel."

"What? Time travel without the trombone? If such a talent exists, I've never heard of it," Frankie said dismissively. "Here are the notes, though. Listen very closely. If either of you vanishes, I'll know I was wrong!"

She whistled the seven notes she had played earlier on the Shagbolt. They sounded almost as awful as they had before, but a little less fart-like. "The last note is the tricky one. Played sharp, it takes us back to the decade we came from. Played flat, it takes us three thousand years further into the past."

"Let's hear the whole thing over," I said.

She whistled the notes again. Then I whistled them, and Tom tried it. Nothing happened. If anything, the posts we were tied to felt more solid.

"If we think those guys have gotten far enough away by now, it's time to start screaming," said Tom. He inhaled, filling his lungs for a long, loud bellow.

"Not yet!" Frankie snapped. "Screaming is a last resort! I'm sure those creeps didn't pick a hideout near anybody who might be helpful. We have to be quiet awhile longer."

Tom deflated.

"Why?" I asked.

"Shh!" replied Frankie. "I'm concentrating!"

I thought I heard a small sound from the direction of the bench. I glanced over but saw nothing. Frankie muttered something under her breath.

Tom whispered, "Why did you want to go to Fourteenth Street on March 20, 1852?"

"You two couldn't be more distracting if you tried!" Frankie hissed.

"Sorry!"

The head of a mouse popped out of a knothole at the foot of the bench. His whiskers twitched, then he wiggled all the way out and scampered up one of the bench legs. After sniffing our cell phones and nibbling a tiny bite from one corner of the *I-Ching* book, he ambled over to Frankie's bracelet and started nudging it toward the edge of the bench with his nose.

"Hey—" I started to say, but Frankie shushed me.

The mouse flattened himself against the bench and quivered, the bracelet forgotten.

"Can either of you do anything about the cat?" Frankie murmured.

"What cat?"

Frankie tossed her head in the direction of a rusted piece of farm equipment. As we watched, a lean and hungry-looking black cat oozed out from beneath it and began stalking the bench. I realized our lives might depend on a mouse who was only seconds away from being eaten.

I rubbed my feet together frantically until one of my shoes came off. Then I hooked the shoe with my toes and tossed it. I was aiming for the cat, but the shoe did a high pop-up and hit Frankie in the head. The mouse squeaked and dodged behind a nearby coil of rope.

"Brilliant!" Frankie snarled.

The cat slunk under the bench and looked up at the spot where the mouse was hiding. I ripped off my other shoe, got a better grip on it, and launched it toward the bench. It came down in front of the cat. The cat looked at it calmly, glanced at me, and yawned.

"Puss puss puss," said Tom in a sweet little voice, and when the cat tilted its head toward him, Tom spat something out of his mouth that looked like a bullet and caught the cat right between the eyes. The cat did a somersault, sputtered and hissed in ten different cat languages, and raced to the back of the barn.

"Not bad," admitted Frankie, and then went into something that looked like a trance, her eyes focused on the bench in front of her.

The mouse crept cautiously from behind the rope and tippy-toed back to the bracelet. He dragged it to the edge; three charms went over the side, and their weight caused the bracelet to drop to the floor. The mouse followed it, scurrying down one of the bench legs. He looked at the bracelet like he was afraid of it. Out of the corner of my eye, I could see Frankie nodding encouragement.

The mouse hunkered down inside the bracelet's loop, took a section between two charms in his mouth, and made a few hesitant steps toward Frankie, like a tiny horse with a bit between its teeth. Frankie closed her eyes and her head lolled, as though she had fallen asleep. The mouse scurried behind the post she was tied to, disentangled himself from the bracelet, and ran for the wall of the barn like someone was chasing him with a broom.

Frankie's head snapped up. She slid down to the base of the post, and the bracelet was in her hands.

CHAPTER 9
First Folio, Now This

"You gotta be kidding," I said.

"You never told us what your psychic talent is," said Tom.

"You can talk to animals," I guessed.

"I can sometimes get simple minds to think things they wouldn't ordinarily think," explained Frankie as the sound of a blade sawing into rope came from behind her. The bracelet jangled a bit as she cut. "It helps if the mind is already inclined to do what I want. Melvin, there, was a mouse just aching to have an adventure."

"His name is Melvin?"

"Possibly. Why shouldn't it be?"

"Couldn't you control the cat?" asked Tom.

"The cat was too intent on dinner. There was no reasoning with it. Once you hit it with...whatever it was you hit it with...I was able to increase its terror enough to send it on its way."

"What was that, exactly?" I asked Tom. "That you had in your mouth?"

"My quarter. I hid it there, because we need it to flip whenever we consult the *I-Ching*. That, and it had a modern date stamped on it. It wouldn't have been good if those guys had found it."

It took Frankie ten minutes of concentrated sawing before the strands snapped and she could pull the rope off her wrists. She massaged her hands, and then she untied Tom and me.

"We have to get the Shagbolt back," she declared, reattaching the bracelet to her wrist. "Otherwise, we're stuck here!"

I tucked my phone in my pocket and handed Tom his. As I put my shoes back on, Tom searched the floor and found his quarter.

"Leave nothing!" Frankie commanded, retrieving the assassinated flashlight from its resting place and gathering up all its shattered pieces of plastic. "We have to be very careful we don't change history. Even a broken flashlight could make a mess of future events."

Tom picked up Frankie's backpack. He curiously unzipped it, and a handful of resealable plastic bags fluttered out.

"Those *hydrostatic* hoodlums stole your sandwiches!" Tom declared, bending to pick them up.

"What?"

"The bags are empty!"

"I didn't bring sandwiches. Those are acid-neutral archival bags. Good for protecting books."

"They are?" Tom brightened. "Can I have one?"

"Take as many as you want. Just so long as you leave me two."

"I only need one," Tom said gratefully.

I eased the barn door open an inch and looked out. There was no one around, and the three of us slipped into late-afternoon sun.

From outside, the barn had a visible lean to it, like it might fall over at any moment. Not too far away was the stone foundation and half-toppled chimney of a house that had apparently burned down. Killbreath had mentioned a place called the Hole. That pretty well described it.

"If slave catching is a legal profession," I asked no one in particular, "why do these guys need a hideout?"

"Because Ohio is the Grand Central Station of the Underground Railroad," Tom answered. "There are enough abolitionists around who want to help escaped slaves get safely north to Canada that Killbreath and his boys could find themselves in a real fight if they did what they're doing openly."

"So you *do* manage to learn things in that mausoleum." Frankie nodded approvingly. "You two know the area. Which way do we go?"

I looked around. There were no recognizable landmarks, not even a road. The ground was rocky and hard-packed; there were no hoofprints to follow. The only sign of horses was a faint aroma.

"Beats me," I said apologetically.

Tom flipped his quarter in the air.

"No," I said.

"Yes," he replied, picking up a stick and drawing a broken *yin* line in the dirt. "The *I-Ching* is talking to us. We should listen to it."

"Those guys could come back at any moment," I said, looking around for the best places to hide.

"Make it quick," Frankie said to Tom.

He flipped his coin five more times and wound up with a hexagram that looked like this:

"'Hexagram twenty,'" Tom read from the index of the *I-Ching* book. "Page seventy-one...the hexagram is called *Observing and Contemplating.*"

HEXAGRAM *20*

OBSERVING AND CONTEMPLATING.

SPOT THE DIFFERENCES. UNDERSTAND
WHAT YOU SEE. PAY ATTENTION
TO WHAT YOU'RE DOING. YOU CAN
REPLACE AN AA BATTERY WITH A
CHAPSTICK, BUT THAT DOESN'T MEAN
THE RADIO WILL PLAY.

"More ancient wisdom," I muttered sarcastically.

"It's two dashes, followed by two dots, followed by three dots, followed by a final three dots. It spells *miss!*" Tom spoke without pausing. "We're *missing* something! We're observing, but we're not contemplating! We have to look around more!"

"How did you figure out the Morse so quickly?" I asked, sensing another mystery.

"Did I? Isn't it obvious?"

"No."

"Well... I don't know. It just came to me."

"Maybe you have more than one talent," Frankie suggested. "Some people do. Maybe you hear phones before they ring, and maybe you see patterns more quickly than the rest of us."

Tom grinned as he tucked the *I-Ching* book into his newly acquired archival bag and sealed it shut.

"I don't know what it is we could have missed," I said. "There's no way of knowing which way those jerks went." I sniffed. "They... *Wait!*" Suddenly it dawned on me. "Road apples!"

"They rode what?" asked Tom.

"Road apples. It's what my father calls horse manure. You can smell it! It's fresh! Look around and find it!"

Frankie located it about ten feet from where we were standing. It had been well hidden by the overgrown grass.

"One big road apple in a line with two smaller ones. The

horse went in the direction of the two smaller ones," I said, feeling like I had finally contributed something.

"How do you know this, Kemosabe?" asked Tom.

"When I was six, I was crazy about the pony rides at Zane Grey Park. I guess they made an impression."

"And here I was, thinking you had nothing to offer," said Frankie.

"What's that supposed to mean?"

She didn't reply and took off in the direction I had indicated. We followed her, and about a hundred yards later there was some soft ground that had picked up fresh hoofprints, proving I was right. Another hundred feet and we found the parallel wagon ruts of what, in that time and place, passed for a road. We jogged along it for what might have been half a mile and finally came to a house.

"That's...familiar," said Tom.

"Yeah," I agreed, studying the white two-story building with its steeply pitched roof. "It's the central part of the old Willets place. I guess they eventually added wings on both sides, and solar panels, but that house is still standing back in our time."

"So, if that's the Willets place, this has to be Davison Road we're on," reasoned Tom.

In our time, Davison Road had some of Freedom Falls' oldest homes on it.

"That guy Bert said something about runners hiding out at the Coopers'," I said. "That's where Killbreath and his boys were going, but before they got there, there was somebody who'd pay good money for a trombone. I don't know of any Cooper family on Davison Road. Maybe they moved away. I have no idea where their house might be."

"Maybe it's not a family named Cooper," said Tom. "Maybe it's a business. A cooper is somebody who makes barrels."

"The Barrelhouse!" I said, and Tom nodded. "It's a restaurant on Davison," I explained to Frankie, "where the road loops down to the river. Or it *will* be on Davison, someday. It's a big rambling brick place that looks like it's been there for ages. It might have been a cooper-maker—"

"Cooperage," Tom corrected me.

"—*cooperage*, way back when. If this is the Willets place, and we stay on Davison, it should take us about fifteen minutes to get there."

"Good," said Frankie, and started walking.

"So," said Tom, catching up to her. "Why Fourteenth Street?"

Frankie pursed her lips and looked up at the sky, like she

didn't really want to discuss it. But she said, "There are lots of bookstores on Fourteenth Street. At least there were in 1852. There's a book I have to get."

"You mean," I said, not believing it, "we stole the Time Trombone so you could go shopping?"

She stopped and whirled on me with her hands on her hips.

"We didn't *steal* the Shagbolt! It belongs to me as much as it does to any member of my family! We're using it so I can replace a rare first edition from my father's book collection, so he doesn't think I'm irresponsible. If he thinks I'm irresponsible, he'll never let me become Keeper of the Shagbolt. I was going to try to convince him before we get to Louisville next week, when I turn thirteen. There was a Keeper in the eighteenth century who was fourteen, and I'm sure I'm much more mature than he was! I mean, his nickname was Barefoot Besnik! The problem is, my father still blames me for what happened to his First Folio. If he finds out I've lost *another* one of his books, he'll never trust me!"

"His first what?" I asked.

"Folio!" said Tom, like she had mentioned the Holy Grail. "A First Folio is a first edition of Shakespeare's plays. That book's, like, four hundred years old! It would be really valuable!"

"Your father has a First Folio?"

"Had. My father collects old books. He's got a trailer full of them."

"What happened to his First Folio?" asked Tom.

"The pigs got it."

"Pigs!"

"The carnival has racing pigs. They're cute, about the size of a football. When I was six, I thought it would be fun if they had a tunnel to run through. So I set the First Folio up like a tent, and they ran through it. Then Iago turned around and ate it."

"Iago is a pig?"

"A total glutton. There was nothing left. And it had been signed by Shakespeare!"

"That's impossible," Tom assured her. "The First Folio was published after Shakespeare's death."

"You really haven't been paying attention, have you?" Frankie gave Tom a pitying look.

"Oh!" Tom's eyes went wide. "Right! You have a time machine."

"Shakespeare actually thanked my father for the loan of the book. He said he couldn't have written the plays without it."

"So now we know who really wrote Shakespeare's plays," Tom said, awestruck.

"Apparently nobody," I said. "And now you've lost some other book of your father's?"

Frankie sighed, and resumed walking. "A mint-condition first edition of Harriet Beecher Stowe's *Uncle Tom's Cabin*, published in two volumes on March 20, 1852. Actually, I only need volume two."

"What happened to it?" I asked. "Did a dancing monkey poop on it?"

"Our carnival doesn't have dancing monkeys. I was reading it as part of my lessons, and two nights ago somebody snuck into my room and took it."

"Really?" I said, trying to keep the disbelief out of my voice. "Are you sure your dog didn't eat it?"

"I don't have a dog! Something woke me around midnight, and there was this tall, thin woman dressed all in black, like a ninja—even her head was wrapped; all I could see was her eyes—and she was taking the book off my desk. Just volume two."

"Maybe she'd already read volume one," said Tom.

"Did you scream?" I asked Frankie.

"I would have, but she turned to me and raised a finger to her lips. That, and the dagger on her belt, made me think I'd be smart to keep my mouth shut. She unbolted my door and let herself out. I lay awake for hours after that. It was very upsetting."

"So a ninja snuck in through a window just to steal the second half of a book? That makes no sense!" There was something wrong with her story. I thought maybe she was covering up some new stupid thing she'd done, and my idea about a pooping monkey might be closer to the truth.

"And I *so* want to be the Shagbolt's Keeper!"

"Does it have a current Keeper?" asked Tom.

"If it does," I said, "they're not very good at it."

"There hasn't been a Keeper for the past three years!" Frankie was indignant. "Ever since my cousin Donka married an outsider, left the carnival, and bought a house in Pasadena. My father thinks the world has changed enough that we no longer need the Shagbolt with us at all times, but he's wrong! There should always be a Keeper of the Shagbolt, who practices with it and is ready to play it at a moment's notice whenever danger threatens."

"What kind of danger are we talking about?" asked Tom, glancing around. The trees loomed close to the road. Anything could be lurking behind them.

"Back in 1940, my great-grandfather was Keeper of the Shagbolt," said Frankie, and there was no doubting the pride in her voice. "The Camlos were camped out in the Ardennes forest in Belgium, and Nazi troops came crashing through the trees and surrounded them. My family would have been killed, or thrown into a concentration camp, but Great-Granddad played eight notes on the Shagbolt, and everybody—forty-three Camlos and eighteen others related by marriage—got whisked away to a safe place five thousand years earlier. They had all agreed to think about the Salisbury Plain in England on the day of the summer solstice, and that's where they went. They stayed for a few weeks and made friends with the local people, and after they left, the locals built a stone monument where their camp had been."

"Stonehenge!" said Tom.

"Actually, the locals, in their language, called it the Blocks o' Fun Adventure Park. But yes. Stonehenge."

"Every one of those Camlos had a psychic talent?" I asked.

"You're not allowed to marry into my family unless you do," said Frankie, and her eyes narrowed. Then she shook her head as if something had upset her. The sound of wagon wheels crunching on gravel came from the bend behind us.

"Off the road!" Frankie snapped, and pushed us into the bushes.

A farm wagon laden with hay trundled into view, going

in the direction we were headed. It was pulled by two muscular gray workhorses and driven by a drowsy-looking farmer. When it was almost past, Frankie launched herself from our hiding place, caught the tailgate, and chinned herself into the hay. Tom and I broke cover the moment we realized what she was doing, grabbed the tailgate, and joined her.

We worked our way into the hay, then stuck out our heads along the wagon's left side, where, sooner or later, the cooperage would come into view. The side-view mirror had yet to be invented, so the wagon's driver had no way of knowing we were there.

"We probably could've gotten there faster on foot," said Frankie quietly. "But the way we look, and the way we're dressed, we're much better off if we stay hidden. Keep your eye out for any place where Killbreath might have sold the Shagbolt."

We passed a tiny house with a ramshackle chimney, and it reminded me of something that had been bugging me.

"*Uncle Tom's Cabin?*" I said. "The slavery book?"

"What about it?"

"My social studies teacher says it's a bad book. He says it shows the slaves as either happy-go-lucky idiots who are always dancing around, or as stupidly loyal to the monsters who think they own them. Why would you be reading that?"

"*Uncle Tom's Cabin* convinced a lot of people that slavery should end," Tom said before Frankie could open her mouth. "It's an important piece of history."

"That's probably why my father put it on my reading list," said Frankie.

Tom pointed at the house we were passing. It was an elegant two-story job with a white picket fence and a neatly lettered sign saying MUSIC LESSONS.

"There might be somebody there who'd buy a trombone," he said.

"Remember this spot," said Frankie. "We'll double back if we don't see any place more likely."

We passed three girls in long dresses who were leaning against a rail fence near the roadside as if they were watching a parade. Their faces were hidden in the depths of their bonnets. One of them started to wave, but the one next to her slapped her hand down. The wagon swayed as it rounded a bend, and they were gone.

"WHOA THERE!" bellowed a gruff and alarmingly familiar voice. We pulled our heads back into the hay and rearranged the strands so we could still look out and see what was going on.

The slave catcher who had originally lassoed Tom—we had later heard Killbreath call him Zack—had stepped out from behind a tree as the wagon approached, and leveled a shotgun at the driver. The wagon came to an abrupt stop.

"What is this?" demanded the driver.

"Jus' hold it right there, Mr. Collins. Stay where you are!" said Zack, dropping the shotgun into the crook of one arm and, with the other, snatching up a pitchfork from where it leaned against the tree.

He strode to the side of the wagon and drove the fork into the hay like he was harpooning a whale.

CHAPTER 10
Runners

Collins slipped from his perch atop the wagon, raised a cloud of dust as his boots hit the road, and approached Zack angrily.

"What the Sam Hill do you think you're doing? You've no right!"

Zack thrust the fork in again, about a foot back from the location of his first poke.

"Got every right, Mr. Collins," said Zack amiably. "I's a *bonny-fide* slave catcher, thanks to that ol' 1850 Compromise. It's the oldest trick in the book, hidin' in a wagonload o' hay!"

I realized something *had* felt familiar, even as we were jumping on the wagon. It *was* the oldest trick in the book. I had seen it many times on TV. Zack lunged at the hay a third time. At the rate he was going, in a few more lunges, one of us was going to be losing an eye, or possibly gaining a nostril. All three of us wiggled deeper.

"I object," growled Collins, catching the fork in mid-thrust and forcing Zack back toward the roadside.

"On what grounds?"

"I don't like my hay all fluffed up and airy. It'll make the cows burp. Nothin' I hate more than the sound of burping cows. Unless it's the self-serving drivel of a slave catcher!"

Zack yanked the fork from Collins's grip and sidled away far enough so he could raise the shotgun. Collins looked down the twin muzzles, put up his hands, and stepped back.

"Sorry 'bout that," snarled Zack. "But I got a job to do!"

He speared the hay again, close to the middle.

"Might be they's people hidin' in here and you know nothin' 'bout it," Zack said generously. "Might be."

He poked the fork in yet again, and this time a voice that wasn't Frankie's or Tom's or mine went, "Oww!"

Zack looked triumphant. He started to pull out the fork, but before he could, it was yanked from his hand and disappeared into the hay. He brought his shotgun to his shoulder and aimed at the spot where it had vanished.

"All right, you!" he barked, but before he could continue, the fork's handle shot out and hit him in the eye. He staggered back, and Collins grabbed the shotgun and tried to wrestle it away from him.

As a test of strength, it was pretty even. The men were in a tug-of-war over the gun, and circled around each other down the length of the wagon and then butted up against the side of one of the horses. The horse barely moved, although its tail flicked as though a fly might be bothering it. Collins and Zack rotated around each other one more time and came even with the horse's head, the shotgun pointed skyward and trembling next to the animal's ear.

I was pretty sure I knew what was about to happen, and it wasn't going to be good. I grabbed Frankie's hand and felt around for Tom's, hoping we'd have time to jump before—

The gun went off.

Zack and Collins were knocked to the ground as the terrified horse reared, whinnying. The second horse reared, too, and then both animals were galloping full speed down the road, the driverless wagon careening madly behind them like a runaway locomotive. I tumbled over Frankie and crashed into Tom, and then the two of us slid back into her, like we were playing Twister in an actual twister.

The wagon lurched violently, half the hay fell out, and we broke the surface of the remaining hay like three swimmers coming up for air. I tried a backstroke to get to the front, but I was tossed to one side instead. My stomach pitched one way, I pitched the other, and I tried not to get seasick, but it wasn't easy.

Once I righted myself, I realized that we were going too fast to jump. If the horses collided with anything bigger than a sapling, body parts would fly through the air, and not all of them would belong to the horses.

"We have to stop this!" I shouted over the deafening clatter of spinning wheels and thundering hooves. We were clutching the wagon's sides—Frankie and me on the right, Tom on the left—trying to keep the vicious swaying from knocking us back down.

"How?" Frankie screamed back at me.

"Do that trick you did with the mouse!"

"With stampeding horses? Are you crazy?"

I decided it was up to me. And the only thing I could think of was completely nuts.

I took a faltering step toward the front, and a hay monster

rose up in front of me. The mound shook itself, sent straw flying, and turned into a broad-shouldered young man in tattered clothing. He had to be a runner—an escaped slave—who had been hiding in the wagon even before we hopped on. He reached into the hay and pulled a woman into the daylight. She was pregnant and dressed as raggedly as he was. Blood streaked her arm along a gash that looked like it might have been made by a pitchfork.

Since I wanted to make our situation crystal clear, I shouted, "We're all gonna die!" and gestured frantically at the flying landscape.

Hay Monster gave one calm glance to the fence posts whizzing by, handed the woman to me and Frankie, and turned to the wagon's front.

"Seth drives Master Landry's coach!" the woman informed us. "He's good with horses!" She pulled a kerchief from her head and started tying it around her pitchfork wound.

I felt a glimmer of hope. As I watched Seth climb from the wagon bed up to the spring-mounted driver's bench, I saw the muscles ripple across his back. If anybody could rein in two insane horses, it would be Seth. He eased himself over the seat, caught up the reins, and stood like a colossus with his legs braced well apart.

Seth might have been good with horses, but he was terrible with trees. A low-hanging branch caught him in the middle and swept him over our heads, and in moments he was disappearing down the road behind us, a surprised look on his face.

"Great," I said under my breath, and returned to my original plan, which involved suicide.

I let go of the woman, who had become hysterical the moment Seth flew past us, and allowed Frankie to support her fully. I floundered through the hay to the driver's seat.

I didn't make Seth's mistake and climb up into the seat. Instead, I braced my knees against the wagon wall and grabbed the reins that had been helpfully stretched within reach by Seth's sudden departure. I hauled back on them with all my might and hollered "WHOA!" at the top of my lungs.

The horses went faster.

"Tree!" screamed Frankie, as if I couldn't see it hurtling toward us.

I yanked the reins to the left and the horses veered, crashing through a picket fence surrounding the yard of a three-story house. Four clotheslines stretched across our path, heavy with dresses, and we broke through all four lines, snapping them like string, the clothing draping itself around the horses and wagon like bunting on a float in the Run for Your Life parade.

An apron plastered itself to my face, blinding me, and I clawed it away. I didn't want anything blocking my view of the barn we were about to hit.

Tom came up beside me and added his strength to the reins. We pulled back on the right side as hard as we could, and the horses turned just enough to miss the barn, the wagon knocking shingles off the corner.

Ahead of us, through the trees, I could see the building that would one day be the Barrelhouse restaurant. It was low and long and made of brick, and there were towers of barrels in the yard around it. Beyond the cooperage, the ground sloped down to a pier that jutted into the river, with a flatboat docked at its end. Men were loading barrels onto the boat.

The horses made a beeline for the pier. If we reached it at the speed we were going, we'd sail right down its length, fly off the end, and crash into the boat. More likely, we'd hit the rocks that formed a breakwater on either side of the pier's entrance. Either way, I was pretty sure we'd be dead.

I let go of the reins and scrambled into the driver's seat. The horses crossed the edge of the cooperage's yard. Ahead of us, Killbreath and Bert emerged from around a stack of barrels. Killbreath raised his hand like a policeman who wanted a car to stop. He might even have said "Halt!"

Then barrels were tumbling down on them as the horses nicked the edge of the stack, and Bert fell beneath a plummeting keg.

Killbreath lunged at us as we passed and caught the side of the wagon.

"No you don't!" shouted Frankie, and raked her bracelet across his fingers.

He dropped off and was almost run over by one of the rear wheels. The wagon barely missed another pyramid of barrels, swerved around a woodpile, and bore down on the rapidly approaching pier.

I grabbed the brake.

I had forgotten that wagons had brakes, although I had known it when I was younger—since Zane Grey Park had a wagon ride as well as pony rides. Unfortunately, the brake isn't used to stop a moving wagon; it's used to keep a wagon from rolling when it's already stopped. Only a lunatic would throw the brake while the horses were running.

I hurled my weight against the lever next to the driver's seat, and hard wood blocks jammed themselves against the metal rims of the wagon's wildly spinning front wheels. The wheels kept spinning. A screeching drowned out all the rest of the world's noises, and the front of the wagon shimmied as the smell of scorched wood filled the air.

The horses thundered onto the pier, narrowly missing the rocks on the right, and the wagon's front wheels locked. I saw the rear of the wagon rise up and I was certain we were about to go end over end. I said a short, end-over-end prayer.

"Not good!" screamed Frankie.

Tom jumped up and planted his feet squarely on the back of the driver's seat, leaned back until he was straight out, and pulled on the reins with his full body weight. The wagon's rear end dropped back, and we skidded behind the horses like a sled. The ringing in my ears turned briefly to "Jingle Bells."

The brake handle trembled in my hands like it was about to explode, and I wrapped myself completely around it until *I* was trembling like I was about to explode. If the brake handle broke, we were done for.

We were slowing. But we were also running out of pier.

The men down the end, loading barrels on the flatboat, looked up, shouted, and dived into the water. The horses dropped from a gallop to a canter to a trot, and then there was no more pier. They dug in their hooves and reared, once, twice, and the third time pushed the wagon back just enough to give them room to stand without tumbling forward into the boat.

The horses did a little side step against each other and finally calmed. Then, like two enormous, revolting Pez dispensers, both tails lifted and a load of road apples tumbled out.

"Is everybody all right?" I asked, and Frankie shook her head and pointed. I turned to see Killbreath and Bert running down the hill, waving guns, heading for the pier.

"Oooh, that was a kick," said Seth's friend, and I thought she was telling us how much she had enjoyed the ride until I saw she was holding her swollen tummy and gazing lovingly down at it. I had seen pregnant ladies do that before. I always found it a little creepy.

"Okay," I said, jumping to the pier and going to my knees when my legs refused to hold me. I staggered to the rear of the wagon and pulled out the pins that held up the tailgate.

The gate dropped, and Frankie and Tom slid out in a cascade of hay. All three of us reached up and, as gently as we could, helped our new friend get down.

"Thank you very much," she said, dusting herself off. "We have to go back for Seth."

I turned and looked at the riverbank. There was no way

we were going to get to it before our pursuers reached the end of the pier and cut us off. I glanced farther up the hill and my heart sank.

"They've got him," I said.

Seth was trudging down the slope, his hands held over his head. Zack was walking behind him with the shotgun. I wondered what had happened to Mr. Collins. It couldn't have been anything good.

"We're going to have to swim for it," said Frankie.

"Can't swim," said our new friend, and she reached up and twisted a piece of her hair around one finger. I felt my heart do a little flip-flop: My mom did the exact same thing with her hair whenever she was upset. Suddenly, I wanted to reassure this woman that everything was going to be fine. I wished I could do it without lying to her.

"My name is Ambrose," I said, looking up into her eyes. "My friends call me Bro. Is it that you can't swim, or you don't want to leave Seth?"

"Both. I'm Dwina. Seth is my man, and I'm staying with him!" She nodded at the shore. "You three should go. Now!" She turned me by the shoulders and gently pushed me toward the water. I could feel her hands trembling. She was terrified but putting on a brave face.

"She's right," agreed Frankie. "The longer we stay here, the bigger the chance is that we'll do something that will change the future. We have to get going!"

"What if we untie the boat and take that?" suggested Tom. "You'd join us in a boat, right?" he asked Dwina.

"No," she said. "Not without my Seth."

A strangely familiar voice over my phone, in a place where reception should have been impossible, had warned me not to let Dwina drown. Trying to teach her to swim, or even taking her on a boat ride, didn't sound like smart choices.

"We're not leaving you!" I assured her, and shot Frankie a glance.

Frankie looked from the shore to the water and grimaced. I could see she was torn. But after a moment she muttered, "All right; have it your way. We stay. But this is exactly the sort of situation the Shagbolt was made for, *and I can't believe we don't have it!*"

Killbreath and Bert could see they had us trapped. They slowed, stopped, and waited for Zack and Seth to join them. Killbreath watched us keenly across the distance, as if he expected us to do something foolish. We were good at that. He was right to keep an eye out.

Tom sat down on the pier and started flipping his quarter.

He laid out a broken piece of hay for every tail and an unbroken piece for every head. I studied the pier and asked myself what it would take to turn the horses and wagon around so that they faced the other way. The answer was—a much wider pier.

Frankie sniffed. "Do you smell something?"

"That's my sweat," I said apologetically.

"No, besides that." Frankie's brow furrowed, and she looked back to a spot on the pier where our flying wagon had dislodged half a dozen planks. "I wonder..."

"Hexagram five," said Tom, waving at his strands of hay.

"The hexagram is called *Waiting*," he continued, and turned the book so we could see.

HEXAGRAM 5

WAITING.

CALCULATED INACTION. BIDE ONE'S
TIME. BE THE BUMP ON THE LOG.

WAIT FOR THE TICK, WAIT FOR THE
TOCK, AND THE NEXT TICK YOU SEE
MAY BE THE OTHER GUY BLINKING.

"Is there a...Morse code message?" I couldn't believe I heard myself ask.

Tom gave a quick nod, like he was a little bit frightened. But then, we were about to be captured by slave catchers, so he had every reason to be. "Yes. It's two dots, followed by a dash and two dots, followed by three final dashes. It's Morse code for *I do*." He swallowed hard. "Don't ask me how I figured that out so quickly. I just did. And I think it's a personal message for me. It's telling me that in this particular situation, I wait. That's what I DO."

"You can wait if you want," I growled. "I say we rush them. We can use the wagon's tailgate as a shield—"

Frankie grabbed me by the wrist, as if she expected me to run down the pier that instant.

"They've got guns!" she hissed. "We're going to wait! We're going to do what the *I-Ching* says. We have to make those creeps come to us."

Zack and Seth had met up with Killbreath and Bert. Killbreath holstered his pistol and used the butt of Zack's gun to deliver a blow to the back of Seth's neck, causing him to fall to his knees.

The nineteenth century had way too many guns in it, as far as I was concerned. Or, at least, the people I didn't like had way too many of them. It occurred to me that this was probably true of the twenty-first century, too. I just hadn't noticed.

Killbreath handed the shotgun back to Zack, then yanked Seth to his feet and shoved him down the slope in front of him. The four of them marched down the hill until they stood at the entrance to the pier.

"That there was a merry chase," hollered Killbreath, twirling his pistol at the end of his finger. "Fun's over. Time we all got goin'. You so much as look like you're gonna jump"—he fired the pistol in the air and we all shuddered—"and I'll use this! Now, get yer tails over here!"

Dwina took a step forward. I snatched her by the elbow and pulled her back.

"You're not going to shoot another man's property, are you?" Frankie called out. "We're all worth more to you alive than dead! And if we're maimed, I'm sure we'd have to be discounted!"

"Well now, don't you jus' talk all ed-you-cated!" Killbreath waggled his head from side to side. "That's enough to get you strung up, and whosomever it was ed-you-cated you as well. You wanna live, where I'm takin' you, you jus' better watch your smart-talkin' mouth!"

Killbreath pushed Seth into Zack's hands, stepped onto the pier, and gestured for Bert to follow. The two men strode purposefully toward us.

"I'm not going back to Tara," muttered Dwina. "Too many flighty womenfolk there."

Behind us, the horses stirred uneasily. The pier creaked ominously. I became aware of the aroma Frankie had mentioned, and was pleased to find it wasn't me.

Killbreath and his sidekick stopped about a hundred feet away from us. They were on the far side of the loose planking.

"I ain't so sure we'd get anythin' for the Chinese kid," Killbreath announced, and aimed his pistol at Tom. "So I'm thinkin' losin' him would be no loss whatsumever." He cocked the gun. "You others got 'til the count of three to get yerselves over here."

"Waiting," said Tom.

"What was that?" Killbreath scowled.

"Waiting," Tom repeated, a little louder, and I could see he was trembling.

"Waitin' fer what?"

Frankie stepped in front of Tom and answered for him.

"Waiting for you to act like a man and not some lily-livered... *bickwidus* and come over here and get us yourself!"

Killbreath stalked toward us, glowering as though he planned to whip us all when he arrived, and Bert trailed in his wake. As they cleared the loose planking, Frankie announced, "I smell a skunk!"

"I been called worse!" Killbreath sneered.

"I'm sure you have, but I wasn't talking about you!"

The pier exploded behind them as the planks erupted into the air and a soaking-wet, nine-foot-tall hairy giant wearing Bermuda shorts and a Hawaiian shirt shot up from the depths below and slapped the guns from Killbreath and Bert as they turned to see what the commotion was.

Both men screamed as Mr. Ganto clutched them by the arms and dragged them down the hole he had punched in the pier. All three dropped from sight, Killbreath and Bert flailing their arms and legs, their screams abruptly ending in a loud *splash!*

The horses went berserk.

CHAPTER 11
Pier Pressure

The horses reared. Their front legs waved in the air as if they were trying to climb an invisible mountain, and their hind legs rippled with muscle as they pushed backward on the wagon. The axle twisted sideways and the wagon jolted back, cockeyed, hitting one of the pier posts and splitting it away from the plank floor. The horses' front hooves came crashing back down, and the whole pier shook.

They reared again, and I felt the pier sway beneath us. Frankie got into her surfboard-riding stance, Tom went down on one knee, and Dwina threw her hands across her belly. I danced two steps to the left, closer to Dwina.

The pier's posts had probably been rotten to begin with. The passage of the runaway wagon had weakened them, and the hole Mr. Ganto had made hadn't helped. When the horses' hooves came down a second time, the pier collapsed.

Everything forward of the hole broke away, twisted to one side, and tumbled into the water, moving slowly at first and then picking up speed like the climax of a log-flume ride. The pier came apart beneath me, and a plank hit me on the side of the head. A horrendous screeching filled the air, and then I couldn't hear because I was underwater.

I spun sideways, thrashing, and the air I had gulped before going under burst from my mouth. I started to drown. I followed my bubbles—they knew where "up" was—and four strong strokes got me to the surface.

I spat out water, sputtered, and looked around for my friends. The only people I could see were Seth and Zack on the riverbank, wrestling the shotgun back and forth. The horses were submerged up to their necks, the water white and churning all around them. I couldn't see Frankie or Tom or Dwina.

I knew Tom could swim. I had no idea whether Frankie could. Dwina had stated flat out that she couldn't, and all I could think of was that finger-in-her-hair thing she had done that reminded me so much of my mom. I tried to remember exactly where she had been standing before the world fell out from under us. I picked a likely spot and dived.

The collapse of the pier had raised clouds of silt from the river bottom, making everything shadowy and misshapen. I wondered if Mr. Ganto and his captives had been pinned beneath the rubble. I didn't think anyone could save them if they had been.

Suddenly I swam into something soft. I backstroked in a panic, at first not realizing what I had hit, but then the silt cleared and Dwina's face appeared in front of me, the way my mother's sometimes does when she's trying to wake me up, all hazy around the edges. Dwina was upright, as though her feet were tethered to the riverbed, her hair floating above her head like her soul trying to leave her body. Her eyes were closed. It looked like her soul might already have left.

My lungs were giving me hints they weren't enjoying themselves. I dropped down to Dwina's ankles near the bottom of the river and discovered her left foot was pinned between two of the pier's planks. I grabbed one of the planks and freed the foot. I expected her to rise, but she didn't— grown-ups almost never do what you want them to—so I dropped into a squatting position, thrust my legs down with all my might, and pushed myself upward, catching Dwina under the arms and taking her with me.

We broke the surface to the sound of a gunshot. Whether it was aimed at us I had no idea, and I didn't have time to look around to find out. I took a deep breath, got an arm around Dwina, and started swimming for the shore.

It was a short distance, but I was beginning to feel the way I do when I run too many laps in gym class. I hit my head against a floating barrel and nearly blacked out, but then hands pushed the barrel out of the way and latched on to Dwina from the other side.

It was Frankie. We linked hands under Dwina—Frankie squeezed my hand in hers, and it somehow gave me an energy boost—and together the three of us got to the riverbank.

We staggered up the bank, hauling Dwina between us as gently as we could, until we were able to lay her out on a grassy patch. Frankie immediately straddled her and started rhythmically pounding the center of her chest, performing CPR. Tom floundered out of the water about thirty feet downriver. He appeared to have a fish in his mouth.

I looked up and saw Seth running toward us, waving the shotgun in one hand. There was no sign of Zack anywhere. I realized with a jolt that CPR didn't exist in the nineteenth century, and to Seth, it probably looked like we were attacking Dwina.

I jumped up and threw myself in front of him.

"We're trying to help! We're trying to help!" I caught the shotgun with both hands and found myself hoisted in the air as Seth raised it over his head. I could tell he wanted to use it to swat Frankie away from Dwina, but he couldn't as long as I was dangling from it. He shook me violently, but I managed to hold on, so he dropped the gun and I fell with it. He took a threatening step toward Frankie.

Dwina coughed and water fountained out of her mouth. Frankie rolled off her, and Seth slid to his knees and scooped Dwina into his arms. Dwina sputtered and shook, and her eyes flew open.

"Lordy!" she exclaimed.

"You folks all right?" I heard a familiar voice and turned to see Mr. Collins, the driver of the hay wagon, approaching at the front of a group of five other men. Seth tensed as they approached, but Collins put up a reassuring hand and said, "It's okay, Seth; they're with me. They're all members of the Friends Meeting. Is the lady all right?"

Dwina was standing, lightly supported by Seth. She patted her prominent tummy, grinned, and said, "Still kicking!"

I had forgotten I was holding the shotgun until Collins eased it out of my hands.

"I sure will see to it that Zack gets his gun back," Collins assured us. "Someday. He was running so fast he's probably in the next county by now. Did you pull the trigger, or did he?"

"He did," said Seth. "Shot went wild."

"Just as well," said a man behind me.

"We'll get all of you north of the river by nightfall," promised Collins, gesturing to include Frankie and me, then nodding toward Tom, who was standing to one side, wringing out his shirttail. The fishlike thing in his mouth turned out to be the plastic bag with his *I-Ching* book in it. "But right now, we've got two horses that need rescuing."

"I swim good," said Seth, by way of volunteering.

"We'd be grateful for the help," said Collins appreciatively.

The discussion turned to the best way to get the horses unhitched and out of the water. Frankie and Tom and I started taking tiny steps back up the hill the moment we thought no one was looking.

"You think the Time Trombone might be at the cooperage?" asked Tom, sounding like he hoped it wasn't.

"Either there or nearby," replied Frankie.

"You need fixing," said Dwina, catching me by surprise

when I nearly backed into her. She took me by the elbow and raised my arm, peeling back the ripped sleeve of my sweatshirt and exposing a wrist that, much to my surprise, was bloody. I had no idea how I had done it. "I'll clean you up," she announced, steering me toward the river. "I saw some *hushpain* growing by the water."

She washed my forearm, exposing a jagged cut that continued to bleed after she was finished. I squeezed it shut with one hand while Dwina busied herself sorting through a tangle of weeds growing on the riverbank, from which she plucked a spiky purple plant. She snapped the stem and squeezed the sap over my cut, and after a brief tingling, the pain went away and the bleeding slowed, then stopped. She tore a strip of cloth from her apron and tied it as a bandage around my wrist, using a knot I had never seen before. It looked like a flower.

"There," she said, and for the first time our eyes met. "Oh. You're just a boy."

"I'm twelve," I said.

"You speak well. Can you read?"

"Yes."

"Never tell anyone who taught you. Miss Butterfield

taught me, and some others, and they found out and punished her by sending her away. Forced her to marry a man she
did not want."

"I don't think that will happen to any of my teachers," I
said. "They have a union."

"You free?" she asked, turning my hands over and studying them. "Never done work?"

I thought I had worked quite a bit. But I understood what
she meant. I had never chopped wood, or dug holes, or done
anything to rough up my hands. All I had was a slight callus
on my lip that said I played the trumpet.

"Yeah," I said, "all three of us," nodding my head to
include Frankie and Tom, who had joined us. "You're free,
too, now."

"Maybe. I'm not one to count chickens. We need to be
farther north." She searched my face. "My Haki would have
been twelve."

"Haki?"

"My brother. He died on the boat, the day before we got
here. They tossed him."

"They . . . tossed him?"

Dwina frowned and looked away. Frankie put a hand

gently on her shoulder and explained, "She's saying the crew of the slave ship got rid of her brother's body by throwing it in the sea. He probably starved on the voyage."

Dwina nodded once, and the silence stretched. Then she looked back at me and somehow managed a smile. "Now you're leaking again! You are just the leakingest boy!" She wiped my cheek with her thumb.

"I promise you," I said, "things are going to get better."

"Oh, yes? You know? You got the Sight?"

It took me a moment to figure out what she was asking. Then my answer surprised me.

"Yes. I do."

Dwina reached out and held me under the chin, searching my eyes the way my mother did whenever she wanted to see if I was telling the truth.

"Might be," she decided. "How better?"

"There's going to be an end to slavery," I said, wishing I could tell her how her own life was going to work out—wishing I knew. "And someday—I'm not saying it will be *total* or anything, but—there's going to be less prejudice."

"I don't know what that is."

"Actually, you do," said Frankie, easing Dwina's hand away from my chin. "But Rose likes using fancy words."

"They call you Rose?" asked Dwina, and she looked so delighted, I couldn't protest. "That's a good name!" She looked down at her belly.

Someone shouted *huzzah!* from the direction of the river and we turned to see Seth and Collins and the others turning the horses toward the shore. Someone—most likely Seth—had managed to swim underwater and unhitch them.

"Dwina," said Frankie, "the three of us have to go. You should be all right with these men. They seem to be good people."

"We can't just leave her!" I said under my breath. "We should at least make sure she gets safely away from Freedom Falls!"

"Seth is here. I will be fine," said Dwina. "You three go do what you need to do. Stay free! Never tell anyone the names of your teachers!"

Frankie squeezed her shoulder reassuringly, and the three of us started up the hill. After two steps, I turned and ran back and gave her a hug. Frankie eventually tugged on my shirt to pull me away.

We didn't look back until we reached the cover of the trees at the top of the hill.

"So, what does Mr. Ganto have?" Tom asked. "A Time Tuba?"

"What's that supposed to mean?" replied Frankie as she bent down to pick up the end of a piece of rope that was lying on the ground.

"How else was he able to follow us through time?"

"He didn't follow us; he came with us." Frankie pulled the rope to her. It was one of the clotheslines the runaway wagon had snagged and then left behind during its mad trip down the hill. Most of the clothing was still attached to it. Frankie started to coil the rope, removing each item of clothing as she got to it, dropping the clothes in a pile at her feet. "Mr. Ganto has a psychic talent, so the Shagbolt affects him. He's clairolfacient."

"He can...change the color of his hair?" Tom guessed.

"He can smell things that are thousands of miles away."

"If he came with us, why didn't we see him, and where's he been all this time?" I asked, forgetting about Dwina enough to join the conversation.

"He was probably outside the school when I played the Shagbolt," said Frankie. "The farther you are from the horn, the longer it takes you to catch up with everybody else. He would have arrived at Nellie's Erratic an hour or two after we did, so he had to track us down and then figure out the best way to save us. I'm sure he loved pulling those bullies through the hole in the floor. *Don Giovanni* is his favorite opera."

"*Don Giovanni* is an opera about people being pulled through holes in the floor?" Tom asked.

"Mostly. Yes. See if this fits you." Frankie handed me a floor-length dress.

"What?"

"Our clothes are attracting too much attention," Frankie explained. "I shouldn't be wearing pants, and your sweatshirts make you look like you're running around in pajamas."

"I'm not putting on a girl's dress!" I protested.

"Listen!" Frankie stamped her foot. "I'm pretty sure I'll get through this all right, but I'm not so sure about either of you! If you two dress like girls, you can wear bonnets, which will hide your faces and make it less likely we'll be bothered by more slave catchers, or even decent people who feel compelled to obey the Fugitive Slave Law just because they were raised to believe every law is good and just. This would be a great dress for you; the color will bring out the hazel flecks in your eyes."

She held the dress out to me and shook it impatiently.

"No!" I said, folding my arms across my chest.

"Look, I'm sorry if this reminds you of your dad—"

"It doesn't!"

"It does, but you won't admit it. You're not the only kid whose parents sometimes embarrass him. Trust me; I know. But I've gotten over it, and you will, too."

She pushed the dress against me. I snatched it from her, gave her an angry glare, and started pulling it over my head.

"Good!" Frankie approved. "These are large sizes; they'll fit better if we put them on over our own clothes."

She handed Tom a dress. I was surprised by how quickly the summer sun had dried out the river water; I was only mildly damp.

"So how did Mr. Ganto join the carnival?" Tom asked as he wiggled into a purple monstrosity that I wouldn't have been caught dead in.

"A couple years before I was born, my family took a vacation in the Pleistocene. An hour or so after they returned to their own time, Mr. Ganto showed up. He's been with us ever since."

"The Pleistocene is a prehistoric epoch," Tom informed me.

"I didn't think it was a town in New Jersey," I said as I tried to pull the dress's waist down from my armpits.

"Does this make me look fat?" Tom asked, turning so I could see him from the rear.

"No. You're fine," I lied.

"The apron has a pocket I can keep the *I-Ching* book in," he said happily, reaching behind his back to tie the apron's strings.

I finished buttoning my dress and found I was annoyed by how well it fit. Frankie handed me an apron similar to Tom's, and I added that to the getup.

"Not bad!" declared Frankie. She had found a dark red dress for herself with a white apron and some sort of frilly collar that I was grateful my dress didn't have. She turned me from side to side, pulling and smoothing the gray fabric, and then flipped a green cloth bonnet onto my head and tied it tightly under my chin. The bonnet stuck out on either side of my face so I could only be seen from straight on. I admitted grudgingly to myself it was a good disguise.

She fidgeted with Tom's outfit a bit, then slapped an equally concealing bonnet on him.

"Do you think Mr. Ganto got crushed when the pier collapsed?" asked Tom, gazing back the way we had come.

"Mr. Ganto is a very powerful swimmer," said Frankie, starting off in the direction of the cooperage. "By the time the pier collapsed, he was probably halfway across the river."

"Do you think he, like, *killed* Bert and Killbreath?" I

asked, falling into step beside her, wondering how girls could move in full-length dresses without tripping and landing on their faces.

"That's not his way. He probably kept them underwater until all the fight was out of them, then hauled them out on the opposite shore and left them there."

We entered the yard in front of the cooperage, where men were restacking the barrels the hay wagon had knocked over. They glanced at us, but continued their work.

"This is where that Chester guy thought runaway slaves were hiding," I said.

"Yes," agreed Frankie. "It's probably a station on the Underground Railroad. Collins, I think, was bringing Seth and Dwina here. Keep an eye out for Killbreath's horse."

"And Chester," Tom reminded us.

We walked across the yard like we had business there, three young girls looking to buy a barrel, or maybe a set of matching kegs to put around a coffee table. On the far side of a woodshed, beneath a chestnut tree, we found four horses tethered to a hitching rail. One of the horses had a trombone case strapped to its saddle.

"That was easy," I said. "I mean, if you ignore the part with the runaway wagon."

I helped Frankie loosen the buckle on the leather strap threaded through the handle, and together we lowered the case to the ground.

"It's too light," muttered Frankie. She undid the latches and flipped open the lid.

The case was empty.

CHAPTER 12
Some Sort of Bizarre Cutting Implement

Lookin' fer somethin', ladies?" inquired a voice behind us, followed by a whooshing sound and the sudden feeling that a fast-moving snake had just coiled itself around my left wrist. My arm jerked back and I was spun around to face Chester. A bullwhip stretched between us. He was holding the whip's more useful end.

"You shouldn't go pokin' round other people's property," Chester informed us, sounding so much like Killbreath it occurred to me they might be related. "'Specially," he added, leaning forward to peer deep into my bonnet, "if you, yerselves, might *be* other people's property! How'd you all escape? What was all that tarnal commotion with the wagon? Where's my brother, an' Bert, an' Zack?"

"The slide horn is *our* property," said Frankie, standing straight and tall, "and we, ourselves, belong to no one. Take your filthy whip off my friend!"

Chester flicked the whip's handle, and a wave undulated down its length, undoing the coil around my wrist. He raised the whip over his head and snarled at Frankie, "Miss Smart Mouth, is it? Maybe you'd like my filthy whip down the side of yer pretty little face!"

Chester cracked the whip in a motion that looked like it would slash Frankie from head to toe. But the whip's end cut through the overhead branches of the chestnut tree and snagged on something. Chester said "Tarnal!" again, and yanked hard on the handle. Instead of the whip coming free, it jerked higher into the branches, pulling Chester off his feet. He went up about a yard and let go, hitting the dirt and dropping into a crouch, staring wide-eyed at the whip's dangling handle.

"What in tarnation?" Chester sputtered.

The handle dropped a foot, Chester sprang to seize it, and a hairy arm with an enormous hand reached down from the tree, caught Chester by the collar, and dragged him into the branches. Chester started to cry out, but his voice faltered and turned to a mumble.

Leaves fluttered down.

"Mr. Ganto?" Frankie inquired.

"You have not been a good girl," the tree rumbled in response.

"No," Frankie agreed. "I haven't. Could you ask that man you're holding what became of the slide horn?"

Through the branches I could just make out Mr. Ganto perched comfortably, one-handedly holding Chester above a twelve-foot drop. Twigs stuck out of Chester's mouth, making it look like he was eating a hedgehog. Mr. Ganto plucked the twigs out, pulling a spiny cluster of horse chestnuts with them.

"S-s-sold it ta B-B-Brinley," Chester managed to stammer.

"Brinley?" asked Ganto.

"W-w-white house, g-g-green shut-shut-shut—"

"Shutters?" Ganto suggested.

Chester nodded and pointed vaguely up the hill.

"Thank you," rumbled Ganto, reinserting the chestnuts like he was putting a cork in a bottle.

"What did you do with the others?" Frankie asked the *Gigantopithecus*.

"Left them. Other side of river. Told them not to come back. I will bring this one to them."

"You're going to swim across the river *again*?" I asked, dumbfounded.

"Trash should be kept together," said Ganto, shaking Chester as if he were a dust rag. "If we let this one run loose, he will cause more trouble. Better he should join the others. I will signal when I return. Please do not leave without me."

The branches of the tree shook, raining down more leaves, as Ganto swung himself and his captive into an adjoining tree and disappeared into the forest.

"Nothing in the fossil record suggests *Gigantopithecus* could talk," said Tom.

"What?" asked Frankie, picking up the trombone case and handing it to me. "You want a jawbone with a comic-book speech balloon coming out of it? They could talk. It's singing you don't want them doing."

We trudged back up the hill to the road where we had first encountered the hay wagon. Houses were spaced out unevenly on either side, and after a few minutes we found the one we had seen with the sign advertising music lessons. The house was white with green shutters.

"This must be the Brinley place," I said. "Should we peek in a window or go up to the door and knock?"

"I think you two are going to hide in some bushes while I go get the Shagbolt back," Frankie said. "You don't look entirely convincing in those dresses."

"No," I said. "Whatever we do, we're doing it together."

"Why don't we see what the *I-Ching* thinks?" asked Tom, pulling the book out of the pocket of his apron. He dug deeper and found his precious quarter.

"The *I-Ching* doesn't *think*," I said irritably. "It's not a person."

"It's talking to us," he replied, jiggling the book in my face. "I shouldn't be the only one listening. This is important!"

I looked to Frankie for support. I could tell she wanted Tom and me to stay out of sight, while she took the risks, but she gnawed on her lip for a moment, then shrugged. "My mother is a crystal-gazer. Who am I to judge?"

"Good!" said Tom, squatting and picking up a stick. "I want us all to concentrate while I flip. Ask yourselves, what is our current situation, and what is the best way out of it?"

He flipped the quarter six times and used the stick to draw a hexagram in the dirt.

" 'Number three,' " Tom read, and I looked over his shoulder to reassure myself he wasn't making stuff up.

HEXAGRAM 3

DIFFICULTY.

A CHALLENGE TO BE OVERCOME.
PROBLEMS AT THE BEGINNING.
WHAT IS THE POINT OF BEING
AHEAD OF YOUR TIME IF SOMEBODY
ELSE IS SO FAR BEHIND THEIRS, YOU
CANCEL EACH OTHER OUT?

"We already know we're having difficulty," I said disgustedly. "We don't need a hexagram to tell us that!"

"Is there a Morse code message?" Frankie asked.

Tom nodded vigorously. He ticked off the parts of the hexagram with his stick. "There's two dots, a dash, and a dot—that's an *F*—followed by two dots, which is *I*, followed by three dots—*S*—and then a final dash, which is *T*. The message is *fist*!"

"You decoded that without looking at your paper," I said. I knew I wouldn't be able to do it as quickly, even if I had memorized the code.

It was a clue, and I missed it.

He pulled the code paper from his book and offered it to me. "You can check it if you want, but I'm sure I'm right."

I ignored the paper.

"What's *fist* supposed to mean?"

"Isn't it obvious?" Tom responded. "We were trying to decide whether to look in a window or knock on the door. Which do you do with your fist?" He clenched his hand and mimed rapping.

"Maybe it's telling us to break a window," I countered.

"Door it is," said Frankie. "And the two of you might as well come. Just remember, making a fist, in this century, wouldn't be ladylike."

"Did I ever thank you for helping me save Dwina?" I asked as we filed through the gate and up the porch steps.

"No, you didn't. Not that you have to. It was the only thing to do. But—you're welcome."

We got to the door and she raised her hand to knock, but before she could, I reached across her and pulled a cord hanging from the doorframe. A bell jangled inside the house.

"Maybe this isn't what *fist* meant," I said. A little smugly.

The door was opened by a short, chubby man in a plaid vest and a pumpkin-orange tie. He was wearing stemless eyeglasses that clung to his nose with a metal clip. One arm cradled the Time Trombone against his shoulder, the way a soldier might carry a rifle.

"Yes?"

"Hello," said Frankie. "My name is Shofranka Camlo, and these are my adopted sisters, Rose and Thomasina. We were robbed earlier today of a valuable family heirloom, and we have reason to believe it may be in your possession."

"Why on earth would you think that?" sputtered the man.

"You're holding it in your hand."

The man frowned and took a step back. He held out the trombone and stared at it as though he had never seen it before.

"The slide horn? I just bought it from a man who swore it had been in his family for generations. Said he had to give it up because it was chapping his lips. Surely I haven't paid good money for stolen merchandise!"

"We have the case that was custom-made to fit it," I said, holding open the lid so he could see the shape indented in velvet perfectly matched the horn he was holding. His frown deepened.

"May we come in?" asked Frankie.

"What? Oh, yes, of course; I've quite forgotten my manners. I am Colonel Josiah Brinley, late of the Fourth Ohio Volunteer Infantry. Served under Taylor in Mexico. Come in here to the music room; we'll see if we can't clear this up."

We followed him into a room with a small keyboard instrument at one end and, at the other, a fireplace with a bugle hanging off a cord from its mantel. Sheet music and a deck of playing cards covered a table in the room's center. A bookcase crowded with books stood by the door.

"I had seen the man once before—we had played cards together in town not two days past—he seemed honest enough. Said he needed the money quickly, to pay off a gambling debt, which I thought proved him honorable." Colonel Brinley tapped the deck of cards with a pudgy finger. "We couldn't agree on a price, so it was decided I would cut the cards and whatever card turned up, I would pay its value in dollars for the horn. It was a good risk; my highest offer had been eight."

"What card did you draw?" asked Thomasina.

"The ace of clubs."

"You only paid a dollar for the trombone?" I squawked.

"Fourteen dollars, actually," said the colonel, with a grimace. "Aces were high. It was more than I wished to pay, but what could I do? A gambling debt is a debt of honor."

"Who shuffled the cards?" asked Frankie.

"He did."

Frankie nodded, as if this explained everything.

Thomasina leaned in close to the bookcase to examine something, and the protruding edge of his bonnet swept a small blue vase from its shelf. He caught it, tossed it from one hand to the other, and put it back on a different shelf.

"Can we have our trombone back?" I asked, holding the case out to the colonel, in the hope that he might chuckle jovially and slip the horn into it.

"I'm afraid not. Stolen it may be, but then again, it may not be. I've paid for it; it's mine. If you children would care to fetch your parents, I'm willing to discuss it with them. On the other hand, I'd be very interested in buying the case from you."

I slammed the lid. "It's not for sale!" I snapped.

Frankie burst into tears. "We were having a picnic," she whimpered convincingly, like she was terribly upset, "and our father forbade us from bringing the slide horn, but it is so lovely to have music, and Thomasina was playing it ever so delicately, and this man galloped by on his horse, and snatched it out of my poor Tommy's hands, and I am sure it will mean a spanking in the woodshed for each of us if we do not get it back!"

"You're not from around here," the colonel said coldly. "My wife teaches melodeon to some of the children of Freedom Falls, and I've never seen you among their number. You're itinerants, passing through, possibly even Gypsies—"

Frankie's head popped up, instantly dry-eyed—

"—so I doubt there's any woodshed involved. You're trying to play on my sympathy, but it's not an instrument easily strummed! I think it's time the three of you were on your way. I will be keeping the trombone!"

I thought furiously, trying to come up with a way to get the Shagbolt back. I could see from the way the colonel was clutching it that he half expected us to try to snatch it from him, so making a grab for it wouldn't work.

I glanced around, searching for inspiration. My eyes roved

from the playing cards to a picture on the wall of puppies playing poker. My dentist had a similar picture in his waiting room—the dogs were much older, of course—and immediately I knew I had to gamble.

"Do you really want the trombone case?" I asked the colonel.

"Would you be willing to sell it?"

"No, but I'd be willing to wager for it."

The colonel looked at me shrewdly. "Women do not wager. Nor do children."

"But maybe Gypsy children do," said Frankie, with a touch of ice in her voice.

"What kind of wager?" asked the colonel.

"Would you honor it, even if you lost? Even if we are children?" I demanded.

"Are you implying I am not a gentleman?"

"Is that a yes?"

"Of course it's a yes!" the colonel exploded. "I honor all my debts! What kind of wager do you propose? It is not seemly for children to play cards with adults, outside of the nursery!"

"No card games," I said hastily. "Are you familiar with rock-paper-scissors?"

"Some sort of bizarre cutting implement?"

"No. It's a way of settling disagreements," I explained. "We stand facing each other. Each of us makes a fist. We shake our fists three times at each other."

"Sounds pointless."

"I'm not done. On the third shake, you do one of three things with your fist. If you spread out all your fingers, that's called paper. If you stick out only two fingers, it's called scissors. No fingers out, it's rock. If you've got scissors and your opponent has paper, scissors cut paper—you win. If you've got rock and he has scissors, rock breaks scissors—you win. If you've got rock and he has paper—"

"Rock rips paper—I win!"

"No. Paper covers rock—you lose."

"Makes no sense."

"That's the way it's always been, ever since the game was invented, back in—?"

I turned to Thomasina, thinking he might know when rock-paper-scissors had been invented. He surprised me by looking up at the colonel and asking, "What's today's date?"

"August twelfth."

"Eighteen fifty-two?"

"Of course!"

Thomasina turned to me and answered my question. "August 12, 1852."

I was stunned. "You think...I just...invented rock-paper-scissors?"

He shrugged, as if to say it was entirely possible.

"I like it," said the colonel. "It's a way of settling a dispute without recourse to cards or dice. What is your proposition?"

"We do rock-paper-scissors once, winner take all. If you win, we give you the trombone case. If we win, you give us the trombone."

The colonel stroked his chin thoughtfully.

"You appeal to the sporting man in me! Let us perform the contest! Do we stand in a special way?"

"Yes!" I didn't want to disappoint him. "Plant your feet well apart, with the rear foot at a ninety-degree angle to the front." I gave him the same instructions Frankie had given us for staying upright during time travel. I put the trombone case down near the bookcase and faced him in the same way. He placed the trombone on the table.

"What if we both make the same gesture?"

"It's a tie and we go again. Are you ready? You do the count!"

He nodded nervously and licked his lips. We both hunkered forward.

"One!"

We threw down our fists.

"Two!"

Again.

"Three!"

He threw out two fingers. I kept my fist.

"Rock breaks scissors! I win!" I crowed.

The colonel's hands both became rocks and they quivered briefly at his sides. Then he unclenched them, shook himself, and forced a thin smile. "Bested fair and square," he admitted.

I picked up the case and held it open before him. He squared his shoulders and placed the trombone with great longing into its velvet bed. Before he let go he said, "It's a fine and unusual instrument. Do you have any idea where and when it was made?"

"Prague," said Frankie, gently easing his hands off the horn so I could close the lid. "Late sixteenth century."

"That old? It seems so modern."

"Its maker was extraordinary," Frankie assured him, snapping the latches and taking the case by its handle.

"Excuse me," said Thomasina, adjusting his apron and keeping his voice soft and girlish. "But I see you have a copy of *Uncle Tom's Cabin*." He pointed to the bookcase. The blue vase marked the spot. "Have you read it?"

"It belongs to my wife, actually," replied the colonel, and I had to admire his effort to be polite. I could tell he was seething. "I, myself, do not read fiction. Waste of time."

"Is she still reading it?" Frankie asked excitedly. "I see there's a gap where volume two should be."

"These personal questions border on the impertinent. But, yes, Mrs. Brinley is still reading it. She's over to Ethel Mordred's house at this very moment"—he waved at the window toward the house across the way—"with a number of the other village ladies, discussing it. They call it a book club, but it's really just a reason to drink lemonade and gabble. I miss the old quilting bees. At least those produced a quilt. No good will ever come of women reading fiction—you mark my words! They should confine themselves to cookbooks and almanacs."

"Oh, I quite agree," Frankie said, giving him the least sincere smile I had ever seen in my life. "Well, we really *must* be going!"

Frankie swept out into the hall, and Thomasina and I

quickly followed. The colonel was a few steps behind, but we waited for him to open the door for us.

"If you ever reconsider, and wish to sell the horn—"

"We'll keep you in mind," Frankie assured him, and a few moments later we were off his porch and through his gate.

Frankie gave me an odd look, like she was seeing me in a new light, and said, "That was very good."

"Thanks," I said, feeling a funny warmth in my chest. I figured the dress was too tight.

"What made you choose rock?" Tom asked.

"You did," I said.

"Me?"

"Well, it was really the hexagram you came up with. What was it called?"

"*Difficulty.*"

"Right. And the Morse code that went with it was obviously telling us how to get out of difficulty."

"How?"

"By making a fist!"

CHAPTER 13
The Emperor's New Matching Handbag

That was completely awesome!" Tom announced, looking back at Colonel Brinley's house. "He totally believed we were nineteenth-century kids. Girls, even!"

"Don't flatter yourselves on your acting ability," Frankie warned him. "I could smell rum on the colonel's breath. He's obviously not the sharpest key on the piano."

"Shouldn't we be playing the trombone and returning to our own time?" I asked as we stepped into the road.

"So soon?" asked Tom, sounding genuinely disappointed. "Look at that mounting block! It's built right into the fence!

It's so a lady can get in and out of a carriage easily! Very nice design."

"I'm glad you find this all so interesting," I said. "But I've had way too much of the nineteenth century. This isn't a safe place for us."

"We can't leave yet," said Frankie. "I've been listening for Mr. Ganto's signal that he's within range of the Shagbolt, and I haven't heard it. The windows were open back there and there wasn't a sound, so he's still on the far side of the river. And I still need a copy of *Cabin*."

She hiked up her skirt and crossed the rutty road to the house across the street. Tom and I followed, without hiking our skirts, and tripped.

The Mordred place was bigger than the colonel's, with a wraparound porch and fancy columns supporting the roof. It was the sort of house my mother would call "upscale."

"It's pretty amazing that the first place we visited," said Tom, "had a copy of the book you were looking for."

"It's not amazing at all," said Frankie, stopping at Mordred's gate. A nearby tree had a WANTED poster tacked to it, offering a three-dollar reward for information leading to the capture of a fugitive slave who could be recognized by the pattern of whipping scars on his back. "I researched *Uncle*

Tom's Cabin on the Internet after my father's book was stolen. A hundred and fifty years ago, practically everybody had a copy. In America, it was the second-bestselling book of the entire nineteenth century."

"What was the first?" asked Tom.

"The Bible."

"You wouldn't know it," I said, tearing down the poster.

Frankie pushed past the gate, and we followed her up a yellow brick walk to the front door.

"Couldn't we just go back to the twenty-first century, and you can buy a copy of the book online?" I said, searching for any reason not to meet more nineteenth-century people. "I've got five bucks I'd be happy to chip in."

"I looked into that," Frankie admitted. "The cheapest first edition I could find was sixteen thousand dollars."

"*Colonoscopy!*" cried Tom. "No wonder Ninja Lady stole your father's copy!"

"Oh, I'm pretty sure the reason she stole it had nothing to do with its value," Frankie said mysteriously. She looked straight at me as she said it. Again, something I should have picked up on went right over my head.

"Why else would somebody steal an old book?" I asked.

"Maybe to force whoever they stole it from to go looking

for a replacement," Frankie said. "Of course, I didn't think of that until after we got to the nineteenth century. But then, she would have expected that."

"Who? Ninja Lady?" I was totally confused. "Is there something you're not telling us?"

"If I told you, you'd both start acting weird, and it would jeopardize the mission."

"We're already acting weird," Tom pointed out.

"Weirder, then!" Frankie clarified. She turned to the door, lifted the ring in the brass door knocker's nose—the knocker was the face of the wind, with puffed-out cheeks and puckered lips—and rapped loudly.

"The two of you shouldn't say anything," she said over her shoulder. "These are women. They'll be more likely to spot boys in girls' clothing than the colonel was. Let me do the talking."

She rapped several more times and nobody answered. We heard laughter from the far side of the house and followed it.

Around back, in the center of a garden, five women sat at a table under the shade of an enormous oak. Books were scattered on the tabletop around a punch bowl and plates of tiny sandwiches. The women looked up at our approach, and the largest—she looked like an opera singer—stood and faced us.

"May I help you?" she asked.

Frankie curtsied. Tom didn't realize we were stopping and collided with me. I shoved him back to keep my balance, and we flailed at each other until we realized we might not be making a good first impression. We froze.

"I am so sorry to bother you," said Frankie, "but I am Shofranka Camlo. I am working my way through boarding school by representing the American importers of a wonderful new Parisian fashion sensation that promises to be the must-have accessory of the fall season. Since you ladies have the reputation of being the trendsetters of the town of Freedom Falls, we have searched you out before making our offer to any of your neighbors. I hope we are not intruding."

"You are...selling something?" Opera Singer sounded intrigued.

"I prefer to think of it as providing a once-in-a-lifetime opportunity."

"What boarding school? And who are *they*?" Opera Singer waved her hand at Tom and me.

"Miss Evangeline's School for the Gifted but Destitute. This is Thomasina, and this is Rose. I speak for them."

"Have they no command of English?"

"Alas, madam, no one knows. They are mimes."

"Mimes?"

"Yes. They do not speak."

Tom and I shook our heads sorrowfully. Tom pretended to zip his lips, which made absolutely no sense, since I was pretty sure the zipper hadn't been invented yet.

"Mimes!" gasped Opera Singer. "How awful! You poor dears!"

Tom bugged his eyes and nodded enthusiastically, and I realized he was imitating the silent comedian Harpo Marx, from the old Marx Brothers movies that he loved but his mother couldn't see the value of. He raced over to the table and acted like he was eating an invisible hamburger.

"Are you hungry?" asked a lady in a lavender dress, who held up a plate full of sandwiches. Tom held out his apron and emptied the entire plate into it. Then he threw in some cupcakes. He sat on the edge of the table and began eating out of his apron, flashing Harpo's squirrelly look from the depths of his bonnet. A couple of the women looked appalled, but the others raised fans to their faces and giggled.

"You said something about an opportunity?" Opera Singer asked.

Frankie, who didn't look all that pleased by the demon she had unleashed, flashed a forced smile and said, "We are taking pre-orders for the biggest advance in fashion since the crinoline! I am talking about nothing other than the Fantastic Transparent *Plasteek* Clutch Purse!" Frankie dramatically waved a Ziploc bag over her head.

There was a sharp intake of breath from around the table. I sat down in Opera Singer's chair and helped myself to the sandwiches, which turned out to be cucumber. Everybody else's eyes were on Frankie. She moved close to the table and displayed her plastic bag. The ladies stared as if she were showing them diamonds.

"Tired of rummaging in your reticule for that thing that always seems to be at the bottom?" Frankie asked. I supposed *reticule* was an old-time word for *handbag*. "Rummage no more, with this miracle of the age! See where everything is at a glance! Let others know the high quality of your combs and brushes; the size of your homes by the number of keys on your key rings; how beautiful your embroidered handkerchiefs are without ever having to sneeze!" She plucked a butter knife off the table, placed it inside the bag, zipped it, flipped it, and shook the sealed bag to show the contents wouldn't fall out. The ladies gasped and said "Oh!" as if she had done a magic trick.

Frankie handed the bag to Lavender Lady. "Feel it. Hold

it to the light. It is waterproof down to two fathoms, and you know how your river loves to flood!"

"It's so smooth!" declared Lavender Lady. "And the weave is so fine, I can't even see the thread!"

"The thread is silk from silkworms owned by mystic men of the Far East who breed their worms to have great clarity of mind. This clarity can be seen in the silk. Or *not* seen, perhaps I should say," Frankie explained, with a remarkably straight face.

I couldn't help but enjoy Frankie's performance. I suspected she was showing off her carnival-schooling.

As the bag got passed around the table, I ladled myself a lemonade from the punch bowl. A glance around the garden reminded me how far back in time we had traveled. The ceramic gnomes were beardless.

"This, of course, is a salesman's sample," Frankie explained. "Pre-order price is only two dollars per purse. In Scupperville"—she named a town farther up the river—"twenty-seven of the town's most refined ladies pre-ordered a total of thirty-three purses. One of those ladies, I should perhaps not mention, bragged about how Scupperville is always ahead of Freedom Falls when it comes to fashion."

Opera Singer bellowed "Marigold!" at the house, and a parlor maid bustled out.

"Marigold! Please bring me two dollars from the top drawer of my vanity."

Marigold turned, but Frankie raised a hand and stopped her.

"That will not be necessary. We are accepting no money at this time. You will pay upon receipt. I will take down the names of any of you who wish to place an advance order."

A portable writing desk sat on one corner of the table. Frankie helped herself to a piece of paper, dipped a handy feather pen into an inkwell, and looked up expectantly at the ladies. All of them gave their names, and two of them wanted to pre-order more than one bag.

"You ladies are *ever* so much more gracious than the ladies of Scupperville." Frankie sighed. "It seems such a pity they will be receiving their purses before you."

"Is that absolutely written in stone?" asked Opera Singer, who turned out to be Ethel Mordred. "Just because they ordered before we did?"

"I am afraid that is how it works," said Frankie, in a voice full of regret.

"Perhaps if we offered you a little more money per purse? Or if we gave our money in advance? You might move us to the top of the list?"

"Alas, I would not be comfortable doing that," said Frankie. "However..."

"Yes?"

"Is that the new book everybody is talking about?" Frankie pointed to the table. "The one about the evils of slavery? I have been meaning to read it, but all the booksellers seem to be sold out."

"Why, I've finished reading mine," said Lavender Lady, who had identified herself as Lavinia Moon. She picked up both volumes of the book and handed them to Frankie. "Please take it as a gift. I am sure you would find it particularly edifying. Considering." She waved a hand at Frankie's face. Frankie cocked her head to one side.

"Why, thank you *so* much! You know, I do believe the Scupperville orders might accidentally find their way to the bottom of the pile!"

The ladies beamed. Frankie placed volume two of *Uncle Tom's Cabin* into her Fantastic Transparent *Plasteek* Clutch Purse and sealed it shut. That's when an unearthly howl came from the direction of the river. The eeriness of it raised the hairs on the back of my neck.

"Oh, dear!" cried Mrs. Mordred. "I do hope Joe Sawyer has not gotten his cravat caught in the lumber mill's band saw again!"

I squirmed, wondering what part of Joe Sawyer's body his cravat might be.

"Well, ladies," said Frankie, "we will not take up any more of your time. We have miles to go before we sleep. You can expect your new purses to arrive from Paris sometime before Christmas. I will deliver them personally and you can pay upon receipt. It has been *such* a pleasure to have met you!"

Frankie gave meaningful glances to Tom and me, and we followed her out to the road.

"That was absolutely amazing," I conceded. I was genuinely impressed. "You sold those women something anybody else would have thrown away as trash."

"You'll notice I didn't take any money from them," Frankie said primly, sticking the other volume of *Cabin* into the second of her two Ziploc bags and putting them both into her tiny backpack. They fit with very little room to spare. She took the trombone case from me, jammed it against my chest, and popped the lid. "That howl we heard was Mr. Ganto, signaling he's back in range. I want to use the Shagbolt before he gets too close."

"You don't want Mr. Ganto arriving at the same time we do?" Tom guessed, echoing my own thought.

"No, I don't," admitted Frankie. "It would be better if he showed up a few minutes after we do. If we all arrive at the same time, the first thing he'll do is take the Shagbolt away from us."

"Because he's under orders from your father," I said.

She nodded and raised the trombone to her lips. "I want all of us thinking of that ghastly middle school of yours, about ten minutes after we parked the golf cart behind the Dumpsters. If we do this really well, we'll wind up sitting in the cart. I'll drop you two off at home, and then I'll take the cart back to the carnival."

"Wait!" said Tom, putting his hand up.

"What?"

"I don't suppose you could leave me here?"

"Are you kidding?"

"I don't mean forever," Tom hastened to explain. "I just mean for a day or two, and then you could come back for me. I love this stuff—it's what I really *want* to study—and

I could use a break from Puma Ma. I'd like to look around some more."

Tom ran away from home, on average, every two weeks. The first few times it happened, his mother had called the cops. As it got to be a regular thing, she grew less concerned. At first, he had hidden out at my house, but when that became the first place his mother would look, he found other places he could disappear to. His favorite was the back room of the Freedom Falls Historical Society, which had a window with a loose latch.

"No," said Frankie. "I like history as much as anybody, but this particular time and place is way too dangerous for us. Besides, neither of you can imagine how leaving somebody behind could totally screw up the future. We're all going back together!"

She gave the trombone's slide a loosening wiggle. "Now, don't distract me. The last thing I want to do is play that final note flat." She grinned. "You'll know I've messed up if we all get run over by a herd of buffalo!"

She put the mouthpiece to her lips and pumped out the first six of the seven notes she had taught us earlier, and I was pleased to find I remembered them perfectly. The seventh note was an F, and she played it clear and sharp.

For the second time in my life, I felt myself turn to dust in the wind. The individual grains of me blew away, spiraled through a tunnel, and put themselves back together in a brand-new place.

It was not the place we were trying to get to.

CHAPTER 14
Not the Middle School

We were not outside. And we were definitely nowhere near a golf cart. We were in a large, high-ceilinged room that somehow felt familiar. A massive desk in front of a throne-like chair occupied the center, with benches facing the desk on either side of a wide aisle, and I was reminded for a moment of the courtroom set for *The Crucible*, until I noticed the statues.

There were two of them, one on either side of the aisle farthest from the desk, near the double-door entrance to the room. We had arrived closest to the statue on the left. It stood on a pedestal engraved:

JUSTICE
SEES THE DIFFERENCES

The statue was a woman holding a set of balance scales. She was wearing an ankle-length dress, a pearl necklace, and the kind of eyeglasses I had once heard my mom call cat's-eye, which flared up at the top corners. With her free hand, the statue held a pair of binoculars halfway to her face.

HARMONY
DISPELS THE DIFFERENCES

declared the pedestal on the right side of the aisle, which supported a statue of a man in a business suit, striped tie, and narrow-brimmed hat. He was holding a briefcase in one hand and a rolled-up newspaper in the other, and stared blindly into space with a self-satisfied look on his face.

"Where are we?" I asked, getting a very bad feeling about it all.

"Look at the ceiling," said Tom, a touch of fear in his voice.

I looked, and I knew where we were. The ceiling was tarnished tin, with the image of an eagle hammered into its center. The bird's wings were spread, and lightning bolts shot out from between its talons, like really painful toe fungus. We were in a room I had been in numerous times before, but it had never looked like this.

"We're in the school library," I said flatly.

"This is your *library*?" asked Frankie. "It's not big on books, is it?"

No shelves, no worktables, not a book in sight. No sign of Ms. Butler, our helpful school librarian, either.

A buzzer went off and the lights got brighter. Footsteps clomped on the other side of the door. We scrambled and hid behind Justice.

The doors flew open and two men entered, dragging another man who had been stripped to his T-shirt and under-shorts. He was handcuffed and had a gag in his mouth. The two men quick-marched him down the aisle and stopped in front of the desk, then did their best to stand at attention as their prisoner struggled to break free of their grip.

Tom nudged me frantically, and I nodded to show him I had seen the same thing he had.

The prisoner was our school principal, Clyde McNamara.

Nothing happened for a moment. Then a door behind the throne opened and Quentin Garlock walked out. The man we knew as a substitute teacher was wearing a suit identical to the one Harmony was wearing and had an annoyed look on his face. He made a big show of consulting his watch and snarled, "You're almost ninety minutes late! I've sent staff home, waiting for you! This facility does not—should not—accept new inmates past the hour of five. You could have put him in a holding cell in town and brought him here tomorrow."

I climbed up on the pedestal and peeked around Justice to get a better look. Tom tugged urgently on the hem of my dress, like he thought maybe this wasn't the smartest thing I had ever done.

"Holding cell's full of drunks, celebrating Killbreath's fourth inauguration," one of the men said apologetically. "Your clerk said—"

"My clerk said you could bring him here, but that was almost two hours ago! All right, let's get this over with." Garlock snatched a sheaf of papers off the desk and glanced at them. "Clyde McNamara, this is your second offense. Court trial is waived as superfluous; you've had the one—no need to burden the system and the taxpayers any further. You have been caught once again wearing a garment called a kilt."

The man on McNamara's left produced a piece of plaid

cloth and tossed it onto the desk. Garlock glared at the guard. "I just said—*there is no trial*. Meaning there is no need for evidence. Take that filthy rag away!"

Before the guard could retrieve it, McNamara lunged forward and snatched it up with his cuffed hands. He clutched it to himself like a security blanket.

At first I had hoped they were rehearsing some sort of skit, but then I decided they wouldn't have cleared the library for it, and the red on McNamara's cheek looked too much like real blood. I chinned myself up on Justice's binoculars to get a better look. Tom sputtered below me.

"Certainly an admission of guilt," said Garlock. "Remove his gag. Do you have anything to say before I pass sentence?"

McNamara spat out the gag the moment it was loosened.

"This is the tartan of my people—the clan McNamara!" he said defiantly. "We have worn it proudly for centuries! I wear the kilt only once a year, in the privacy of my own home, every January twenty-fifth, on the anniversary of the birth of Angus McOffal, the inventor of haggis, the national dish of Scotland. It is a tradition!"

"Haggis is a football stuffed with sheep's guts," said Garlock, looking a little queasy.

"You think it was easy coming up with a recipe like that?

Only my people could have done it! I have a right to wear the kilt!"

I remembered that my father owned a kilt. He wore it sometimes, but he said it was too modern for him to be truly comfortable in. It was news to me that McNamara wore one. It shouldn't have been something you got beaten up over.

"Wearing it makes you a trans-temp—a cross-time dresser—wearing the clothes of an age other than your own. It is disruptive to the society in which we live, and it is expressly prohibited by the Uniform Uniformity Act of 1964, except in the case of sanctioned theatrical performances glorifying the state."

"The kilt has never gone out of fashion!"

"Only in your head, sir! The world eagerly awaits the day when the kilt will be eradicated and join the burnoose, the kimono, and that abomination known as lederhosen in the dustbin of history! Some might pity you, but I say you're sick, and it makes me wish capital punishment wasn't reserved only for the genetically inferior! As it is, I sentence you to the maximum for a second offense—three years in the prison laundry, where every day you will be subjected to proper, if revoltingly dirty, apparel. May it rub off on you!"

I leaned a little too far to the left and lost my grip on the binoculars. I found myself hanging by a single nocular. I swung out into plain sight.

Garlock consulted a chart on his desk.

"As far as accommodations are concerned..." He stabbed a finger down. "There, perfect! Cell one eighty-six, right next door to our worst offender, Hannibal Brody, a three-time loser! Maybe you can learn a lesson from someone *serving a life sentence*! Take him away! Turn him over to the guards in block B, and next time you bring me a prisoner, make sure you do it during normal business hours. You've made me late for a very important inaugural dinner!"

Nobody was looking in my direction. I grabbed Justice by the nose and got myself back under cover.

"No!" McNamara started to protest, but the gag was yanked back in his mouth. Garlock tossed the case's paperwork into his top desk drawer, turned on his heel, and left the same way he had come.

The guards dragged McNamara past Justice and out the door. I swung around the statue to stay out of sight, then dropped down to where my friends huddled behind the pedestal.

"My father's in prison! For life! Because of the way he dresses!"

Frankie sprang up and put her hand over my mouth.

"Shh!" Her eyes rolled toward the door Garlock had left through, reminding me we didn't know if he was still close enough to hear us.

"Over here," Tom said in a loud whisper. He had crossed to Harmony's side of the room and was holding open a door that, when the place was our school library, had led to the media room.

It was now a large office, as we discovered when we slipped into it, and Tom closed and locked the door behind us. I ran to the room's one window and looked out.

What had been the athletic field behind the school was now a prison exercise yard, fully enclosed by additions to the building that formed a box around it. Loops of razor wire decorated the roofs like hellish Christmas garland, and a guard tower loomed at the opposite corner like a gigantic troll.

"What's *wrong*?" I demanded. "Where are we? What's happened?"

"Isn't it obvious?" Frankie sighed as she put the Shagbolt case down on a desk next to a computer monitor. "Something we did in the past somehow changed the present. We have to figure out what it was, and go back and fix it!"

She sat down at the computer and began tapping away at the keyboard.

"Maybe we should get out of these clothes," said Tom, plucking at his skirt.

"Don't bother!" snapped Frankie. "We're only here long enough to find out what we did to mess things up, then we're going straight back to 1852 and making it right!"

"I want to see my father!" I circled around to the far side of the desk. "He's next door to cell one eighty-six! We have to find it!"

"No, we don't!" Frankie barked. "We're dressed as nineteenth-century girls in a prison dedicated to locking up people dressed as nineteenth-century girls! Don't leave this room! They'll put you in the cell next to his!"

"We have to get him out of here!" I declared. "I mean, I hate it that he dresses as a samurai to go grocery shopping, but he shouldn't go to prison for it! I have to get to his cell! At the very least, I have to see him!"

"It's too late," said Frankie. "He wouldn't know you."

"I'll take off the dress!"

"That's not what I mean. In this timeline, you probably don't exist. Neither, in all probability, do I. He literally wouldn't know you, because he never had you as a son." She waved her hand at the monitor. "Minorities were eliminated in North America during the Great Purge of 1933. It was a WPA project. 'We're Purifying America.' The Gypsies went first, then everybody else who didn't meet certain standards. Then, even those who met those standards but who followed alternative lifestyles that made the majority uncomfortable found themselves in the so-called cleansing camps. Certain types of religions. Certain types of families."

"That's awful!" I said, running up behind her and looking over her shoulder. The photo on the monitor showed people being led away in chains.

"Those are Asians!" Tom growled, coming up next to me.

"They could just as easily be Romani or Indian or African—" said Frankie.

"Or dressed in togas or tricornered hats," I said, suddenly seeing little difference between exterminating people for the way they looked to locking them up for how they dressed.

Tom had started nervously flipping his quarter. He took a pencil off one of the desks and began scribbling down the results.

"What could *we* have done that caused this much damage?" I said in disbelief. "We were there for less than a day!"

"Anything that happened because we were there that wouldn't have happened if we hadn't been!"

"You could have warned us this kind of thing could happen!"

"I told you to be careful!"

"Maybe it wasn't Tom and me. *You* showed those ladies plastic!"

"They weren't chemists! They couldn't have made their own plastic! You, on the other hand, went and invented rock-paper-scissors!"

"Oh, like that could have caused all this?"

"*Apophenia!*" said Tom, trying out a new curse.

He held up the *I-Ching* book, open to one of the hexagram descriptions.

"What did you ask it?"

"I wasn't thinking too clearly," Tom admitted, chewing anxiously on the pencil's eraser. "I just wanted to know what our situation was. That's the hexagram it gave me."

I looked.

Hexagram 18

Decay.

SPOILAGE. PUTRESCENCE. ALL-
ROUND YUCKINESS. SOMETHING IS
ROTTEN IN THE STATE OF DENMARK,
AND YOUR OWN STATE ISN'T SMELL-
ING ALL THAT SWEET, EITHER. SNIFF
YOUR ARMPITS: IF THAT ISN'T THE
SOURCE, FIND IT!

"Is there a hidden Morse code message?" I asked, pretty sure there would be.

Tom nodded.

"A dash and two dots, followed by a dot, then a dot and a dash, ending with a dash and two dots."

"What does it spell?

"*DEAD!*"

CHAPTER 15
T for Torture

I got a shiver, thinking about how appropriate it was for a hexagram called *Decay* to contain the Morse code for *dead*. Tom was right; it wasn't a coincidence.

"Is that it?" I asked Frankie. "Is somebody dead who shouldn't be? When we were in the past, did we accidentally kill somebody without noticing? What if Chester died of fright when Mr. Ganto took him away? Getting grabbed by Mr. Ganto would have scared me to death. At the very least, I would have needed clean underwear. Or, what if that book they gave you"—I waved at Frankie's backpack—"was supposed to save somebody's life, and it didn't because it wasn't there when it should have been? Like, maybe someday somebody was supposed to be holding it, and it was supposed to stop a bullet?"

"I'm thinking it might be the opposite," replied Frankie. "We didn't accidentally kill anybody, but we *did* deliberately save somebody's life. What if Dwina was supposed to die then, but because we saved her, she lived to do something—or her children went on to do something—that eventually caused all this?"

Her fingers typed furiously.

"Are you crazy?" I exploded. "That nice lady? How could she possibly do anything that could mess things up as bad as this? The best thing about our trip was saving her! I'd do it all over again if I had to!"

"You'd probably even save Killbreath under the same circumstances," Frankie said gently. "I'm beginning to see that's the kind of person you are."

"I wouldn't put that to the test," I said, not comfortable with a compliment coming from her.

She leaned in and squinted at a blurry PDF file.

"Okay—I did a search for Edwina Landry. The only thing that came up is a genealogical record from 1910."

"Why *Landry*?" I asked.

Tom was quick to slip in the answer; it was right up his nineteenth-century alley.

"Because former slaves sometimes kept the last names of their onetime captors, and Dwina mentioned a Master Landry!"

"Yes," Frankie agreed. "It was a long shot, but here it says Edwina and Seth Landry were married and had a daughter Rosella, who grew up to marry a man named David Stemplehill, and then Rosella and David had three daughters: Violet, Columbine, and—if you can believe it, Morning Glory. The record takes the family up to 1910, but beyond Morning Glory, the original document is too damaged to read."

"Morning Glory Stemplehill!" I exclaimed, hardly able to believe it.

"You've heard of her?"

"My mother used to say that her favorite name of all her ancestors was Morning Glory Stemplehill! She was my mother's great-great-great-something-grandmother, maybe there should be another *great*, or a couple less, but I'm a direct descendant!"

"Then, if you add two more *great*s, you're directly descended from Dwina herself," said Frankie thoughtfully. "If you hadn't saved her, you would've ceased to exist!"

My head was starting to hurt, and it wasn't just from lack of sleep.

"I don't know about that," said Tom. "This is a classic Grandfather Paradox. If you traveled back in time and accidentally knocked your grandfather off a cliff before he ever met your grandmother, your father or mother would never have been born, and you wouldn't exist. But then you couldn't have gone back in time and accidentally killed one of your ancestors. It's not possible."

"It's like in the old Gypsy rhyme," Frankie added.

> *"Your time-travel tales can be thrillers,*
> *'Bout time-traveling grandfather killers,*
> *But with Granddad destroyed,*
> *There is often a void,*
> *And limericks do make good fillers!"*

"That's an old Gypsy rhyme?"

"We also have a nice one about werewolves. So, obviously, Dwina was supposed to live so you could be born and go back in time to save her. It has to be something else we changed that's made all this mess."

"Wait," I said. "If what we did caused that purge thing, where they eliminated a bunch of people in 1933—like, probably, our great-grandparents—why are we still here?"

"We shouldn't be," Tom admitted. "Maybe it's because we're visiting from a different timeline. Or maybe it's because we somehow *do* manage to fix this thing!"

"There's another computer over there!" Frankie pointed and snapped her fingers. "And there's a tablet on that table! Help me figure it out! We have to know what we did before we go back!"

Tom went to the other computer and began tapping at the keyboard.

"What, exactly, is it we're looking for?" I asked, picking up the tablet and watching it spring to life at my touch. It was only 6 percent charged.

"The point where history starts running amok," said Frankie, rapidly scrolling through documents. "The point where it deviates from the history we know."

"It would help if we knew more history," I muttered to myself, looking for a news feed.

"Obviously," continued Frankie, "it had to have happened after we were there. What was that date again?"

"August 12, 1852," said Tom as he studied some nineteenth-century photographs. "A very important date in Chinese history."

"Was it?" Frankie looked up from her scrolling.

"Totally. On August 12, 1852, in San Francisco, the Chinese first introduced chopsticks to America. Two days later, we opened the first Chinese laundry, to clean the shirts of Americans who tried to eat with chopsticks. It was the most brilliant piece of marketing ever, although we try not to brag about it."

"Did you just learn this?" asked Frankie.

"Gee Gee Pa told me over breakfast the other day."

"Gee Gee Pa?"

"My great-grandfather. He tries to teach me one new thing about China every morning. Every Friday, he gives a quiz. It makes Puma Ma furious. She says it's irrelevant."

"So the date was in your head." Frankie returned her attention to the screen. "That's probably why, of all the available dates in the 1850s, we went to that one. Your thoughts overrode mine." She didn't sound happy about it. Tom just grinned.

"Hey!" I blurted. "According to this, Lenny Killbreath's father has been president of the United States for twelve years now! He was just re-elected for a fourth term—the inauguration was today! His son Lenny—eighteen-year-old Lenny!—is Secretary of the Inferior, a department that decides what to do with U.S. residents who fail their annual citizenship tests! Am I going crazy?"

"No, it's the world that's gone crazy," Frankie assured me. "Lenny's father, Bruno Killbreath, is the fourth member of the Killbreath family to be a president of the United States, starting with Horace Killbreath, who was elected in 1884. Horace's son, Montgomery Killbreath, was president in 1933 and is considered 'the architect of the Great Purge.'" She waved her hand at the monitor, as if we might be wondering where she was getting all this from. "After he was elected for a third term, some people started calling him King Monty. Or, at least they did before they were hanged."

"What could have made the Killbreath family so powerful?" I wondered.

"*We* did, apparently!" Frankie clenched her fists in frustration. "I haven't dug far enough yet to figure out what it was—"

"Hey, guys!" Tom's voice was full of alarm. He pointed with his pencil to the far corner of the room. Just below the ceiling, aimed in our direction, was a TV camera. The little red light on it glowed brightly. "*Acrimonious!* We're under surveillance," he said woodenly. "The *I-Ching* was right. We're dead!"

"Maybe not," said Frankie, renewing her efforts at the keyboard. "There must be a camera in practically every room of this place. Meaning there's a control booth somewhere with hundreds of TV screens in it. And what? A single guard, maybe two, trying to watch them all? While they also keep an eye on the portable TV they've probably got hidden at their desk to watch the football game?"

"Assuming football still exists," I said.

"They may not have noticed us," Frankie said, with forced optimism. "One of the guards may be asleep; the other might be in the bathroom; maybe the game's gone into overtime."

Something snicked in the lock of the room's only door.

"Or maybe the guards aren't football fans," I said, giving a second look to the room's window. It was barred, and the space between the bars was too narrow for even a kid to squeeze through, no matter how flattering and slimming the kid's dress might be.

The door burst open, and two men with machine guns flew into the room. They skidded to a halt, leveled their guns at us, and barked, "Nobody move!"

We didn't. We locked ourselves into whatever position

we were in and stared up at them, wide-eyed. Nothing happened. Long seconds dragged by, and I was almost about to ask "Can we help you?" when Quentin Garlock appeared at the door.

He was wearing a gray winter coat and a gray woolen scarf and gray leather gloves, and even the snowflakes on his shoulders were gray, unless it was dandruff. He leaned wearily against the doorframe and, as he skinned off his gloves, said, "I was almost to my car. A five-hundred-dollar-a-plate dinner, and I've already missed a hundred dollars' worth of fruit cup. What nonsense has called me back?"

He studied us, his expression growing more sour as his eyes roved from Frankie to Tom to me.

"This is a prison!" he announced. "People try to break *out* of prison. NOBODY breaks *into* prison! Are you insane? What is wrong with you? Who are you?"

All three of us made the decision not to speak. Garlock turned purple. It was a nice contrast to all the gray.

"Three cross-time dressers! Of three ethnic types that haven't been seen in these parts since sometime in the last century! Two of you not even wearing clothing proper to your gender! This has to be some kind of sick joke!"

Our bonnets were hanging down our backs by their chin

straps. I was, ridiculously, relieved that Garlock had realized Tom and I were boys.

"And children, on top of it all! Who helped you get in here? It wasn't Gnuteson, was it? He's wanted my job for years! He probably thinks this will somehow embarrass me politically. I hate people who scheme to get the jobs of others! ONE OF YOU SHOULD ANSWER ME!"

We all clenched our lips a little tighter.

"Really? Don't trifle with me! I'm in no mood to waste time!"

Garlock gestured, and one of the guards pulled Frankie away from her computer while the second guard pulled Tom away from his. I slipped the tablet into the pocket of my apron as the guards jammed the three of us shoulder to shoulder in the center of the room.

"Now, I'll ask you again. What are you doing here?"

We refused to answer. None of us even made eye contact.

"Right! If you want to play it that way, there's an easy way to make you talk! Millard!" Garlock addressed the bulkier of the two guards. "In the top drawer of that filing cabinet, you'll find a thin wooden case containing stainless steel implements designed to cut, crack, break, and sever. Be a good lad and fetch it here."

Millard slung his weapon over one shoulder and rummaged in the drawer.

"We'll soon have you singing like little birds," Garlock promised us.

"Uh, where, exactly, would it be?" asked Millard.

"Look under *T*, for *torture*," suggested Garlock.

"Uh, time sheets...tax forms...a recipe for tuna casserole. Nothing to do with torture."

"Try *P* for *pain*."

"Personnel records...payroll forms...a jar of peanut butter...no wooden case. Maybe under *O*?"

"*O* for what?"

"*Ouch?*"

"Ouch? I'll give you ouch! Out of my way!"

Garlock shoved Millard aside and ransacked the drawer himself, finally slamming it and pulling open the drawer beneath it.

"There!" he said triumphantly, waving the case around. "Totally misfiled! Heads will roll in clerical, unless they've also misplaced the portable guillotine, in which case I'll have to content myself with a strongly worded memo. Now—"

He flipped open the case and displayed its contents to us.

It was full of brightly shining surgical tools. I particularly didn't like the one that looked resembled a can opener.

"—whom shall I interrogate first? Or would you prefer to reconsider and simply tell me everything?"

"Hey, boss?" said the guard who wasn't Millard.

"Not now, Alphonse; I'm busy."

"Why is there a trombone case on the desk?"

Garlock turned and regarded the case. I decided we had reached the point where one of us had to speak.

"You should open it," I said, because opening it was the last thing I wanted him to do.

"Oh, I should, should I?" Garlock stepped over to the desk and put his hand lightly on the Shagbolt's case. "Nobody breaks into a prison and brings a trombone with them. A harmonica, possibly. In an extreme case, an ocarina. But nothing this size. What is it, really?"

"It's a trombone," I answered honestly.

"It is the symbol of our cause," said Frankie. "You've heard the expression 'bold as brass'? *We* are BRASS. The trombone is our symbol. And we are your worst nightmare!"

"BRASS? Never heard of it!" Garlock drummed his fingers on the trombone case. I made a great show of ducking my head and wincing, like I expected something horrible to happen, and he stopped, yanking his hand back like he'd been stung. "What does it stand for?"

"What does what stand for?" asked Frankie.

"BRASS!"

"Boys—" I said the first word beginning with *B* that popped into my head.

"Brotherhood—" Frankie overrode me.

"Right!" I agreed. "The Brotherhood of—"

"Brotherhood Rebuilding—" Tom corrected me.

"A Saner Society!" Frankie finished. "Brotherhood Rebuilding a Saner Society! BRASS! Hear it and tremble!"

"You're one of those sick little protest groups that will stop at nothing to make some wrongheaded, meaningless point?" Garlock goggled in horror at the trombone case. "IS THIS... A BOMB?"

"Why don't you open it and find out?" I asked.

"Want I should call the bomb squad?" asked Alphonse, reaching for the nearest phone.

"NO!" Garlock caught Alphonse's hand before it could get to the receiver. "We'll handle this ourselves. If this is some trick of Gnuteson's, I will not be made a laughingstock!"

"But, boss, what if it really is a bomb?"

"Then one of these clever children will disarm it." Garlock

took a scalpel from his collection of razor-sharp flatware. "It's time we stopped fooling around!"

Two strides brought him over to us. He gathered Frankie's hair in one hand and tilted her head back. "Stay perfectly still," he advised her. "If you so much as raise your hand, or try to kick me, I can guarantee things will go very badly for you and your friends. Now, which one of you offensively dressed young men cares enough about this young lady to save her from getting a very nasty scar across her neck?"

He raised the scalpel to Frankie's throat and pressed the tip against her skin.

CHAPTER 16
Erase Trouble

W hat do you want to know?" I asked, prepared to tell Garlock everything, even though I knew he wouldn't believe it. I tried desperately to imagine a lie that he would.

"For starters, and most importantly," he said, repositioning the scalpel below Frankie's left ear, so I could have a clear view of what he might do if he didn't like my answer, "the question is, who are you working for? *That* is the eight-hundred-pound gorilla in the room!"

"No," rumbled a voice behind Garlock. "*I* am the eight-hundred-pound gorilla in the room. Let go of the child!"

Garlock and the two guards spun around and were slapped across their collective faces by a hand the size of Michigan. Guns got yanked from grips and thrown across the room, a scalpel got tossed aside, and within moments, Alphonse, Millard, and Garlock had been neatly stacked on the floor and Mr. Ganto was sitting on them. They struggled to free themselves, but Mr. Ganto bounced once, and they stopped.

"What took you so long?" asked Frankie.

"Someone played the Shagbolt while I was still quite distant from it," said Mr. Ganto, sounding hurt. "Almost as if they did not wish to travel with me."

"We would never leave you behind; you know that," cooed Frankie, patting one of his hairy wrists.

We had seen Mr. Ganto materialize silently behind Garlock and the others a few seconds before he made his presence known. If anyone had been paying attention to our faces, no doubt our expressions would have betrayed him. Several recent swims by the *Gigantopithecus* across the Gustimuck River had washed away any lingering trace of skunk.

"Am I sitting on Nazis?" asked Mr. Ganto. "They feel as though they might be Nazis. There is a bumpy sort of arrogance to them."

"Mr. Ganto has a very sensitive tush," Frankie explained.

"Sensitive enough to feel arrogance?" I was surprised. Mine was only sensitive enough to feel awful, usually after I had eaten too much peanut brittle.

"They might as well be Nazis," replied Frankie, ignoring me. "Something we did in the past has changed the present so much that there's virtually no personal freedom. You can't even wear a kilt without going to jail."

"We have to go back to the past and straighten things out!" Tom chirped happily, and the *Gigantopithecus* scowled.

"He's right!" agreed Frankie. "And the longer we stay here, the more danger we're in!" She began an end run around Ganto to get to the Shagbolt. Ganto reached casually behind himself and pressed a hefty index finger down on the case's lid.

"Your father does not want you using this," he said, in a voice like sorrowful gravel.

"What's wrong with Nazis?" demanded Garlock from somewhere in the middle of the pile. "They were our allies— *mmpht!*" Ganto bounced twice and Garlock shut up.

"My father doesn't want me using it, but my mother thinks I'm destined to become the Shagbolt's Keeper! And she's the one with the crystal ball! If I'm ever going to be the Keeper, I need more practice with it!"

"Your mother and father do not talk," said Ganto.

"Well, *duh*!" snapped Frankie, and I thought it was a weird response.

"It is childish to play one against the other."

"Gantsy, we don't have a home here to return to," Frankie explained. "The Romani are gone; anybody who was even the least little bit different is gone; we have to go back to 1852, figure out what we did wrong the first time, and undo it! We have to use the Shagbolt!"

"Undoing mistakes so rarely goes well for you," replied Ganto, shaking his enormous head sadly from side to side.

"This sort of thing has happened before?" I asked, feeling a flash of anger. "What is *wrong* with you, Frankie? It's like your father locked a gun in a safe and you don't understand why he doesn't want you to have the combination. The Time Trombone is dangerous! It just wiped out hundreds of thousands of people!"

"The trombone didn't wipe out those people; *other* people wiped out those people! Trombones don't kill people; people kill people. And we can bring them back!" Frankie tugged on the case and Ganto lifted his finger, releasing it. She staggered backward with her prize. "If you had your own time machine, you would use it, too. Believe me!"

"I don't think I would, if I knew how dangerous it was."

Frankie handed the case to Tom, opened it, and withdrew the Shagbolt. She looked at Ganto, who shrugged and stood, his head almost grazing the ceiling. He opened a supply closet and shoved his prisoners into it, jamming Alphonse and Millard in first and then, when it became obvious there would be absolutely no room for Garlock, stuffing him in, too. Then he upended a desk and stuck it under the closet's doorknob.

"It'll help if we're all thinking about August 12, 1852," said Frankie. "And the place should be *here*, rather than San Francisco, no matter how badly one of us wants to see the American premiere of chopsticks."

Tom nodded to show he understood.

Frankie raised the mouthpiece to her lips and played the same flatulent notes that she had the very first time we had time-traveled. Again, I felt myself disintegrate and turn into tiny particles, and I realized it must be the way sand feels when it's passing through the narrowest part of an hourglass. The office in the prison that had once been my school vanished, and I was never happier to leave a room in my life.

We were instantly surrounded by hay, and at first I thought we were back in the runaway wagon before the horses bolted, but then I saw the roof, and I realized we were in the hayloft of a barn.

"This is the place where they held us prisoners!" declared Tom, peering over the loft's edge at the barn's floor. "I recognize the corn shucker!"

"You would," I said, a little tired of his knowledge of strange antiques. I looked where he was looking. Eyes gazed up at me from the top of a rusty contraption.

"And I recognize the cat," said Frankie. "So we're in the right place. But what time is it? Is it after we escaped, or before they brought us here?"

Bright daylight flooded the loft as Mr. Ganto swung wide a door in the back that opened into thin air.

"Midday," he rumbled.

"That doesn't answer my question," Frankie muttered.

I whipped the tablet out of my apron pocket, thinking all I had to do to find the time was turn it on, but then I realized I was being foolish. A tablet had to be connected to a network to know what the local time was, and there was no way an 1852 barn was going to be a hot spot.

The black surface of the tablet glinted.

The noises around me faded to a distant buzz.

The glint on the glass expanded and became a blurry

picture, then sharpened in the center where human figures moved. *Oh*, I thought. *Somebody downloaded a movie. It looks like a Western.*

I watched, mesmerized, as people walked up a gangplank and boarded an old-time paddle wheel steamboat. The name *Buckeye Beauty* was painted on the boat's side. I recognized two of the passengers. The boat was chugging up a river, and arm in arm, looking eagerly toward their destination, were Dwina and Seth. I broke into a big smile, seeing Dwina again.

Then the boat exploded.

I shouted, threw the tablet into the air, and staggered backward. Sound came flooding back, and the first thing I heard was Tom saying, "Bro! What? Are you okay?"

Frankie retrieved the tablet from the hay and glanced at it. I could see the screen was blank. "What?" she demanded.

"Dwina!" I gasped. "And Seth! They were on a steamboat called the *Buckeye Beauty*—and it blew up!"

"You saw that on the tablet?"

"Yes!"

"What app were you using?" Tom asked. "It wasn't SimCentury Nineteen, was it? That's only in beta; it's full of bugs!"

"The tablet wasn't turned on!" I explained. Behind me, Ganto snorted.

"He was scrying," said Frankie. "That's what Rose's kind of precognition is called. He can glimpse the future in shiny objects."

"So you think I saw the future? You think Dwina and Seth are going to be on an exploding steamboat? I didn't save her life just so she could die trying to get across the river! She's supposed to live and have kids!"

"I don't know what it means, or why it's the first thing that's happened now that we're back!" Frankie ran both hands through her hair as though things were getting to be a bit too much for her. It was the first time, in all we had been through, that she showed signs of losing her cool. It made me like her a little more.

"First things first!" she decided, regaining control. "We figure out what we did to ruin the future, and we fix it! Then we decide what to do about this new thing."

"We find Dwina and Seth," I said, "and we keep them from getting on any steamboats!"

"Possibly. But not before we work out what we did to cause the future to change so radically!"

"We should consult the *I-Ching*," said Tom, digging the quarter out of his apron pocket.

"The last time we did that, we got *dead* as a Morse code message," I said. "But nobody died."

"I'm pretty sure *dead* was a description of the society we found ourselves in. It looked pretty dead-end to me." Tom balanced the coin on his thumb. "Everybody think about our current problem and the best way to solve it." The coin flew in the air and Tom caught it.

"Tails!"

He slid the pencil he had gotten from the prison out from behind his ear and looked around for something to write on.

"Here," I said, taking the pencil from him and drawing a broken *yin* line on the post I was standing next to. Tom tossed the coin five more times, until I had drawn this:

"It's the forty-sixth hexagram," he said, and showed us the page.

HEXAGRAM *46*

RISING. ASCENDING.

LIFE HAS ITS UPS AND DOWNS.
BUOYANCY IS A VIRTUE. ONLY AFTER
YOU'VE HIT BOTTOM CAN YOU TRULY
GO OVER THE TOP. WHAT GOES
AROUND, COMES AROUND. THE DUTY
ROSTER FOR TORNADO WATCH IS,
APPROPRIATELY, ROTATIONAL.

"More gobbledygook," I decided. "Is there a message in Morse?"

"Do you have to ask?"

"I wish I didn't. Just once, it would be nice if the word in Morse turned out to be *stupid*, or *inane*, something that proved whoever is sending these messages knows how idiotic this all is."

"Inane?"

"Vocabulary word in Richardson's class last week. You were out sick. Means 'silly.'"

"The Morse here," explained Tom, poking at the hexagram with his finger, "is four dots followed by one dot, followed by a dot and a dash, followed by a dash and two dots. Morse code for *head*."

His decoding was even quicker than usual.

"Meaning what?" I wondered. "That we're supposed to use our heads to solve our problem? Isn't that obvious? How is that a help?"

"Phone," said Tom.

"What?"

"Foe-un," Tom repeated, turning it into a two-syllable word.

My phone rang.

It was the ringtone I used for my wake-up alarm. My phone thought it was six o'clock on Thursday morning—I had been up for twenty-four hours. It was a good thing I had dozed off during social studies. I slapped the places where my pockets usually were, remembered I was still wearing a dress, and scooped the phone out of my apron. I shut off the alarm, glanced at the phone—and froze.

"It says I've got perfect reception! That shouldn't be possible, should it? In 1852?"

"Cell phones only work if there are cell towers," said Tom. "You should have zilch."

"Unless..." I tried puzzling it out. "This phone is here

right now in two places. I've got one, and my past self has one, but it's the same phone. Maybe it's in touch with itself. Maybe...holy cow!" I finally recognized the voice that had called me just before Killbreath had captured us. "Nobody recognizes their own voice when they hear it over a speaker! That was me! I have to warn him!"

I punched my number into the phone. The phone rang once, twice, three times, and on the fourth ring a voice said, "Hello?"

I knew I had very little time, but at least I knew what I was supposed to say.

"Listen to me," I said, as rapidly as I could. "Whatever you do, don't let Dwina drown! You got that?"

"What?"

"Don't let Dwina drown! Repeat it!"

"Who is this?"

"Repeat what I just said!"

"Uh, don't..."

"Let Dwina drown!"

"Let Dwina dwown. I mean, drown."

"Good. Now duck!"

"What?

"DUCK!"

The phone went dead.

"All right," I said. "About how long did it take, after Killbreath captured us, before we all arrived here at the barn?"

Frankie thought for a moment. "About forty-five minutes, tops."

"Then we have forty-five minutes to figure out what we have to undo."

"Assuming we didn't do it between getting captured and arriving here," said Tom.

"Let's hope we didn't. I don't remember us talking much. Not with burlap bags over our heads."

Frankie thumbed the tablet to life.

"If we're lucky, this thing's got an encyclopedia, or something similar, stored in its memory," she said, searching through the apps.

I pointed at the tablet's upper right corner with Tom's pencil.

"Watch out for that," I said, tapping the spot. It showed the battery life was down to 2 percent. "What the—?" I looked closely at the pencil for the first time. "This pencil has *KILL-BREATH* printed on it!"

"Yeah," agreed Tom. "I noticed that. It's probably a campaign pencil, the sort of thing they give away before an election. Puma Ma's got a sponge with our congressman's name on it. She says it's ironic."

"No," I said. "Then it would say something like *VOTE FOR KILLBREATH*. This just says *KILLBREATH No. 2*."

"Maybe the opposing candidate paid for it," suggested Tom. "Maybe they were comparing Killbreath to a big load of the old number two." Tom held up two fingers and grinned.

"No," I disagreed. "It's more like it was made by the Killbreath Pencil Company!"

"'Killbreath Graphite Novelties,'" Frankie read from the tablet. "'Founded 1853. The most successful pencil-making company in the history of the world. It made its founder, former slave catcher Archibald "Kill" Killbreath, a millionaire by the time he was thirty, and enabled the start of the Killbreath political dynasty.'" Frankie looked up at us. "Ask me what made Killbreath Graphite Novelties so successful."

"What?"

"It was the first company to put an eraser on the end of a pencil!"

Tom fell to his knees and clutched his head. "Oh no! The pencil I had been using to write out the hexagrams—that's what gave Killbreath the idea! And the *Trouble* hexagram contained the Morse code message *erase!* That's what it meant! This is all my fault!"

"No, it isn't," I tried to reassure him.

"It is! If I'd only made more mistakes, the eraser would have been worn down, and he wouldn't have noticed it!"

"Okay, then," I couldn't resist saying. "Maybe it is your fault. He never would have gotten the idea from one of *my* pencils."

"So what we have to do"—Frankie enunciated slowly and deliberately, as if she were talking to children—"is make sure Killbreath never finds the pencil. Then his family will never become rich and powerful, and the future will go back to being what it was when we first left it. We can fix this!"

"I can't believe something as simple as a pencil is at the bottom of all this," I said.

"Oh, I don't know," replied Tom, recovering quite quickly from his guilt trip. "I once read a book where a zucchini-colored crayon was at the bottom of a plot to take over the world."

"Sounds awful."

"It wasn't that bad. A little loony at times—"

"Focus!" Frankie hissed. "Our best chance of getting the

pencil is between the time they brought us into the barn and the moment Killbreath took it to write down our names."

We joined her, looking over the hayloft's edge at the barn floor below.

"They dragged us in," said Tom, reviewing what had happened. "I managed to kick one of them in the shins—"

"That was me," I said.

"Oh. Sorry. And then they tied us to the posts, left the burlap sacks over our heads, and frisked us. They spread our stuff out on that bench down there. The pencil was tucked into my *I-Ching* book for at least half an hour before Killbreath found it."

"So, it's during that time that we'll have to get it back," said Frankie. "Any ideas?"

"Yeah," I said. "Mr. Ganto jumps down, knocks their heads together, unties us, and we get the pencil back."

"Do you remember that happening?" asked Frankie.

"No. Of course not."

"Then it didn't happen. Whatever we did, our earlier selves didn't notice. If they had noticed, they would have behaved differently afterward, and we wouldn't be having this conversation right now."

"My head hurts!" Tom complained.

"It's lack of sleep," I assured him.

"It's time-travel nuttiness," he corrected me. *"Paradoxical!"*

"Whatever we do to keep that pencil from Killbreath," said Frankie, "we have to do it so cleverly that our earlier selves are unaware that we're doing it."

"Okay," I said, eyeing a coil of rope hanging off a peg on the opposite side of the barn. "How about this?"

My friends huddled around me as I explained my plan.

CHAPTER 17
Thunk! Clangity-Clank! Thzzzt! and Klonk!

M y friends, of course, didn't like my plan, so we came up with two alternate plans and they voted unanimously to make my plan THE LAST RESORT. We barely had time to set up a few necessary props before the barn door flew open and our earlier selves were dragged in by Killbreath and his boys.

Frankie, Tom, and I were well hidden, watching from above, as our earlier selves, with bags over our heads—or maybe over *their* heads—got tied up below us. And that was strange. It would have been worse if I had been able to see our faces—that would have been *really* freaky—but it was bad enough knowing the scrawny kids being bullied below us were...*us*. I had seen prisoners with bags over their heads on television. I tried to imagine what it would be like to see one of those bags pulled off and the face beneath it turn out to be mine. It would definitely make me think of prisoners differently.

Killbreath warned our twins not to speak unless spoken to. He spread out their possessions—including the Time Trombone and the book containing the history-rewriting pencil—on the bench. He and the other two creeps, Bert and Zack, got into a huddled conversation about whether or not there might be other "runners" in the area.

I remembered hearing their conversation during the time my head had been in the sack. I also remembered some odd noises—*thunk! clangity-clank! thzzzt!* and *klonk!*—along with an argument about somebody getting drunk. Maybe those noises had nothing to do with our trying to snatch the pencil. Then again, maybe they did. I would have paid more attention if I had known there was going to be a quiz.

Killbreath and his boys didn't notice the mouse.

The mouse was plan A. He moved stealthily up the leg of the bench and raised his head just high enough to see over the top. Then he ducked back down, and waited.

Frankie insisted the mouse's name was Melvin. She warned us that if anything scared Mel, she would lose what little control she had over him, and he would need time to calm down before she could use him to retrieve her bracelet later on.

Mel's head once again came up over the bench's side. The rest of his body followed, and he flattened himself against the wood, crawling commando-style toward the pencil. He got as far as Tom's flashlight, hid behind it, and peered cautiously around it.

Killbreath and Bert had their backs to the bench. Zack sat down on a grain bin and started picking his teeth with a bowie knife. He took a swig from a little brown jug he held in the crook of one arm.

Mel broke from cover and ran the length of the Shagbolt. He peeked around the end of the case, less than a foot away from his goal. He took a hesitant step forward.

Thunk!

The bowie knife embedded itself in the bench only a whisker's width ahead of him. Every hair on Mel's body stood on end and, looking more like a hedgehog than a mouse, he dived off the bench, hit the floor, and disappeared down a knothole. Zack ambled over, grinning, and wiggled his knife out of the wood.

Plan B, I said to myself.

Tom glanced at me, gave a thumbs-up, then turned and headed for the back of the loft. He grabbed a rope we had tied to a nail, and lowered himself out the door to the barnyard below.

Plan B involved Tom causing a commotion outside and, we hoped, drawing all three slave catchers out to check on it. During the frantic few minutes before the arrival of Killbreath and his boys, we had scoured the barnyard for usable noise makers. We left some rusted pots and pans from the remains of the farmhouse piled up behind one of the bigger trees. Tom was supposed to make a racket with these, then run for his life. If the slave catchers took the bait and left us by ourselves, Frankie would drop down and grab the pencil.

Clangity-clank! Clangity-clank!

The sound matched what I remembered. I hadn't been sure it would—otherwise, I would have told Frankie to skip her experiment with Melvin. It wasn't too loud, though, and I wondered if it was enough to trick everybody into going out.

The rest of what I remembered hearing at the time didn't give me a clue. I had been too scared to wonder about the noises around me.

All three of the men looked in the direction of the noise. Killbreath raised a finger to his lips, nodded Bert toward the door, then tapped Zack on the chest and pointed to the floor, indicating he should stay. Killbreath followed Bert out.

So plan B got rid of only two of them.

Plan C.

THE LAST RESORT.

Me.

Zack wasn't happy about being left behind. He jammed his hands in his pockets, kicked a corncob across the floor, and returned to the jug he had left on top of the grain bin.

Frankie threw a pebble across the length of the barn. It rattled in a horse stall and Zack crouched, pulled out his knife, and crept over to investigate.

The moment his back was turned, I rolled off the crossbeam I had been hiding on near the ceiling and plummeted toward the bench directly below me.

Thzzzt! went the rope that circled my waist and looped over the beam as Mr. Ganto, who had the rope's other end, let it out from his place near the back of the loft. He could raise and lower me, like I was a human piñata. I hoped I didn't get clubbed—I didn't want to see candy bars burst out of my butt.

I was in my underwear. A dress—or even jeans and a sweatshirt—might have snagged on something and given me away. My boxer shorts had little blue elephants on them. I decided, if we managed to save the future, I would try to have more say in underwear purchases.

I descended rapidly and then lurched to a halt about two feet above the bench, like a burglar dropping down from a skylight in a movie—a burglar who had forgotten to put his pants on.

I reached for the pencil. My fingers grazed it and then I was swinging away from it, twisting wildly at the end of the rope. I made swimming motions with my hands, trying to get back to where I wanted to be, but that only made me spin faster, like one of the midway rides at Camlo's carnival, the kind that make you puke. I shouldn't have thought of puke. It's not a good thing to think of when you're spinning. The barn whirled around me and I felt myself getting ready to spew.

I tried to remember if, when I was tied up with a bag over my head, I had smelled vomit. The bag had smelled like rotten potatoes, so it was difficult to tell. But nobody had said, "Hey, where did all this puke come from?" so I guessed I had managed to keep it to myself. I didn't remember the sound of upchucking, and that's not something you quickly forget.

I lunged for the edge of the bench, caught it, and pulled myself hand over hand down its length. I touched the pencil, but before I could get my fingers around it, I was shooting back into the air even faster than I had dropped—*tzzzht!* the sound was reversed—and I saw Zack turning around below me. Mr. Ganto was pulling me up so I wouldn't be seen.

This, then, I decided, was the *Rising*, the *Ascending*, the *I-Ching* hexagram had mentioned. I wondered how my *head* figured into it. Zack passed directly beneath me, glancing this way and that, knife at the ready, like one of the bad guys from the video game *Grand Theft Stagecoach*.

The rope around my waist slipped. Grabbing for it, I clutched my shorts instead, keeping them on even as the rope passed over them and cinched itself tight around my feet. I was dangling upside down by my ankles, like a tea bag about to be dropped into hot water. The hot-water part was pretty accurate. I looked toward the floor and found myself staring into Zack's upturned face.

The rope broke.

I dropped six inches, hung there for a split second, then plummeted headfirst onto the slave catcher. *Klonk!* The last of the mysterious sounds was explained as our heads hit with a resounding crack. Just before I lost consciousness I thought, *So that's what the* I-Ching *meant by* head.

I awoke on my back, staring toward the rafters. The broken rope was still swinging, so I knew I had only been out for a few seconds. Sitting up, massaging my scalp, and rolling to my knees took only a moment. There was something urgent I had to do, but I was foggy about the details. Writing was involved. Maybe I had to take a test. Zack was lying next to me, blinking rapidly, mumbling something that sounded like "flying boy."

When I got up and tried to take a step, I fell over, since my feet were tied together. Loosening the knot, I pulled the rope up around my waist and tightened it like a belt. I probably thought it *was* a belt, I was so groggy. I got up again, staggered over to the bench, and picked up the pencil.

Still not thinking terribly clearly, I stuck the pencil between my teeth, bit off the eraser, and swallowed it. Then I put the eraser-less pencil back in the book.

The voices of Killbreath and Bert came from outside the

barn door, while Zack was rubbing his eyes and shaking his head. Frankie leaned out of the loft and waved frantically at me. I wobbled over to the grain bin, lifted its hinged lid, and fell forward into a mound of musty oats. The lid fell shut over me.

"You 'n' Zack'll stand watch," said Killbreath, to the sound of the barn door opening and footsteps on the threshing floor. "Until we hear from Chester. Jus' in case it's bobolitionists."

I looked out through the crack between the bin and its lid. Zack was getting to his feet, and Killbreath and Bert were approaching him. The end of the rope I was tied to snaked across the floor from the bench to the bin where I was hiding, like a neon sign saying LOOK HERE.

I started to reel it in. Before it had moved six inches, Zack had staggered upright, lurched forward, and stood on it with both feet. I stopped pulling.

"What in tarnation's wrong with you?" Killbreath demanded as he got closer to Zack. "You reek!"

The front of Zack's shirt was wet. I could see the jug had fallen and rolled beneath the bench.

"Boy," muttered Zack, pointing upward.

"*Boy* is right!" snarled Killbreath. "Didn't I warn ya 'bout drinking moonshine from Luther Owens's still? Stuff'll kill ya! I have a cousin tried some—he was blind for three days! No one works for me drunk!"

Zack threw his shoulders back and tried to stand without wavering.

"I am not drunk!"

I yanked on the rope as hard as I could. Zack flailed his arms and fell over. I reeled in the rest like it was spaghetti and the bin was starving, and I got it all inside without anyone seeing.

"Not drunk, are ya?" Killbreath hauled Zack to his feet and shook him like a dirty doormat.

"I seen somethin'!" Zack protested. "There was blue elephants!"

"And my cousin seen dancin' dill pickles, afore he couldn't see nothin' at all! You 'n' Bert get outside, an' watch for bobolitionists. Some un' was nosin' round out there!"

Bert took Zack by the arm and assisted him out the door. I watched as Killbreath found a rickety-looking chair near the opposite wall and positioned it near the bench. He picked up one of our cell phones, scowled at it, put it back, then went over and one by one yanked the sacks from the heads of our twins.

"Don't mean you can talk," he warned us. "You ain't been spoke to yet!"

There was a funny taste in my mouth. I wondered if I had eraser breath. I would have thought eating an eraser would make your mouth all fresh and clean.

"Let's jus' say I'm a naturally curious cuss," said Killbreath, beginning a speech I remembered only too well, "so I would like to know whose house it was you broke into, an' why, of all the swag you coulda taken, you stole a slide horn and some gutta-percha pitcher frames."

I coiled the excess rope around my waist. My movements caused a loose board in the back of the bin to loosen even further, and with the soft hiss of breakfast cereal pouring into a bowl, moldy oats began spilling out of the bin onto the floor behind it. The opening looked just wide enough for me to fit through. I slid out with the oats and crawled on all fours to where the barn's side door hung half-open.

I peered out cautiously, looking for any sign of Bert and Zack, and when I saw the coast was clear, I slipped into the barnyard.

Frankie stepped out from behind a tree and waved me urgently over to her. She and Mr. Ganto had gotten out through the loft door, which wasn't far from the tree, and a rustling in the branches overhead told me where Mr. Ganto was. Bert and Zack were on the other side of the barn from us.

"We have a problem," said Frankie when I reached them. She had my balled-up clothing tucked under one arm. "Tom wasn't waiting for us. Mr. Ganto found this on the ground." She held up Tom's apron. There was blood on it. "I'm afraid something's happened to him!"

CHAPTER 18
I Am a Yo-yo

I took the apron. A dark red streak near the pocket glistened. I sniffed it. It was definitely blood.

"The moment I saw you hide in the grain bin, I figured we were all right," Frankie whispered. "Mr. Ganto and I got out of the barn and did a quick look around. There's no sign of Tom. Somebody or something may have gotten him; he may have been chased by an animal; maybe he had an accident. The thing is, we can't call out for him; otherwise, those goons will hear us. If he's someplace close, but injured, he knows he can't call out, either."

"We have to find him!"

"Mr. Ganto wants me to use the Shagbolt and take us back to our own time. He's got it up in the tree with him. If Tom is close enough to hear it, he'll come back with us."

"And if he's not?"

"He must still be in range. Not much time has passed."

"What if he's unconscious?"

Frankie blinked. "I honestly don't know. For the Shagbolt to work, I think the conscious mind has to hear the notes and somehow process them. Being unconscious may be a deal breaker."

"I'm not leaving without Tom," I informed her. "He's my best friend." I looked up into the tree, where I could see Mr. Ganto's face gazing down at us. "And I'm not leaving until I've checked out a riverboat called the *Buckeye Beauty*. Dwina's and Seth's lives may depend on it. Mine, too."

"Excuses," said Mr. Ganto.

"I'll give you one more excuse," I replied, thinking clearly for the first time since butting heads with Zack. "If we play the Shagbolt now, there are three kids tied up in that barn who will hear it and go back to the future with us. Wouldn't that complicate things?"

Ganto gave me a sour look, then nodded.

"I had forgotten all about them," Frankie admitted.

"Taking ourselves back to the future with us would mess things up royally."

"Yeah," I agreed. "I'd hate to have to share my toothbrush. Even with myself."

Gunshots resounded from inside the barn, announcing the death of an innocent flashlight.

"So what do we do?" asked Mr. Ganto.

I shook Tom's apron and caught the quarter as it fell from the pocket.

"We can ask the *I-Ching* where Tom is," I said, tossing the coin in the air. It came down tails. I picked up a twig and drew a broken line in the dirt.

"I got the impression you didn't believe in the *I-Ching*," said Frankie.

"I've changed my mind," I said. After a moment I added, "About a lot of things."

Five more coin flips and we had a hexagram that looked like this:

I dug the *I-Ching* book out of the apron, slipped it from the Ziploc bag, and looked it up. It turned out to be the forty-eighth hexagram.

HEXAGRAM 48

THE WELL.

RESOURCES. SUSTENANCE. A HOLE
IN THE GROUND CAN EITHER TAKE
LIFE OR SUSTAIN IT. WATCH YOUR
STEP. STAY GROUNDED. YOU CAN SEE
STARS FROM THE BOTTOM OF A WELL
IN BROAD DAYLIGHT, BUT ONLY IF
YOU REMEMBER TO LOOK UP.

"Is there a well around here?" I asked.

"Haven't seen one," rumbled Ganto. "Odd."

"Where would an old-time farm have its well?" I asked Frankie, as if it were the kind of information she might have.

She shook her head and guessed. "Near the house?"

"Yeah," I agreed. "But probably nowhere near the out-house, right?"

I pointed. South of the farmhouse was a tiny building with

a missing door; a bench with butt-sized holes in it was just visible inside. I remembered Tom once telling me that before the invention of toilet paper, one of the things people used was corncobs. It was the kind of useless but interesting fact he was always coming out with. I suddenly missed him a lot.

"So maybe on the north side?" said Frankie.

"But not too far from the barn," I reasoned. "Cows and horses need water, too. So somewhere there?" I pointed to what I thought was the most likely area, glanced to make sure neither Bert nor Zack was in our line of sight, and headed for it.

The area was overgrown with weeds. Thistles scratched at my bare legs. Frankie and I fanned out, looking for some trace of a well. Mr. Ganto crouched low behind Frankie, trying to be inconspicuous.

I stubbed my toe on a low rock wall and almost fell headfirst into a hole in the ground. At one time the wall had circled the hole, but most of the wall had fallen in, leaving an unprotected pit that some safety-minded person had placed wooden planks across. The planks had rotted, and it looked as though someone had recently fallen through.

"Tom?" I said his name softly, not wanting the slave catchers to hear me. I moved an unbroken plank to one side, allowing more light into the hole. A big hand reached around me and cleared the well's mouth completely. Mr. Ganto sidled past me to get a better look.

"Bro?" said the well.

Tom was at the bottom, knee-deep in water, looking forlornly upward.

"Are you all right?"

"I lost my book!"

"We have it," I assured him. He didn't appear to be broken.

"I can't climb out—the walls are too slick!"

"I'll come down for you," I said, looking around, trying to figure out how I might do that without getting trapped myself.

"It's a good thing you're dressed as a yo-yo," said Mr. Ganto.

"Dressed as a what?" I wasn't sure I had heard him correctly.

He picked me up, held me above the well, and dropped me.

"Yo-yo," he repeated.

I fell, spinning, as the rope around my waist uncoiled. Mr. Ganto was gripping the rope's end, and as I realized what was happening, I hoped he had it tightly. The wall of the well flashed by around me, and I caught the rope before it ran out, lurching, straightening, and dropping the final few feet at a speed that was a little less stomach churning. I wound up dangling about a foot above Tom's head.

"I was running, looking behind me to see if they had seen me—" he began.

"And you fell through the boards," I finished for him. "I get it. Grab my hands."

"I cut myself on the edge of one of the pots I was banging."

"Bad?"

"It took a while to stop bleeding."

The rope jiggled impatiently.

"Give me the hand that didn't get cut."

I used both hands to clutch the arm he extended, grabbing him above the elbow with one and tightly by the wrist with the other. The place on my arm that Dwina had bandaged throbbed painfully.

"Ready?" I asked him, but before he could answer we were ascending, Mr. Ganto rapidly hauling up the rope. We were over the edge of the well in moments.

"We are too exposed here," said Ganto, setting us down on our feet. He turned and loped away, heading for the cover of a grove of trees. Frankie flapped her apron at us, as if we were barnyard geese, and we stumbled after him.

"You were in a well," muttered Frankie a few minutes later as she bandaged Tom's hand with a strip of cloth she had ripped from the bottom of my dress, "but you couldn't take a moment to wash your cut?"

"I didn't know how clean the water was," answered Tom. Quite reasonably, I thought.

We were safely away from the barn and Killbreath's gang, concealed amid pines with low-hanging branches. Mr. Ganto sat cross-legged on a bed of pine needles, the Shagbolt case open on his lap, as though he fully expected the Time Trombone to be used at any moment.

"Yo-yo?" I said to him. "Was that supposed to be a joke?"

"Yes." He grinned at me with teeth the size of tombstones.

"Mr. Ganto," explained Frankie, "being from the Pleistocene, has a primitive sense of humor. He likes slapstick. Clever wordplay doesn't amuse him, and he always looks grave at a pun."

"I felt my apron fall off as I ran," said Tom. "I was so afraid I had lost the *I-Ching* book. But you found it! And my quarter!"

"We used the *I-Ching* to find you," Frankie informed him, tying off her bandage and letting his arm drop.

"You did? Which hexagram?"

"*The Well*," I said. "Apparently, there isn't a hexagram called *Clumsy Idiot*."

"*The Well*," Tom repeated, thumbing through his book. "Did you do the Morse?"

"I don't know Morse," I reminded him. "And hiding from slave catchers seemed more important."

"Here it is," said Tom, finding the page and studying it, moving his lips silently as he worked to decode it. Then he went, "Ha!"

"'Ha'? What, 'ha'?"

"This time it's a message for *you*."

"Me? Like, me, personally? What?"

"Two dots, followed by a dash and a dot, then a dot and a dash, followed by another dash and dot, ending with a single dot."

"Spelling?"

"*Inane*."

"*Inane?*"

"That's one of the two words you asked for, isn't it? I can't remember what the other one was."

"It was *stupid*."

"That's probably why I can't remember it."

"How is that possible?" My voice went up an octave. "How could this three-thousand-year-old *I-Ching* thing contain, in Morse code, a word I specifically asked for?"

"Apparently it takes requests."

"Are you saying *it's watching us*?"

"What're you, crazy?"

"Then how—"

"It's *listening* to us." Tom gave me a look as if that explained everything.

"Are you going to spend the rest of the day in your underwear?" Frankie asked. She handed my clothes back to me. I gave Tom an exasperated look, then wiggled into my jeans and sweatshirt.

"And the dress," Frankie reminded me.

"You ripped it," I said accusingly, showing her the ragged place where she had gotten Tom's bandage.

"So?"

"I don't want to go around in tatters. What will people think?"

"You *have* changed." Frankie nodded approval, as if she thought I was serious. But I put on the dress and jammed the bonnet back on my head.

"Time to go," said Mr. Ganto, lifting the Shagbolt from its case and extending it toward Frankie. "It would be best if we arrived at the carnival shortly after you borrowed the golf cart."

"We can't go back yet," responded Frankie, putting one hand gently on the trombone but not taking it. "We have to go to the town docks and check out a boat called the *Buckeye Beauty*. There's a chance it may explode, killing one of Rose's ancestors, meaning Rose would cease to exist."

I got a sudden warm feeling, realizing Frankie was concerned about me.

"But he is standing right there," murmured Mr. Ganto. "Obviously, whatever you fear did not happen."

"It may not have happened because we are about to prevent it," Frankie explained, and I felt the start of a headache. I had trouble following the ins and outs of time travel. "If we leave now, it won't be prevented, and Rose may silently vanish away. Or maybe pop like a soap bubble."

"Excuse me?" The idea was scary.

"If Dwina dies before her time," Frankie continued, "it could cause other changes to the future, even more serious than the loss of Rose. We might return to a future just as bleak as the one in which the Killbreaths are in control. Rose had a powerful premonition. Romani don't ignore premonitions! We might have to save Dwina to make sure there's still a future for us to go back to."

"Your father sent me after you," Mr. Ganto reminded Frankie. "I am supposed to return you to him as soon as possible. He is my boss, and my friend. We should go."

"You didn't, by any chance, talk to my mother about it?"

"She was unavailable."

"Of course she was. But you're *my* friend, too, you know. That should count for something!"

Mr. Ganto scowled a scowl the size of a punch bowl. "All right, then. Let the book decide," he said.

"What book?" I asked, even though I knew full well. The *I-Ching* was beginning to creep me out big-time.

Mr. Ganto waved his hand at *If You Have an I-Ching— Scratch!*, which was still open in Tom's hands. "Toss your coin. Ask if we should continue here or go home. I will abide by the answer."

Tom nodded agreement. Six tosses later we were looking at yet another hexagram. I recognized it as the one Tom had on his sweatshirt.

Hexagram 32

Perseverance.

Stay the course. Ride it out.
Endure. Constancy is a virtue.
Prayers are answered in the
order in which they are received
(you can imagine the backlog).

"Sounds to me like we stay," said Frankie.

"It's three dots, followed by a dot and a dash," said Tom, "followed by two dashes and a dot, ending in a final dot. That would be an *S*, and an *A* . . . it spells the word *sage*."

"What?" I asked. "Those smelly green flakes my mother sprinkles in her turkey stuffing?"

"It also means 'wise,'" said Frankie, "as in 'sage advice.' The *I-Ching* is saying we would be wise to persevere."

We all looked to Mr. Ganto. He slipped the trombone back in its case, snapped the latches, and stood.

"Let's go find your riverboat," he said.

CHAPTER 19
Coffins and Hogsheads

FINEST BOAT ON THE GUSTIMUCK!

DOUBLE BOILERS! QUICK PASSAGE!

THE *BUCKEYE BEAUTY*

DEPARTS FREEDOM FALLS

MCCOY DOCK

FORTNIGHTLY THURSDAYS

5:00 O'CLOCK IN THE AFTERNOON

ARRIVES JORDAN 7:30

"Is that supposed to be Fort Nightly?" I asked. "Like Fort Shawnee? Is it a town?"

"'Fortnightly' means 'every fourteen days,'" said Tom. "It takes the boat two weeks to go down the Gustimuck to the Ohio and then on to Louisville and come back again, stopping at two dozen towns along the way. Freedom Falls is its other turnaround point. It keeps shuttling back and forth between Freedom Falls and Louisville. This is so cool! Look at all the old-time fonts!"

He was scrunched down, reading the faded print on the poster's bottom. The poster—Tom called it a broadside—was plastered to a wall on a shed near the docks, surrounded by other broadsides advertising local merchants.

"That must be McCoy Dock over there," said Frankie, pointing to a remote pier where bales of cotton were being unloaded from the only steamboat in sight. The boat had the layered wedding-cake look of the traditional river steamer, with a paddle wheel on its end and a wheelhouse set behind twin smokestacks on its top deck. It matched the exploding boat in my vision perfectly.

The hours following Tom's rescue from the well had been uneventful. At the first house we had come to, pies had been cooling on the sill of an open window and, seeing no one around, we had snuck under the window and pretended the pies were trying to escape from a burning building and our aprons were firemen's nets. The pies jumped (or, the more suspicious might guess, were pushed) and we saved them from the hard, cruel ground.

Later, sitting on the far side of a hedge, licking the plates clean, we had heard a woman with a strong German accent shout, "Hans! Fritz! Vot has you done mit za pies?" Her question was followed by what sounded like two small boys being spanked simultaneously. We had guiltily left the plates under the hedge and tiptoed out the gate, past a post bearing the name Katzenjammer.

Sometime after that, looking for the best road to take into town, we had seen ourselves go by in the hay wagon. It had come around the bend unexpectedly and, with no time to hide, we had thrown ourselves against the rails of a fence and struck nonchalant poses as though we had been there for hours. I caught myself looking at me through a gap in the hay and started to wave to myself, but Frankie slapped my hand down and held it to my side.

"This is no time to flirt," she had hissed under her breath.

"Did you see the way I was looking at me?" I replied, indignant. "I was checking me out! I should be ashamed of myself!"

"You are very weird," Frankie informed me.

From a safe distance, we watched Zack stop the wagon and begin the events that would end with the collapse of the pier and my saving Dwina from drowning. We had watched until the horses had bolted and Zack had gotten the better of Mr. Collins, finally regaining his shotgun and knocking Collins into some brambles—and then we had eased on past them and followed the road into town.

Mr. Ganto kept to the trees, and when we had gotten to the outskirts of town he had leaned out from a low-hanging limb and said, "I must keep out of sight. I will stay within earshot. Here"—he handed Frankie the trombone case—"do your best to save your friend. Should anything go wrong, play the Shagbolt. Get us out of here." A branch had snapped back into place and Mr. Ganto had vanished.

"So what do we do?" asked Tom. "Wait at the gangplank and make sure Dwina and Seth don't get on the boat?"

"That's not the worst idea," said Frankie.

We walked along the waterfront, passing storage buildings and taverns. The sign at a shipyard declared they built everything, FROM FRIVOLOUS YACHTS TO STERN-WHEELERS. We reached McCoy Dock and strolled out to the *Buckeye*

Beauty's gangplank. We stood self-consciously, trying to look as though we had some sort of business there.

I could see the town clock tower from where we were. It said four fifteen. If Dwina and Seth were going to board the *Beauty*, they had forty-five minutes to get there. I was hoping they wouldn't show and my vision would turn out to be a meaningless dream.

As we watched, the riverboat hands finished off-loading the cotton and began taking on new cargo. They used dollies and skids to move bulky crates from the dock, until most of the boat's main deck was full. A crane lifted coarse nets full of kegs and wooden boxes to a spot on the middle deck.

"It's hard to say good-bye to a friend," said a man in a green coat as he walked alongside a cart with a coffin on it. He patted the coffin, and the man pushing the cart brought it to a halt opposite the gangplank. The three of us stepped respectfully out of the way. Before we did, I saw a brass plate on the coffin lid engraved with the name ISHMAEL DINKLEHOOPER.

" 'Call me Ishmael,' he said, the first day he walked into my pawnshop," Green Coat continued. "What a one he was for telling the stories!"

"He owed me money," grumbled a man in a battered top hat, who had been walking to the left of Green Coat.

"He was a whaling man," replied Coat.

"Cried a lot, did he?" asked the cart man.

Coat ignored him. "His last voyage ended badly. The entire ship was lost. He wrote a book about it, published last year, but it sank quicker than the ship did. It made him nothing. Otherwise, you'd have your money. Now he's headed downriver to the family burial plot. Sad."

"Bah!" The man in the top hat spat into the river, turned, and stomped away.

Coat looked around for more audience, spotted us, and said, "Considering the harrowing events of his final whale hunt, it was rather ironic the way he died."

"Ironic?" asked Tom, taking the bait.

"He choked to death on a shrimp."

Coat shook his head. "Foresaw it, too," he added. "Always was one for prophetic dreams, was old Ishmael. Yet it didn't stop him from ordering the scampi."

We watched the coffin get loaded aboard the *Beauty*.

"Shouldn't we warn the captain that his boat is going to explode?" I said, feeling just a little bit guilty to be worried only about my ancestors and no one else.

"You'd probably want to warn the captain of the *Titanic* his ship was going to hit an iceberg, too," Frankie said disgustedly.

"Well, yeah, *duh*," I replied.

"If you're a time traveler, you can't go running up and down the *Titanic*'s decks shouting 'Iceberg!' the moment the ship leaves the dock," said Frankie, shaking her head sadly. "You can't take the bullet for Abraham Lincoln, and you can't strangle Hitler in his crib."

"You could wait until he was five," suggested Tom, and Frankie glared at him.

"Some events are too major to change," she continued. "The alterations to the future would be too drastic. You'd return to a place you would never recognize."

"Maybe it would be better," I suggested.

"More likely, it would be worse. We've already seen the trouble an eraser can make. I think the only reason we were able to fix that was because it was such a tiny thing. But a riverboat blowing up is big-time. I don't want to sound cold or anything, but my family knows more about time travel than anybody. We have to limit ourselves to saving Dwina and Seth. If the *Beauty* exploded, and people were killed, it was a tragedy, but it could be a bigger one if we stopped it."

"Does the tablet say anything about it?" I asked, suddenly remembering we had future tech with us.

Frankie gave me a look that said she had forgotten about it, too, and she pulled the tablet from her apron. We huddled around her so no one could see what we were doing, and she tickled the screen to life.

"Fortunately," she said, "the thing *does* have a built-in encyclopedia. But that doesn't mean it has information on every— wait, here's something..." She read aloud. " '*Buckeye Beauty*, stern-wheeler built in 1848 in Marietta, Ohio... one hundred ten feet long... under the command of Captain Cyrus Mishrag...' blah, blah, blah—ah! 'Boiler exploded at ten minutes to six on the evening of August 12, 1852, resulting in—' "

The tablet's screen went black, except for a small box containing the words:

BATTERY CRITICAL.
RECHARGE IMMEDIATELY.
SHUTTING DOWN.
BYE.

Then that, too, winked out, and we were left with a shiny, black, totally useless piece of glass.

"Ten to six," I said. "That's, like, ninety minutes from now!"

I pressed the dead tablet to my face and stared into the darkened glass, trying to see the future. Frankie immediately understood what I was attempting. After a moment she asked, "Anything?"

"I see a cross-eyed guy with a squashed nose," I reported.

"That would be you, and it isn't the future," she said glumly. "Scrying never works when you're trying too hard. It may take years of practice before you can do it at will."

"Is that a canoe?" Tom asked, off topic as usual.

He was staring into the river. Frankie and I followed his gaze and I climbed up a bale of cotton for a better look.

"No," I said. "It's an uprooted tree, with some kind of knobby thing down one end. It looks like the Lesser Gustimuck's got it."

The Gustimuck River split in two when it hit the spit of land where the town of Freedom Falls was located. The larger, calmer part of the river—the Greater Gustimuck—flowed southward along the west side of town. The narrower, more turbulent part—the Lesser Gustimuck—flowed southward along the east, until it became a forty-foot waterfall that tumbled down into a rocky pool that knocked it so senseless, it split into numerous streams and wandered off in all directions. In modern times, only boats equipped with engines used the docks on Freedom Falls' east side; canoes and kayaks used the west side docks. In 1852, it was steamboats to the east, and unpowered flatboats, like the one we had seen near the cooperage, to the west.

"Clear the way, ladies!" a tall, bearded man carrying a trunk bellowed as he stepped around Frankie and Tom and proceeded across the gangplank. I jumped down from the cotton bale and tripped over my skirts as I landed. Floor-length dresses were not designed for an active lifestyle.

Passengers were starting to arrive. Two women with parasols followed the man with the trunk, and a family of five came up behind them. The town clock said 4:40. I turned my back, made sure no one was watching, and punched seventy minutes into my phone's timer. It would count down to the boiler explosion.

Two young boys from the family of five argued over a toy pistol; they settled it by doing rock-paper-scissors. "I invented that," I told them, pleased it was catching on so quickly. The kid who had won the pistol ran off with it, and the one who had lost made the sign of "rock" at me and then chased after him.

In all, we counted fourteen passengers getting on the boat. There was no sign of Dwina and Seth.

"That's a phaeton!" said Tom enthusiastically, identifying a large-wheeled carriage drawn by a single horse that had stopped at the end of the dock. "Phaetons were built for speed. And, do you hear that?" A sound like somebody strangling a cat drifted through the air. "That's a barrel organ! Probably with a warped barrel! Isn't that great? Man, I would love to live in this town!"

"You do," I reminded him.

"No, I mean in 1852! It would be so cool!"

"You really think so?" I said, aghast. "We've had nothing but trouble since we got here!"

"But it wouldn't always be trouble! Things would calm down eventually. And it would be better than practicing piano, and going to medical school, the way Puma Ma has planned for me. I would get to San Francisco somehow, and I would blend right in!" He stopped and looked pleadingly at Frankie. "Are you sure I have to go back with you guys?"

"You can't be serious," I said, watching an approaching wagon. It was full of barrels, and the fancy lettering on its side said DAVISON ROAD COOPERAGE. "Even if you could survive here, think of your family. They would go nuts if you disappeared."

"Puma Ma would still have Dorcas and Yvette. She always liked them best, anyway. Maybe I could write her a message and you could take it to her."

"She'd hand me my head!"

"*Nobody* stays behind," Frankie declared. "You saw the trouble just leaving a pencil here caused. Leaving a twenty-first-century *person* behind could be so much worse!"

"But—"

Frankie held an imperious finger in front of Tom's face. "We do *not* even discuss this!"

The cooperage wagon stopped at the *Buckeye Beauty*'s gangplank. Mr. Collins and one of the men from the Friends Meeting jumped down from the driver's seat and began unloading barrels. A crewman on the boat hollered at them to "stow 'em in the boiler room—we're full up on deck!" and we watched as the two men rolled a dozen small barrels up the gangplank. The town clock said five to five.

The final two barrels were bigger than the others, and Collins and his friend were more careful taking them down from the wagon.

"Those are hogsheads," said Tom.

"What? In the barrels?" I pictured it. "Eww!"

"A large barrel is called a hogshead," Tom muttered, like it was something I should have known.

Collins lost his grip, and the first hogshead struck the deck.

"OOF!" said the hogshead.

That *oof* sounded awfully familiar. "Dwina is in that barrel!" I whispered.

Instead of rolling the hogsheads, Collins and his friend carried them upright. The boat whistle was blowing and the crew was preparing to cast off as the two men finished their last-minute delivery and climbed back on the wagon.

Collins picked up the reins but paused to stare up at the boat's wheelhouse. He shook his head. "Captain Mishrag's family owns slaves in Kentucky, and he's friends with Killbreath and that lot. If he knew he was transporting contraband, he'd be real put out. It's a good thing we've got a friend on the crew!"

"Sure is," agreed his companion. "I always did like Clarence."

Collins made noises at the horses and the wagon backed

up. The gangplank swung away, and the boat began to pull into the river.

"We gotta get aboard!" I shouted, and broke into a run.

I hiked up my skirts and leaped the widening gap between the dock and the boat. A crewman had just jumped aboard after undoing one of the heavy ropes that had been holding the *Beauty* in place. He bellowed at me but I ignored him, turning to catch the Shagbolt case that Frankie tossed before she, too, crossed the gap, and then we both turned and caught Tom as he jumped and almost missed.

"Hey, you kids!" A second crewman joined the first and came running at us.

We sprinted in the opposite direction, dodged into a passage, and ran until we were on the other side of the boat.

"Split up!" Frankie ordered as she jackrabbited up a stairway.

Tom pelted toward the stern and threw himself into a pile of ropes. I flipped myself over the railing, dropped down, and hung off the side of the boat with one hand, clutching the Shagbolt with the other. The river lapped at my feet.

Our two pursuers popped out of the passage, looked

around, and scrambled up the stairs. I hauled myself back to the deck, hoping Frankie had a big enough lead, and gave my phone a quick glance. It was six minutes past five.

We were on a riverboat that was going to explode in forty-four minutes.

CHAPTER 20
Something Going Ka-Boom

"D o we have a plan?" Tom asked two minutes later as we wedged ourselves between some crates on the foredeck in a desperate attempt to stay hidden.

"Don't get caught," I answered, wondering what had happened to Frankie. "If they catch us, they'll hold us as stowaways. We won't be able to save Dwina and Seth."

"We won't be able to save ourselves," Tom added, beginning a familiar series of coin flips. I watched the quarter warily each time he tossed it in the air.

"The hogsheads are in the boiler room," I said. "We should

find them, get Dwina and Seth out, and tell them they have to get off the boat."

"Dwina can't swim."

"Seth can, and he can get her to safety. Should I be thinking of a question?"

"I'm wondering what's going to happen next," said Tom, using his pencil to draw the sixth and final *I-Ching* line—a broken *yin*—on the side of the crate next to him. "The same thing you're wondering."

The completed hexagram looked like this:

"Two *yins* above four *yangs*." Tom consulted his book. "Page one oh eight."

I read over his shoulder.

HEXAGRAM 34

GREAT POWER.

A FORCE TO BE RECKONED WITH.
THUNDER MEANS LIGHTNING.

Explosive energy. Is that a
vacant lot or the home of Con-
solidated Antimatter? How
could you tell?

"Sounds like something going *ka-boom*, to me," I said
uneasily. "What's the Morse?"

"Four dots, three dashes, and a final dash," said Tom. "It
spells *hot*."

"Great power? Hot? It's telling us the steam boilers are
going to explode. It's telling us stuff we already know! What
good is it?"

"If Dwina and Seth are in the boiler room, they're at
ground zero. It's telling us we have to hurry!"

I raised my head above the crates. The coast was clear. We
squeezed out of our hiding spot and, crouching low, headed
for the sound of machinery.

I glanced toward the water and stopped.

"Something's wrong," I said.

We weren't going in the right direction. The boat had
entered the Lesser Gustimuck instead of the Greater. It was a
dead end. I swept my gaze toward the bow, and then I understood. The boat was maneuvering to intercept the floating

tree we had seen earlier. The enormous log was closer, and I could see that the knobby thing down one end was a man, clutching the tree's roots and waving frantically for attention.

"That's—" said Tom.

"Archie Killbreath. I guess he figured out a way to get back across the river from wherever it was Ganto dumped him and his boys. And the boat's going to pick him up. And he's friends with Captain Mishrag. One more reason we can't afford to get caught!"

More and more of the *Beauty*'s passengers and crew were gathering at the bow, waving at the bedraggled man on the log and shouting words of encouragement. One crewman had a long pole with a hook on the end; another was waiting for his chance to throw a rope.

"Come on," I said, "while they're distracted."

We headed for the stern and the loud *thumpa-thumpa* that cried *steam engine*. Just before we got to the paddle wheel, we found a long room open to the air on both sides, full of machinery and two enormous boilers. A man with his back to us was throwing logs into a furnace. Two huge pistons went alternately up and down, turning iron wheels attached to rods that stretched through the back wall and connected to either side of the paddle wheel. Scattered here and there were the barrels Collins had delivered. We found the two hogsheads together near the back wall.

"Hello?" I rapped on the top of one. Close up, I could see holes drilled in the sides for ventilation, cleverly made to look like knots in the wood. I decided this wasn't the first time the barrels had been used to transport people. I hoped that meant there was some easy way to open them.

"Hello!" I shouted again, trying to make myself heard above the racket of the engine. "It's okay! It's me, the kid who pulled Dwina out of the water when the pier collapsed. You have to get off the boat!"

The top of the hogshead dropped two inches, then twisted sideways out of the way. The sweat-streaked face of my great-great-ancestor Dwina looked up at me. "Are we there already? Steam is so fast! It's not natural!"

Seth climbed easily out of the other barrel, ignoring the hand Tom offered him, and helped me lift Dwina from the cocoon of quilts that surrounded her.

"What's goin' on?" Seth asked warily.

"It's hard to explain," I said. "You have to trust me. This boat is going to blow up in half an hour. We have to get off!"

Seth looked like he was going to argue. Dwina stopped him with a touch to his chest.

"Rose has the Sight. If he says *get off*, we get off!"

"HEY THERE!" a new voice shouted, and I spun around to see the guy who had been feeding the fire coming at us, clutching a piece of wood. Seth stepped in front of me with his fists clenched.

"Get back in those barrels!" the man cried. "We ain't nowhere near Jordan yet!"

I leaned around Seth. "Is your name Clarence?"

"Yes, yes, Clarence Whiffletree! They can't be seen! It'll cost me my job! And who are you? Are you with them? How many people did they stuff in them barrels, anyway?"

A number of people shouted "Huzzah!" from the front of the boat, cheering something, and I feared it was Killbreath's rescue.

"There's been a change in plan," I said. "We weren't in the barrels. Mr. Collins sent us. Seth and Dwina have to leave the boat now."

"Are you crazy? We're in the middle of the river!"

Raucous laughter, barely audible above the noise of the engine, came from the bow.

"What on earth?" Clarence Whiffletree gave in to his curiosity and walked out to the railing. He leaned over and looked to the front of the boat. I followed.

"It's Archibald Killbreath," I said. "He just got pulled from the water."

"What, that slave-catcher varmint?"

Clarence walked farther up the deck for a better look. I stayed behind him, allowing him to shield me from view.

"You know him?" I asked.

In answer, Clarence spat in the river. I thought I felt the boat pitch to one side from the force of it.

"Lowlife!"

"Killbreath knows there are runaway slaves on board," I lied, seeing it as a way to get Clarence to help us. "He's figured out the trick with the hogsheads. He'll tell your captain—"

Clarence spat again, this time causing a definite lurch.

"—and they'll search the boat. This is why Dwina and Seth have to jump ship."

"Well, they can't do it here. Don't matter how good they can swim—this here's the Lesser Gustimuck; current's too strong. They'd be over the falls and dashed to death on the rocks afore they could as much as blink. The *BB*'s gonna swing around—and it better start doin' it mighty soon—and head the other way. When that happens, it'll come in real close to the far bank. Shallow water, current not as swift— that'd be the time to jump."

"IT WAS A GIANT APE!" Killbreath's voice rang out, and I peeked around Clarence to see what was going on. Clarence took a few steps closer, and I quickly closed the gap.

"It had EYES O' FIRE 'n' musta been FORTY FEET TALL!" Killbreath stood shakily in the center of a circle of crew and passengers, dripping like a rain cloud. The log he had been clinging to was hitched to the side of the boat. His clothing hung in tatters. Beneath his suit and pants, he was wearing a nineteenth-century woman's frilly corset and pantaloons. A day earlier, I would have found that funny.

"It had GREAT, BIG"—the crowd leaned in close, so as not to miss a single terrifying word—"FLOWERS ON ITS SHIRT!"

One of the women fainted. Her male companion caught her and lowered her gently to the deck.

I craned my neck, looking for some sign of Frankie. She knew Dwina and Seth were in the boiler room. With everybody's attention focused on Killbreath, I figured she would have used the diversion to get to us. But there was no sign of her. I was seriously worried.

"Wait a minute, Kill," said a man in a captain's uniform. "The giant ape was wearing a *shirt*?"

"An' short pants DOWN TO ITS KNEES! Hadda be

escaped from a menagerie or a circus! Left the boys stranded on Chubb Island an' me on Fidget's Point!"

The man I assumed was Captain Mishrag glanced at the river, raised a megaphone to his lips, and shouted, "Mr. Bixby! Bring her around! Get us out of here!"

From overhead there was a cry of "Aye, aye, sir!"

The boat shuddered and began a turn that I could see would be a wide one. I cupped my phone in my hand and checked the time. It was nineteen minutes until the boilers blew.

"Cap'n!" shouted a new voice from the overhead deck. "We caught one of the stowaways!"

Everything inside me turned to ice. I leaned out over the water and looked up. One of the crewmen had Frankie by the scruff of the neck and was holding her against the upper railing, waggling her back and forth like he was doing a puppet show.

"Good work, Stevens!" Mishrag called back.

"That there's my property!" Killbreath declared. "She's a runner! We had her all caught fair an' square, her an' her two friends! That's Dorothy Gale! Don't let her go!"

Mishrag raised the megaphone to his lips, and even though they were separated only by ten feet, bellowed at Stevens,

"Take her to the wheelhouse! We'll be up in a moment. This requires privacy." He aimed the megaphone at the crowd. "Break it up, please! Crew, back to work! The rest of you, give this man some breathing space! He's been through an ordeal! Shipwrecked! Hallucinating!"

"None o' them things!" protested Killbreath. Mishrag threw an arm around his shoulders and hustled him toward a stairway.

I plucked at the back of Clarence's shirt. "C'mon!" I pulled him back to the engine room.

"They've got Frankie!" I told Tom, finding him and Dwina and Seth gathered around a barrel, where Tom had obviously been flipping his quarter and consulting the *I-Ching*. "We have less than twenty minutes to save her! Otherwise, she's going sky-high with everybody else when the boilers blow!"

"That would explain the hexagram."

"What hexagram?"

Tom held it in front of my face.

HEXAGRAM 54

THE WELL-REGARDED MAIDEN.

A GIRL OF SUBSTANCE. MAY NOT
KNOW HER PLACE, SO MAKES EVERY
PLACE HER OWN. APPROACHABLE,
BUT BE PREPARED TO DUCK. A
WOMAN TO WALK THROUGH SAND
FOR, AND BY THAT I MEAN SAND
THAT HAS BEEN HEATED BY THE SUN
UNTIL IT'S BORDERLINE UNCOM-
FORTABLE. USE YOUR JUDGMENT.

"Yeah," I agreed. "That sounds like Frankie. What's the Morse?"

"A dot followed by three dots, then a dash followed by a dot and another dot, ending in two dashes. It spells *esteem*."

"Meaning what?"

"That we're supposed to ESTEEM this girl. Value her and respect her. And, I suppose, rescue her."

"Really?"

"Either that, or it means she's going to die in ESTEEM explosion."

I punched him on the shoulder. "What?" I demanded. "Now it's making puns?"

"Yeah," he admitted sheepishly. "But not very good ones." As if that made it okay.

"More steam, Mr. Whiffletree!" came Mishrag's voice, sounding tinny through a brass speaking tube that hung down from the ceiling between the double boilers.

Clarence shouted "Aye, aye!" and started throwing more logs in the furnace.

"Won't that make it too hot?" I said, coming up beside him.

"These boilers ain't blown in fifty trips," he informed me cheerfully. "They'll only blow if there's a flaw in the plates, which more 'n' more, I'm thinkin' there ain't! At least, I hope there ain't!"

He grinned and threw another log in.

I adjusted my bonnet for maximum concealment and went back outside to check on our progress. The boat had the turn-radius of a *Brontosaurus*, but it was finally swinging around toward the Greater Gustimuck. The shore opposite the town of Freedom Falls was getting closer and closer. The current seemed less swift. I figured there would be plenty of time to get Dwina and Seth safely away from the doomed boat. Rescuing Frankie was the bigger problem.

A plan popped into my head.

Immediately, I didn't like it.

As soon as we had seen Seth and Dwina safely on their way, I would play the Time Trombone. I was pretty sure I could hit the right notes to take the three of us home. Mr. Ganto had said he would be within earshot, so he would come, too. We would be whisked away, just before the boat exploded.

And everybody else would die in the explosion.

The two little boys who had used rock-paper-scissors on the dock ran past me, the one with the gun chasing the other and shouting "Ka-pow! Ka-pow!" The one being chased turned, aimed his finger, and shouted "Ka-pow!" right back.

I looked at my phone.

Fourteen minutes.

I had seen two other kids on board, one of them a baby. Clarence seemed like a nice enough guy, helping runaway slaves and all, and I was sure there were other good people on the boat as well.

Frankie had said we couldn't interfere. What had happened in the past couldn't be changed, because it would put the future in peril. You couldn't deflect the bullet intended for Lincoln, you couldn't warn the *Titanic*, you couldn't save the crew and passengers of the *Buckeye Beauty* if it was their fate to be blown sky-high.

"Oh yeah?" I said.

And I came up with a better plan.

CHAPTER 21
That Which Does Not Kill Me Will Probably Try Harder Next Time

The boat started, at last, to come out of its turn. Straightening, the bow began to point downstream into the Greater Gustimuck, the riverbank on the right about forty feet away from us. The water looked shallow, so I figured it was time for Dwina and Seth to be on their way.

I took two steps toward the engine room and was thrown to the deck.

A grinding roar like boulders rubbing against each other filled the air, and the boat slowed, shook, and shuddered to a halt. I wondered if the boiler had exploded. Tom came running out of the engine room with his arms and legs still attached, so I decided it hadn't.

"We've run aground!" shouted Clarence, following Tom. Behind him, Dwina and Seth peeked cautiously around the corner. Clarence ran to the railing and surveyed the situation. "We're stuck on a sandbar! I have to stop the wheel!" He raced back to his machinery.

"This is perfect!" I announced, getting back to my feet. The foggy plan I had was suddenly much clearer. I grabbed Dwina's hand and Seth's shoulder, gave them both a reassuring squeeze, and nodded toward the shore. "You get ready to swim! We're going to create a diversion so nobody sees you escaping! When you hear me shout, uh, 'Mark Twain,' that'll be the signal to jump!"

I took Tom by the sleeve and pulled him back into the boiler room with me. "Get the trombone!" I told him.

"Full reverse!" Mishrag commanded distantly, through the tube. "Mr. Whiffletree—get us off this! I don't care how much steam we have to pour on!"

Clarence threw himself against levers as tall as he was and changed their positions. Steam vented from valves above us and the pistons started to slow.

"What are you doing?" I shouted at him.

"Stopping the wheel! Then I can start it again in reverse. Cap'n's gonna back us off the bar!"

"Will that take long?"

"Couple minutes."

It sounded exactly like the sort of thing that might put an extra strain on the "plates" Clarence had mentioned, and send us all on our way to Kingdom Come, which was a small town twenty miles inland. I ran to the railing and shouted "Mr. Ganto!" at the top of my lungs.

The paddle wheel came to a halt just as Tom joined me with the trombone. After a grinding noise and two loud *clunk*s from the engine room, the wheel began to turn slowly in the opposite direction. It picked up speed as I watched, even as the engine noise grew louder.

"MR. GANTO!" I shouted again, alarmed that he hadn't shown up yet.

Killbreath's voice bellowed through the captain's megaphone. "Attention, stowaways! We got your friend Dorothy Gale! If you care one teensy ounce 'bout her well-bein', you jist get yerselves up here to the wheelhouse, double pronto! She ain't been hurt none—at least, not yet!"

Something wet, hairy, and Hawaiian passed by us on the

outside of the boat, climbing out of the water on its way to the deck above us. I grabbed Mr. Ganto's leg to get his attention.

"Shofranka is in trouble," he rumbled. "I must go to her."

"I want to scare everybody off this boat!" I told him. "Frankie gets saved at the same time. Tom and I run ahead, screaming in terror, you come up behind us, looking vicious—"

"I don't do vicious."

"Try."

"YOU HAVE 'TIL THE COUNT OF TEN." Killbreath's voice came through the megaphone. "ONE... TWO..."

"There may be guns," said Mr. Ganto.

"There always are," I said. It didn't seem to matter what century we were in.

"THREE...FOUR..."

Ganto scooped me up with one hand and cradled me in the crook of his arm. He clambered up the side of the boat, past the second deck to the top deck, and dropped me at a spot about thirty feet behind the wheelhouse. Then he slipped back down and fetched up Tom.

"FIVE...SIX..."

I could see the top of the paddle wheel. It was turning faster and faster, churning up fountains of water and sand, and although the *Buckeye Beauty* was starting to rock back and forth, the boat wasn't budging from its spot.

"More steam!" I heard Mishrag shout.

"SEVEN...EIGHT..."

"Run for your lives!" I screamed, and ran at the wheelhouse with Tom at my side. Ganto was about ten steps behind us, waving his arms in the air and acting like a deranged, homicidal orangutan.

Killbreath, who was standing near the wheelhouse with Mishrag's megaphone, turned in our direction and gaped. A door in the back of the house flew open, and Mishrag stared out at us in disbelief. He was clutching Frankie.

She snatched the megaphone from Killbreath, swung it up, and hit Mishrag in the head with it. As he staggered back, he lost his grip, and Frankie broke away.

Killbreath's hand shot out to catch her, but she funneled it into the megaphone and it stuck, two of his fingers popping out of the mouthpiece like a snake's forked tongue. As he struggled to yank it off, Frankie ran to us.

"The killer ape's escaped!" I shouted to everyone who could hear. "Get off the boat!"

Mishrag was wearing a pistol, and Killbreath pulled it out and pointed it in our direction. He leveled it straight at Mr. Ganto and squeezed the trigger.

Nothing happened. Killbreath looked more closely at the gun.

"You're still usin' a *flintlock*?" he said to Mishrag incredulously.

"I've got powder and shot here, someplace," responded Mishrag, digging into his pockets.

Mr. Ganto grabbed both men by the neck and lifted them off their feet.

"We're saving your lives!" I informed them. "I have no idea why. You're a disgrace to humanity," I told Killbreath.

"Now, don't go judgin' a man jus' 'cause he likes to wear frilly pantaloons," he snarled.

"I'm not," I snapped back, waving my apron for emphasis. "I don't care how you dress. Neither should anyone else. But you're a mean, nasty person, and *that* does matter! Bye!"

Mr. Ganto tossed them over the side. They made a satisfying splash.

I picked up the fallen megaphone and ran to the opposite side of the boat. I leaned out as far as I dared and repeatedly shouted "MARK TWAIN!" until I saw Seth and Dwina climb over the railing. They labored across the thin strip of sand closest to the boat, then waded into the water beyond. I was glad to see the water was no deeper than Dwina's shoulders.

I looked at my phone. Only six minutes remained.

I went into the wheelhouse and found the speaking tube that connected to the engine room. "FULL STOP!" I bellowed into it.

A moment later Clarence Whiffletree's voice came back at me.

"We *are* stopped!"

"I MEAN, ER, SHUT DOWN THE ENGINE! TURN IT OFF!"

"Who is this?"

"It's me. Ambrose Brody. The boy, I mean the girl—I mean the *boy* who's friends with the runaway slaves."

"Where's the captain?"

"Overboard."

"Where's the pilot?"

"Stepped out."

"Stop joking."

"I'm not joking! This is an emergency! If you don't shut down the engine, we're going to blow up!"

"I only take orders from the captain. If he catches you playing around, he'll tan your hide!"

I had been hiding my tan all day. Tanning my hide didn't sound like much of a threat.

"You have to believe me!" I shouted.

The line went dead, or whatever speaking tubes do when no one is speaking. I put my ear to it and thought I could hear Clarence throwing more logs on the fire.

"We have to get down there and stop him!" Tom announced, as if it was news. "Mr. Ganto can grab him and force him to shut down the engine!"

I started for the ladder, but Frankie clutched me by the arm and wouldn't let go.

"NO!" she screamed. "We can't do this! We know the boat exploded. It's part of history. We have to let it happen. Otherwise, who knows what will happen to the future!"

"Maybe something good!" I said.

"And maybe something awful!"

I thought furiously, hearing a clock ticking faster and faster in my head. "All right—we know the boat exploded. But we don't know how many casualties. I say—there were none! And it was because of us!"

Frankie looked confused and dropped my arm. I turned

to Mr. Ganto. "Okay—time for you to chase us all over the boat like you're trying to kill us. If you don't do vicious, try ferocious! We have to scare everybody into the water. Come on!"

I jumped off the side, catching the edge of the deck with one hand and swinging, Ganto-like, to the deck below us. I landed a few feet away from a group of passengers who were arguing loudly about what they thought might be going on.

"The ape has escaped! Save yourselves! Get off the boat! Head for the shore!" I shouted at them, waving my arms over my head like I had gone insane. They stopped, studied me, then continued their conversation.

Mr. Ganto landed with a thud behind me. The group screamed in unison and ran down the deck. Frankie and Tom came down the ladder from the top deck and joined me at playing terrified children, something we were getting really good at.

"You better have guessed right!" Frankie hissed at me as we scrambled from one side of the boat to the other, stampeding crew and passengers before us.

Most people froze at our approach, like they had no idea what to do. When we suggested they "jump overboard! Swim for your lives!" and Mr. Ganto added a helpful "BOOGA-BOOGA-BOOGA!" they seemed grateful for the direction and took it.

As soon as the first two or three people jumped ship and set an example, more and more were willing to follow, like cartoons I had seen of lemmings throwing themselves off a cliff. (My science teacher, Mr. Dawkins, says lemmings don't really do this. I'm pretty sure they would, though, if a crazed giant gorilla were chasing them.)

A crewman stepped out of a cabin in front of us and aimed a rifle at Mr. Ganto. Tom grabbed it by the barrel and shoved it to one side, shouting, "No! No! Bullets only make it stronger! It comes from a planet where they eat lead!" That gave Ganto the time he needed to pluck the weapon from the man's hands and throw it over the railing. A moment later, the man joined it.

We descended to the main deck just in time to catch Killbreath trying to climb back aboard.

I put my foot on his forehead and pushed him back into the water.

"I'm saving your life, you despicable scumbrain!" I apologized.

Mr. Ganto picked up a barrel and threw it at him, reminding me of a very old video game where an ape threw barrels at people. The barrel missed, but Killbreath got the message and started swimming away from the boat.

We rounded the bow and came upon a defiant group of passengers who were waving pitchforks and brooms. They had broken open a crate labeled ACME PITCHFORK AND BROOM.

"He tore off a guy's head!" I screamed, pointing behind me in Ganto's direction.

"And dribbled it like a basketball!" Tom embellished, although I was pretty sure basketball—and, therefore, dribbling—hadn't been invented yet.

A few of the men made halfhearted lunges with their pitchforks. One, confused with terror, started sweeping the deck with his broom. Mr. Ganto roared, picked up another barrel, and used it to fend off the pitchforks. He plowed five men over the railing with it, and everybody else scrambled to follow, the men helping the women until there was no one left on deck but us.

The *Buckeye Beauty* was shuddering and shaking like a dog in a thunderstorm. It lurched to one side, then to the other, and pulled free of the sandbar. It shot backward, with all the pent-up energy of a car that had been spinning its wheels on ice abruptly finding a dry spot. The unexpected motion threw us to our knees. The paddle wheel spun crazily.

"Clarence is still on board!" I shouted, getting up and sprinting for the engine room.

Clarence was doing a victory dance in front of the boilers. The engine pistons were moving so fast, they were a blur, and the needles on two big gauges were pressed as far to the right as they could go. Steam hissed like a chorus of rattlesnakes.

I snatched Clarence by the wrist and tried to pull him out of the room. He resisted, and Mr. Ganto scooped him up, swept him to the railing, and sent him sailing into open water. He splashed and sputtered, and then he fell behind as the boat swept into the channel.

"WHERE IS THE SHAGBOLT?" Frankie was shaking Tom by the shoulders.

Tom jerked his thumb at the deck above us. "I put it down! I kept banging it against things! I was afraid it would get broken! *Fiduciary!*"

Frankie gave me a wild look. "Time?" she demanded.

I pulled out my phone. "Plenty!" I assured her. "Three minutes!"

"Assuming the clock you set that thing by was accurate!" Frankie screeched. To Tom she barked, "GET IT!"

We followed as Tom raced to the nearest stairway and cat-apulted up it. At the bow end of the middle deck, cushioned on a pile of cargo netting, was the Shagbolt in its case. Tom stretched out his hand for it. Frankie shoved him aside and reached for it herself.

Unfortunately, she was right.

The clock I had set my phone by had not been accurate.

The boat exploded.

CHAPTER 22
Night of the Floating Dead

With an earsplitting *BOOM!* loud enough to be heard in Toledo, the deck rose up and came apart around us, the center of the boat flying into the air as though an angry whale had hurled itself against the hull from directly underneath. Steam billowed and fire blossomed, and everything seemed to break into pieces and hang there in space. Then the pieces were spinning in all directions, at first up and to the sides, and then down and into the river.

I was hit by things hard and blunt, then things sharp and stinging, and then I was hurled about thirty feet, struck the water, and blacked out.

I awoke to the sound of somebody screaming. I was draped over a small piece of shattered deck that bobbed beneath me like it would really rather sink. I wiggled my way to a better position, moved my limbs to make sure they were still there, and pulled from my shoulder a splinter big enough to kill a vampire. I had cuts and bruises all over my body, but I was more or less intact. I raised my head and looked around.

Frankie was the one who was screaming. I could see her ahead of me, straddling an oblong box, trying to hold a big hairy mass up out of the water. I looked closer and realized the big hairy mass was Mr. Ganto's head. I prayed it was still attached to his body.

I looked around for Tom.

I couldn't see him anywhere. Debris covered the river. Some of it was on fire. Boxes and bales and barrels bobbed by, caught in an increasingly swift current. But there was no Tom. Behind me, the twisted remains of the *Buckeye Beauty* blazed brightly, partially sunk, but still drifting downstream.

I began swimming frantically, floundering toward Frankie and Ganto. Fortunately, they were downstream, and I didn't have to fight the powerful current. Five or six strokes brought me to them.

I caught the bigger end of the oblong box and realized it was the coffin of Ishmael Dinklehooper. I would have shivered if I hadn't already been trembling.

"Where's Tom?" I gasped as soon as I could catch my breath.

Frankie shook her head. "Missing!" she cried. "Mr. Ganto is hurt! Unconscious! He could drown!"

I grabbed a hank of Ganto's shoulder hair and pulled. His head came out of the water another two inches, enough to clear his mouth. The coffin sank an inch from the added weight, so it was almost a draw.

"We have to get to the shore!" I said. "We'll never survive the falls!"

"I'm not leaving my oldest friend!"

"Then you'll go over the falls together!"

"You don't really think we can swim against this current?"

"Not against it—diagonally, with it. We aim for Picnic Spit, that little piece of land that juts out just before the drop. If we start now, we might be able to make it!"

I didn't believe a word I was saying. There were several hundred yards of white water on the side of the river just before Picnic Spit. Even if we could get that close, we'd be dashed against the rocks.

Frankie let go of Ganto with one hand and slapped him with it.

"Wake up! Wake up! Please wake up!"

His head lolled. I wondered how badly he was injured.

I raised myself up and looked around. The river was narrowing, and the land was sliding by more and more quickly. Not far ahead of us, a curtain of spray marked the rapidly approaching waterfall.

"BRO!" shouted a log to my right.

It was the same log Killbreath had been clinging to. Cargo netting was tangled in its roots and trailed in the water behind it, tugging a snared barrel in its web. I saw Tom riding the trunk, waving frantically.

"Tom! Are you all right?"

He nodded emphatically.

"WHAT'RE WE GOING TO DO?" he hollered.

"Mr. Ganto's unconscious! We're trying to wake him up!"

Tom glanced uneasily in the direction of the falls. "HURRY!"

Tom knew as well as I did that our only chance of making it to shore was with the help of a swimmer stronger than we were. Mr. Ganto was the only person around who met that description.

Knock-knock!

My head swiveled.

Knock-knock!

The noise was coming from inside the coffin. I nearly lost my grip and slid into the surging water.

Knock-knock!

"Who's there?"

"Ishmael!"

"Ishmael who?"

"Ishmael Dinklehooper! Get off the lid!"

The coffin lid was divided in the middle; I moved my grip to the bottom half, and the top half flew open. The weathered, windblown-looking, white-haired man inside sat up. Frankie and I screamed. Ishmael patted the air with his hands in a manner that I imagined he thought might calm us down.

"No, no!" he said. "It's all right! I faked my death to escape from people I owed money to. The book earned squat."

"Are you of the *nosferatu*?" Frankie squeaked.

"No, I'm of the *Pequod*. The *Nosferatu* is a much larger ship. People are always confusing the two."

He looked around and seemed unfazed by the situation in which he found himself. His expression suggested he had seen worse. "What's going on?" he asked.

"Our boat exploded!" I answered, keeping it simple.

"And you saved yourselves by clinging to a floating coffin?"

"Yes."

"How original."

"IN ABOUT TWO MINUTES, WE'RE GOING OVER A WATERFALL!" I shouted. "CAN YOU HELP US?"

Ishmael levered himself out, turned, and stood with one foot inside the coffin and one foot on its edge, shading his eyes in the direction of the falls, like a Tim Burton version of *Washington Crossing the Delaware*.

"The current is very swift," he announced. "But I'm a strong swimmer. There will be enough time to save the girl!"

"I'm not leaving without Mr. Ganto!" Frankie once again declared.

"Mr. Ganto?"

I heaved another inch of Mr. Ganto into view.

Ishmael's jaw dropped. So did Ganto's. River water dribbled out of it.

"Some sort of giant, hairy monkey?"

"Eight hundred pounds, nine feet tall—and he'd probably resent being called a monkey," I said.

"I've had it up to here with larger-than-life animals," said Ishmael, raising his hand to a scar on his neck. "Is it some sort of pet?"

"He's my friend!" shouted Frankie. "And this would never have happened if not for me! I should have obeyed my father and left the Shagbolt where it was! He's still breathing! I'm not leaving him!"

"Then I'll save *you*," said Ishmael, reaching for me.

I drew away from his outstretched hand. If he couldn't save all of us, I wasn't leaving my friends. Besides, I suddenly saw a glimmer of hope.

I remembered the chain.

In the modern world, the town of Freedom Falls maintained a chain stretched from one side of the river to the other, about a hundred feet before the waterfall and about two feet above the surface of the water. It was there, in the colorful words of the town's mayor, "to keep drunken fishermen and idiot kayakers from falling to their probably well-deserved deaths."

I wondered how far back the tradition of the chain went. "Save yourself!" I told Ishmael.

He looked at me as though I had told him to hop on one

foot. "No," he said. "I won't have it said I was the sort to desert children. Or large monkeys. I may still be of assistance. We all might survive the drop."

"Oh, we'll survive the drop all right," I assured him. "It's the hitting I'm pretty sure we won't."

I smelled smoke. I twisted around, and the burning hulk of the *Buckeye Beauty* was right behind us. It had turned sideways and was presenting more of itself to the current. The glimmer of hope I had winked out. If there was a chain, and it caught us, it would save us for only a few seconds. Then the wall of flame that had been the boat would hit us and roast us to a cinder.

"BRO!" shouted Tom. He was pointing at the water behind his log, and at first I couldn't tell what he was all excited about. Then I saw it. Tangled in the cargo net that streamed behind the log, next to the barrel I had already seen, was a trombone case.

I made an instant decision.

"Is it true you sometimes have dreams that foretell the future?" I asked Ishmael, who looked at me like I had gone insane.

"This is hardly the time for chitchat!" he informed me.

"DO YOU OR DON'T YOU?"

"What?"

"HAVE PROPHETIC DREAMS!"

"Sometimes!"

"Good! That's all I needed to know! Hold him!" I dragged Mr. Ganto up another half inch and then I dived away from the coffin.

It was a mistake. I knew I didn't have the strength to swim *against* the current, but I thought I could swim *across* it. My goal was Tom and his tree, but every stroke I swam toward it sent me farther downstream.

I realized immediately I wasn't going to make it.

A powerful hand grabbed me by my dress, and Ishmael was beside me, supporting me roughly with one arm while swimming furiously with the other. We both kicked as hard as we could, and a few moments later Tom was reaching down to help me climb the slippery bark.

I did a fast crawl to the end of the log and hauled myself back into the water, using the cargo net as a line to pull myself along. Twice the current nearly ripped my hands from the net, but I made it to my goal. I faced the oncoming falls, straddled the barrel like it was a fat, wet pony, and hooked one foot into the net's rope-work.

Then I reached down and snagged the Shagbolt.

The log struck a rock straight on and jolted to a halt. I looked up to see pointy tree roots coming at my face, and then the log pivoted to one side and we were moving again, this time with the log lengthwise and Ishmael's coffin, having closed the gap, butting against its side. Ishmael and Tom grabbed Frankie and dragged her onto the log with them.

Mr. Ganto was showing signs of life. He was clutching the coffin, shaking his head as if trying to clear it.

I brought the mouthpiece of the Time Trombone to my lips and blew into it.

Water squirted out.

I blew harder, and more water fountained out, along with something small and silvery that might have been a fish, or one of my tonsils. I moved the slide frantically back and forth, spraying droplets everywhere.

I finally managed to get out a strangled note. Possibly B sharp. I tried again and got something louder and smoother and less wet.

We were almost to the falls. A thundering noise filled the air, and I worried it would drown out the sound I was trying to make. I played the first note of what I remembered as the area code for home. It came out loud and clear. Frankie's head whipped around and she screamed *"YES!"*

The log and the coffin ground to a halt on the chain that stretched across the river's path. My barrel bumped the chain a few seconds later and started to slide under, but then the chain sawed against my waist and the barrel jolted to a halt.

We were stopped a hundred feet from the precipice. Tom cheered, "*Penultimate!*" I lowered the trombone from my lips and heaved a sigh of relief.

Then I felt hot breath on the back of my neck.

A wall of flame was rushing toward us. The chain would hold us in place long enough for us to be crushed against the burning riverboat and roasted like chickens on a spit.

I brought the trombone's mouthpiece to my lips and played three more notes. I couldn't remember the fourth. All I could see was fire.

Mr. Ganto floundered across the coffin and used it as a stepping-stone to the log. He grabbed the chain in both hands and lifted it as high as he could. The log swept under, pulling my barrel with it. Moments later the burning boat slammed against the chain, showering us with sparks.

We had escaped death by fire only to be sent plunging to our deaths over the falls.

I couldn't concentrate. I couldn't remember the fourth note. I was a boy wearing a dress, riding a barrel, about to go over a waterfall while playing a trombone. Nothing they had taught us in school had prepared me for this.

Frankie screamed. It was a single, long, drawn-out note— and I realized she was screaming it for my benefit. It was the missing note. I blasted it out of the trombone and followed it with the fifth and sixth notes. Before I could play the seventh and final one, the log with my friends plunged over the edge, pulling my barrel with it.

The barrel dropped out from under me. I saw myself about to be smashed like a pancake on the rocks at the base of the falls.

I made one last desperate attempt to play the final note.

I was a little bit flat.

CHAPTER 23
Yin Anyang

For the fourth time in my life, I felt like a sand sculpture blown apart by the wind, swept across a desert, and reassembled someplace else. I was lying on my back in a gully full of sun-warmed pebbles, staring up into a vividly blue sky with high, wispy clouds. The thunder of rushing water was gone, replaced by the sound of chirping birds.

Somebody groaned beside me.

I rolled over and there was Tom, soaking wet and gripping his head. He was on his knees, throwing up river water. Beyond him sat Mr. Ganto, with Frankie cradled lovingly in his arms. She slid from his embrace and staggered to her feet.

Ishmael Dinklehooper was sitting on a rock to my right. He may have stretched the truth a bit about being dead, but he hadn't been lying about his psychic dreams.

"Is everybody all right?" I asked, assessing myself and realizing I had escaped with only cuts and bruises, the cuts minor enough to have been washed clean by the river.

"Achy," Frankie announced, limping over to Tom and putting a hand on his back as he spat up the last of his water.

"I've been better," Tom said, letting Frankie help him to his feet. "But I'll survive."

"I can't believe I'm dreaming this all over again," said Ishmael, scratching his head.

"You're not dreaming," Frankie informed him. "You've traveled in time."

"In time for what?"

"We've all gone back to a time about three thousand years before 1852, give or take a few decades." She looked at me. "Or maybe a century. It gets less precise the further back you go. But that's the area code you played."

"I'm sorry," I said. "I did my best. You warned me not to play the last note flat."

"You did great," said Frankie, unexpectedly hugging

me. "You got us out of that mess. And you saved your many-greats-grandmother."

"I also saved a lot of people you didn't think should be saved," I reminded her.

"Yes, well, I'm hoping I was wrong about that. We'll know once we return to our own time."

"Any idea *where* we are?" I asked, looking around.

"Not a clue. It doesn't matter. We're not staying."

I started to hand Frankie the trombone, eager for her to take us back to our own time, but the sound of Mr. Ganto getting to his feet and then unexpectedly sitting down hard on his butt caused Frankie to turn from me and run to him.

"Little dizzy," Ganto murmured.

Frankie touched the back of his head and he winced.

"You have a bump the size of my fist back here," she told him. "And part of your shirt and some of your hair has been scorched away. Your back is all raw and pink."

Mr. Ganto flexed and then shuddered. "There was a blast of steam," he said. "I got in its way."

"I've seen worse," said Ishmael, coming over. He obviously still thought he was dreaming. He was taking everything quite calmly. "I could make up a poultice of aloe and butter; it would help him tremendously." He glanced around. "If we had some aloe and butter."

We were surrounded by low hills with rocky outcroppings and a few scraggly trees. Stretching away from us on either side was a pebble-covered expanse that might have been a dried streambed.

"We have to get to a place where there's modern medicine!" snapped Frankie. "Immediately! Give me the Shagbolt!"

I handed it to her. She raised it to her lips and had a conniption.

"WHERE'S THE MOUTHPIECE?"

She whirled on me and I saw the trombone was incomplete. The brass mouthpiece was missing. I looked down at my feet, then back the way I had come.

"It won't work without the mouthpiece!" exclaimed Frankie.

"It was there when I played the final note, going over the falls!" I said, sounding just as panicky as I felt.

"So it either fell off then, and it went down the falls, and it's still in 1852, and we're doomed, or it fell off here, and it's in with all these pebbles, and we still have a chance! Nobody move! Look around you!" Frankie squatted and squinted at the ground closest to her. The rest of us checked our own areas. "Without the mouthpiece, we're stuck here, wherever *here* is!"

"China," said Mr. Ganto.

"China?" Tom looked up. "Are you sure? How do you know?"

Mr. Ganto inhaled deeply. "One never forgets the smell of one's birthplace. The local trees, the flowers, the scent of the earth itself." He sifted dirt through his fingers. "This is the place I thought of as we went over the falls. When I was certain we were all going to die."

"I was thinking of China, too!" Tom exclaimed, as though he had found a long-lost friend.

"We really should have taken a vote," muttered Frankie. To Ganto she said, "You were born three *hundred* thousand years ago. We've only gone back three thousand. Same trees? Really?"

"Similar. This is the place. A mile or two in that direction is the river now known as the Anyang. We're in Henan province. Near the thirty-sixth parallel." When Frankie just gaped at him, he added, "I have studied your father's GPS. I wanted to learn about where I came from."

"If the Anyang is over there," said Tom thoughtfully, "and we're near the thirty-sixth parallel, we must be close to the ancient imperial city of Yin! It was on the Anyang!"

"That, I would not know." Mr. Ganto frowned and shook his head.

"We'll be *living in* Yin, if we don't find that mouthpiece!" Frankie reminded us, dropping to her knees and raking her fingers through the pebbles in front of her.

We all continued our search, following Frankie's example and getting down on all fours, even Ishmael, who I'm sure had no idea what he was looking for or why he was looking for it.

"The city of Yin?" I asked Tom as we barely missed butting heads. "On the Anyang River? Yin? Anyang? *Yin* and *yang?* Isn't *yin* the name of the broken lines in the *I-Ching* hexagrams? And *yang* the name of the unbroken ones?"

"Quite a coincidence, isn't it?" replied Tom, in a tone that suggested he didn't find it a coincidence at all.

Somebody, at a great distance, shouted. A chorus of shouts replied.

"People!" said Frankie. "We really don't want to run into people! That always leads to trouble!"

"I will investigate," said Mr. Ganto, getting to his feet.

"You're injured!" Frankie protested.

"I am fine. I will climb that hill and have a look."

He stood shakily and started climbing the hill to our right.

"He's very articulate for an ape," said Ishmael.

"He's not an ape," growled Frankie, searching a piece of ground she had already searched.

"No offense. I may have seen him in a dream a few nights back. The same way I had been seeing the white whale during the early days of the *Pequod*'s final voyage. I'm pretty sure I'm having the same dream again, right now."

"You have the gift of oneiromancy," Frankie informed him. "Dream prophecy. Only people with a psychic gift can time travel."

"Oh. You think my dream will come true? Most often, they don't."

"What was it about?" I asked warily, searching so far from where I had landed that I knew I wasn't going to find anything.

"I forget the details. There was the ape—or whatever it is—and this strange place we're in right now, and I was with a party of three other people. Very young, they were."

"And?"

"And, in the end, we lost one of them."

"Find the mouthpiece!" Frankie barked.

"I've looked everywhere!" I snapped back, not wanting to think about what Ishmael had just said.

"Look again!"

"The slide horn is important, is it?" asked Ishmael, earnestly searching the lower branches of the nearest tree. "Music can transport one. Can it transport one through time?"

"Played on the right instrument, it can," said Frankie. "The Shagbolt—the slide horn—was created by this genius inventor back in the year 1592." I could tell she was talking to take her mind off other things. She swept her hands back and forth across the ground in front of her so vigorously she raised dust devils. "He was brilliant. His greatest invention was an automaton made out of clay. And, at the time of his death, he was working on a perpetual-motion dreidel that would have solved all the world's energy problems. But the thing he took the greatest pride in was his Shagbolt. He never fully perfected it, which is why it works only for the psychically gifted. He had hoped to use it to transport his people out of danger in times of crisis, but he did not want to leave any of them behind just because they lacked extra-sensory perceptions. He kept tinkering with it, trying to get it right."

"How did your family wind up with it?" I asked, and got a flashing glance in reply.

"One day the inventor welded a new piece to it, and he

put it on a windowsill to cool. One of my ancestors came along and borrowed it."

"What? The way we borrowed the Katzenjammers' pies? That's not borrowing—that's *stealing*!"

"No, it's not! We *borrowed* it! It's a *time machine*! Eventually, one of us will return it to a time only *one minute* after my ancestor borrowed it, and its inventor will never know it went missing! Then he and his descendants can go about saving his people from persecution throughout history."

"You've had it for over four hundred years! When were you planning to return it?"

"Soon! I'm sure!"

"And I thought it was just you who was irresponsible! It's your whole family!"

"Irresponsible? *You're* the one who lost the mouthpiece! If we never return the Shagbolt, it will be *your* fault!"

"Maybe this gentleman will help us search," said Ishmael.

I looked up. A bony Chinese man with scraggly long hair stood in tattered clothing about twenty feet from us. He darted forward, put something on the ground, then ran back to his original place and fell to his knees, bowing until his forehead touched the earth.

"Oh no," said Frankie.

"Where did he come from?" I asked.

"Popped out from behind those rocks." Ishmael pointed to the only available hiding place.

Tom picked up the object the man had left. It was a balled-up piece of cloth. He opened it and revealed a glob of brown rice.

"He's making us an offering," Tom decided. "This is probably the only food he has."

Tom spoke to him in Chinese. The man looked up, and his eyes shifted nervously from side to side.

"Nope," said Tom. "Mandarin doesn't work."

Tom tried again, using different words that, I guessed, might have been in the rare dialect his great-grandfather used. This time the man replied, Tom answered, and they spoke back and forth repeatedly.

"He says his name is Jiang Ziya." Tom finally went back to English. "He saw us pop out of nowhere. He asked me if we are sorcerers come to free his people."

"And what did you tell him?" Frankie asked, sounding alarmed.

"I didn't say yes, and I didn't say no."

"This is very dangerous," said Frankie. "If he winds up

believing we're sorcerers, it could start a brand-new religion. That's the last thing the world needs."

"He says the name of the current king is Di Xin," Tom continued excitedly, ignoring Frankie's warning. "Do you realize what that means? Di Xin was the last king of the Shang dynasty, just before the Battle of Muye, when he was overthrown, and the slave-keeping Shangs were replaced by the more enlightened Zhou. We've come to one of the most important time periods in Chinese history! *Fiduciary!* This is so great!"

"These Shang guys were slave owners?" I asked, appalled that we had gone from one slave society to another.

"Oh, *yeah*! The Shangs put the 'nasty' in *dynasty*! King Di Xin and his evil wife, Daji, punished people by having their hearts ripped out and their feet chopped off, not necessarily in that order. They were awful. They've enslaved Jiang's people"—he waved at our new friend, who was still groveling—"because they prefer to wear their jerkins with the seams on the outside rather than on the inside. Queen Daji calls that an abomination, and she says it proves Jiang's people are inferior, and fair game for slavery."

"Wait," I said, trying to understand. "A jerkin is a—?"

"Sort of vest."

"A piece of *clothing*? And just because Jiang's people like to wear them inside out, they're persecuted? Turned into slaves? Everybody knows if you accidentally put on a shirt inside out, it's good luck!"

"Not if you're living in the Shang dynasty," said Tom.

Shouts came from the hill to our left, opposite the direction Mr. Ganto had taken. I looked up and three men with spears were running toward us. I looked to the right, hoping to see Ganto, but there was no sign of him.

Jiang jumped to his feet and cowered behind Tom, chattering hysterically.

"He says he's escaped from the palace, and these guys are palace guards sent to take him back," Tom translated.

"So these are the Chinese equivalent of Archie Killbreath and his boys," I said, watching them approach. "How could we possibly have run into more slave catchers?"

"Because no age in human history has ever been free of slavery," Frankie informed us, stepping to my side. The three of us had, without consulting one another, positioned ourselves in front of the terrified Jiang. "The further back you go, the odds actually favor something like this happening."

"Aren't you afraid we'll change history if we get involved

with this?" I asked, surprised at the pride I felt when she stood beside me.

"Yes. Totally. But I like your idea that it might be changed for the better!"

Ishmael joined us, standing next to me with his arms folded.

The three guards halted about ten feet from us and leveled their spears.

Jiang stuck his head out from behind Tom and jabbered at them. The spears wavered a bit and the men looked confused.

"What did he say to them?" Frankie asked stonily.

"He told them we are powerful sorcerers and they should prepare to meet their doom."

"*Fiduciary!*" I said.

CHAPTER 24
Hello Goodbye

I took a mental inventory of all the things we had that might convince the guards we were powerful sorcerers.

We had two waterlogged, almost definitely not working, cell phones.

We had a trombone without a mouthpiece that might be forced to make a tweeting noise if somebody blew on it hard enough.

We had copies of *Uncle Tom's Cabin* and *If You Have an I-Ching—Scratch!* sealed in Ziploc bags.

That was about it.

No, I realized, that wasn't it. We had our looks. Ishmael

was a towering white-haired white guy. That had to be a novelty in this time and place. We had Frankie's olive skin, which had to be equally strange. And then there was Tom and me, wearing tattered and scorched dresses from the far future. To the three guards, we probably looked like demons from hell.

Our difference was our strength.

And we had my new attitude. Which was to beat the brown rice out of anybody who was the least bit intolerant.

I jumped at the guards. I waved my hands over my head and shouted "Hoo-hah!" I landed in front of them, and they jumped an equal distance back.

I bugged out my eyes and threw them a face, and started chanting lines from my favorite hip-hop artist, Kan Sa$s, because I knew the rhymes and rhythm would sound like magical incantations.

Nothing is perfect, and that is that;
I hate three-D movies when the soda is flat—

I laced my hands together, one up and one down, and did that thing where the two middle fingers wiggle back and forth, up and down, in opposite directions, like they're joined at the knuckle. This always makes my four-year-old cousin giggle. The guards looked terrified.

Nothing is perfect, so what can you do?
I shaved my head to save on shamPOO!

I said "POO!" explosively and they fell back another foot. Nothing beats an explosive POO.

I hiked up my dress and did a Michael Jackson moonwalk. They were mesmerized. I parted my legs, grabbed my right knee with my right hand and my left knee with my left hand, then slammed my knees together, crossing my hands so it looked like I had interchangeable kneecaps. I repeated this a few times, until they could see I was no ordinary mortal.

Nothing is perfect, successes and fails,
Go together like boogers and fingernails!

"Your poetry does not scan," said Ishmael.

"Get ready," I said to him as I reached behind the middle guard's ear and pretended to find a small rock, which I showed to the guards and all three of them went "Ooo!" My uncle Leon found nickels in my ears in the same way, so I knew it was powerful magic.

"Trombone, please," I said without turning around, extending my hand behind me. Frankie passed me the Shagbolt.

I did *left shoulder arms* with it; I did *right shoulder arms* with it; I did *present arms* with it. I twirled it in front of me the way I had seen the Freedom Falls high school precision drill team twirl their fake rifles. I raised it and leveled it, as if I was about to play it, and sighted down its length at the forehead of the guard directly in front of me.

Nothing is perfect, that's what I said;
You can't save face when you've lost your head!

I shot the slide forward and hit the guard right between the eyes.

"NOW!" I shouted, knocking the spear out of the stunned guard's hand with the Shagbolt.

Ishmael grabbed the spear of the guard closest to him and yanked it from his grip. He used it to parry the spear of the third guard while Tom and Jiang Ziya tackled the one he had just disarmed. I turned and tossed the Shagbolt to Frankie, then I plowed into the guard I had hit with the slide. He fumbled at his belt for a knife.

I knocked him to the ground, fell on him, and caught his knife hand before he could raise it. Squeezing his wrist with both hands, I beat his hand against the ground until the knife flew from his fingers.

Then I sat on his chest and pummeled him. I pretended he was Quentin Garlock and Lenny Killbreath and Archie Killbreath, and the man was crying by the time Ishmael pulled me off.

The man scrambled to his feet and followed his two friends, who were running back up the hill, disarmed and thoroughly beaten.

Jiang Ziya knelt down in front of me. I patted him on the head.

"How long before they bring back reinforcements?" asked Frankie.

Tom spoke quickly to Jiang, then said, "The city walls are about nine *lis* away. A *li* is about three hundred and fifty meters, so the city's about two miles from here. I would guess we've got at least half an hour."

"Then get busy and find that mouthpiece!" Frankie dropped to her knees and resumed the search.

"I don't think it's here," I said.

"And I KNOW it is!" she snapped. "It HAS to be!"

She stopped raking through the pebbles and looked up at me.

"You don't get it, do you?" she said. "It took me a while, but the more I thought about it, the more I think I understand."

"What?" I was totally bewildered.

"The woman who stole my dad's copy of *Uncle Tom's Cabin* out of my bedroom? Out of my *locked-from-the-inside* bedroom? You just assumed she came in through the window. *My bedroom doesn't have a window!* When she held her finger to her lips to tell me to be quiet? *She was wearing my charm bracelet!*"

"Holy cow!" said Tom. "She stole your bracelet, too?"

Frankie glared at him.

"It's *her* bracelet, every bit as much as it is mine!" she snapped.

"You mean"—I took a wild guess—"that woman was your grandmother?"

"No!" Frankie hit her forehead with the heel of her hand. "She wasn't my grandmother! I haven't told you two everything because it would have changed the way you behaved. It would have made you think that nothing could hurt you, and *that* could have gotten you both killed."

"What haven't you told us?" I asked, still lost.

"The woman who stole the book *had the Shagbolt with her*. She used it to get into the room. I'm positive that woman was *me*. She was *my future self*! Although I can't believe I will ever wear that much eyeliner!"

"Your future self came back through time to steal a book? Why would she do that?"

"After everything we've been through, I can think of only one possible explanation. But, at the moment, it's not important. What I'm trying to tell you is, I *know* I use the Shagbolt in the future! So the mouthpiece has to be here somewhere, because the Shagbolt doesn't stay here! Understand?"

A loud thud and a groan came from the right. We looked over to see Mr. Ganto sliding to the base of the hill on his butt. Frankie jackknifed to her feet and raced over to him, the rest of us close behind.

"I am all right," Ganto assured us sheepishly. "I slipped. Hill was steeper than I thought."

"And you're not as well as you think," said Frankie. "We have to get you home."

"There is an army coming this way," said Ganto, holding up a dented bronze helmet and handing it to Tom. "Souvenir."

Tom showed the helmet to Jiang and asked, "Shang?" and Jiang quickly nodded.

"They are mustering just beyond the hill," Ganto continued. "I will guess thirty thousand men. There are horses and chariots. They are organizing for a march, facing east. The trail will bring them around that bend and through this valley. The vanguard is already moving. We are in its path."

"Okay," said Tom breathlessly, staring at the helmet like it was the greatest of treasures. "This is the beginning of the end for the Shangs. This has to be the start of the Battle of Muye. Idiot king Di Xin sends most of his army to fight some minor enemy in the east, leaving the city undefended. Then his real enemy, the Zhou army, shows up and attacks his city. Di Xin arms his slaves, ordering them to defend the city and, big surprise, the slaves turn on him. So do half of his own guards, he's such a popular guy. The Shang dynasty falls. And we get to see it!"

"NO WE DO NOT!" said Frankie, rushing back to the riverbed and resuming her search. "If thirty thousand men tramp through here, it will bury the mouthpiece! Then it might take us years to find it! And we might spend those years as captives! I don't really want to spend another minute here! Mr. Ganto needs medical care! Help me!"

"It wouldn't be that bad," said Tom. "I can speak the language, and we've already made a friend. If we just hide out for a while, we'll survive the battle, and we could live out our lives in the early days of the new dynasty. The Zhous were pretty good."

"I don't care how *good* they were; we're not staying here!" said Frankie, glaring at me meaningfully, like she thought maybe I had swallowed the mouthpiece and she was considering drastic measures to get it back.

I studied our surroundings. Other than the clump of rocks that had hidden Jiang Ziya, I could see nowhere to hide. I didn't think we had enough time to make it over either hillside. Not if we were going to waste another minute sifting through pebbles.

"Ask the *I-Ching* where the mouthpiece is," I said.

"What?" Tom looked stricken.

Frankie stood up like she had been struck by lightning.

"Yes! Do you still have the book?"

"Um, yeah, but I'm sure it's soaked. The pages are probably all stuck together—"

"You had it in a Ziploc bag," I reminded him. "Why don't you look?"

Tom dug hesitantly in the pocket of his apron. In the far distance, I could hear someone shouting. It sounded like a sergeant drilling his men. I had a feeling the sound was the same no matter what century you were in.

"Dry as a bone!" declared Frankie, snatching the book from Tom's hands and breaking the seal on the bag. "Flip your coin! We should all concentrate on the mouthpiece."

"I—I lost the quarter," stammered Tom, and I knew he was lying. He really and truly hoped we would all stay in ancient China.

"Here," said Ishmael, producing a gold coin from his pocket and handing it to Tom. "Don't mind the hole in it. A crazy man once nailed it to a post."

"Flip it!" ordered Frankie.

Tom tossed the coin. I picked up a stick and drew the six lines his tosses produced.

Hexagram 29

The Watery Abyss.

Stuff gets washed away. Things
go down the drain. You have to
be quick to catch them. If you
use waffles instead of bread
to make a blueberry sandwich,
fewer blueberries will fall on
the floor.

"'*The Watery Abyss*,'" I read aloud from the book, getting a sinking feeling in my stomach.

"It must mean the mouthpiece is at the bottom of the waterfall!" said Tom, barely able to conceal his delight.

"And I *know* it isn't," said Frankie. "What's the Morse?"

"The Morse?" said Tom, as if he had no idea what she was talking about. "Oh, the Morse!" He scowled at the hexagram. He shook his head. "There doesn't seem to be any."

I could hear a series of repetitive thumps, like the sound of many marching feet.

"Tom!" I said, and tried to get him to look at me. He wouldn't meet my gaze. "Tom," I repeated, more gently.

"All right, all right," he muttered miserably, kneeling, and ticking off the parts of the hexagram. "It's two dots, a dash and a dot, followed by a dot, then another dot, ending with a dot, a dash, and two dots."

"Four letters," I said. "What does it spell?"

"*Feel.*"

"Feel?" I was hoping for something a little more specific, like *tree* or *rock*, telling us where to search for the mouthpiece. Even *gut*, if I had, in fact, somehow managed to swallow it. "What's *feel* supposed to mean?"

"Maybe we're supposed to *feel* something," said Frankie, looking around. The marching noise was getting louder.

"I do feel something," I assured her. "I feel panic, like we're all about to get drafted into an army of losers!"

Tom turned away and began flipping the coin again. Frankie stepped up to me and, without asking permission, started to frisk me. She briskly patted my chest and raised my arms so she could pat my armpits. She lifted my apron and started squeezing the cloth.

"I already looked in my apron," I said. "The pocket is empty."

She slipped a hand in the pocket anyway.

"There's a small hole in it!" she said excitedly, and started running her hands along the apron's hem.

The sound of marching feet washed down the dried streambed like the start of a flood. Mr. Ganto stood and positioned himself between us and the approaching noise. I don't know what he expected to do, facing thirty thousand soldiers.

"Ha!" exclaimed Frankie, and ripped the apron's fabric. She triumphantly held up the mouthpiece. "It fell in your pocket and wound up in the lining! We just had to FEEL for it!"

She picked up the Shagbolt and fitted the mouthpiece into place, looking like she was jamming a cartridge into a rifle. As she raised it to her lips, I noticed Tom consulting the *I-Ching* book. At his feet he had drawn a new hexagram:

Seeing the look on his face, I said, "Tom, what is it?"

He glanced my way, his face somehow both happy and full of regret at the same time.

"It's the seventh hexagram!"

Frankie blew the first note of our area code. Tom quickly came over to me and surprised me with a hug. He clutched me like he was never going to let me go. As soon as I got over my shock, I hugged him back.

"Best friends!" he said. "Forever!"

Then he pulled away and started walking up the hill.

"What—" I started to say as Frankie played the fourth and fifth notes. She was facing Ishmael and Mr. Ganto; she was paying no attention to us.

A column of armored men swung into view, way up the streambed, so distant they looked like toy soldiers. It might take them a minute or two to notice us. By then, I knew, we'd be gone.

Frankie played the sixth note.

Tom raised his arms and covered his ears with his hands. I heard him start humming loudly to himself. It sounded like a Beatles song.

Hello Goodbye.

"WAIT!" I shouted.

Frankie played the final note.

CHAPTER 25
Transformations

I was flour going through a sifter; I was grass seed being spread. The atom-sized pieces of me clumped back together and I was sitting on the lawn next to the parking lot of Ambrose Bierce Middle School in Freedom Falls, Ohio.

Frankie and Ishmael were to the right of me. Mr. Ganto was to my left. I leaped to my feet and spun, searching in every direction.

Tom Xui wasn't with us.

"Tom's missing!" I exclaimed. "We have to go back for him! Those soldiers could kill him!"

I snatched the Shagbolt from Frankie's fingers and raised

it to my lips. A large, hairy hand wrapped itself around the slide before I could move it. Mr. Ganto gently, but irresistibly, pulled the instrument from my hands.

"No," he said, in a voice that didn't invite argument.

I argued anyway.

"We can't leave him three thousand years in the past! He's got a math test on Monday! He's my best friend! We have to go get him!"

"He covered his ears," Mr. Ganto stated. "He hummed. It was his decision to stay."

"What if he changes his mind?"

"I am returning this to Shofranka's father." Ganto hefted the Shagbolt. "You can petition him. Perhaps he will grant your request. There is no rush. It is, after all, a time machine." He turned his penetrating gaze on Frankie. "But there can be no further unauthorized trips. It is way too dangerous. We are lucky to have returned to a time and place almost identical to the time and place we first departed from. It would not be wise to imperil success."

"*Almost* identical?" asked Frankie suspiciously.

Mr. Ganto inhaled deeply, held it, considered it, let it out. "There are more chrysanthemums in bloom. I would guess it is about a day after our original departure."

"Is that the only difference?"

"As far as I can smell."

I looked around. The school was the way I remembered it. No new wings enclosed a prison exercise yard, no razor wire edged the roof. We had returned everything to normal.

"I will take the Shagbolt back to the carnival," said Mr. Ganto, slipping into a shadowy area beneath some trees. "I will also visit Dr. Lao in the infirmary. I have need of his skills. Perhaps Mr. Dinklehooper would be so good as to accompany me."

Ishmael was staring wide-eyed at the cars in the parking lot.

"Metal huts?" he asked. "Do people live in those things?"

"Practically," I said.

A minivan with its headlights blazing pulled into the parking lot's far end. Ishmael jumped. Ganto reached out and put a reassuring hand on his shoulder.

"Horseless carriage," I tried to explain, but I could see the phrase didn't help.

"It will take getting used to," Ganto acknowledged. "But if I could do it, you can do it. Come. I may need a shoulder to lean on."

Ishmael, moving like a sleepwalker, turned to follow

Ganto. With a rustle of branches, they disappeared into the grove bordering the school property.

"So. No harm done," Frankie said, more to herself than to me.

"I've lost my best friend!" I reminded her.

"He made a choice. He knew what he was doing. We should respect his decision. If you really feel strongly about it, maybe we can convince my father to let us use the Shagbolt to go back and get him. Don't be surprised, though, if he puts up a fight."

"Your father?"

"Your friend. I think Tom is exactly where he wants to be."

"Maybe if we spoke to your mother and father together," I said. "I mean, it's your mother who thinks you're destined to be the Shagbolt's Keeper."

Frankie sighed. "We can't speak to them together. I have a single parent."

"What? You mean—they're divorced?"

"No. I mean my mother is dead."

"DEAD?"

"She died when I was eight months old. In a fortune-telling accident."

"A *fortune-telling* accident?"

"She failed to foresee the oncoming bus. Her death totally messed up my dad. He had a nervous breakdown. He got over it quickly, though. I think, deep down, he knew I needed him. And he knew I needed *her*." Frankie paused, like she wasn't sure she should go on. But then she took a deep breath and said, "So he developed a split personality. Not intentionally or anything. He's not aware that he does it."

"Does what?" She had lost me.

"The scientific name for it is dissociative identity disorder. DID. He became my mother. I mean, he really...DID. He still becomes her. He spends about half of each day as her. She even has set fortune-telling hours on days when the carnival is open. His glammering ability makes it easy. When he's her, he believes it so completely, even his face changes. At least, that's the image he projects. Usually, glammer is all in the clothes."

"That's nuts!" I exclaimed.

"That's what Dr. Lao said. But he got his psychiatry degree many years ago, when they had different words for things."

"I *heard* your mother looking for Twizzlers!"

"Yup. You did. He was her at that particular moment. Sometimes he even flickers back and forth, one to the other, like a lightbulb about to burn out. He's totally unaware he's doing it. Madam Janus and Orlando Camlo are one and the same person, but they have two distinct *personalities*, with different knowledge and different opinions. Neither has any memory of what the other one has said or done. They leave notes for each other on the fridge. When they're having an argument, you can barely see the door."

"I saw your dad only a few minutes later on the midway."

"What part of *glammering* don't you understand?"

"All of it."

I tried to imagine missing somebody so badly that you took their place. I wondered if I would start dressing like Tom Xui. Then I remembered we already dressed alike.

Frankie sighed. "And here you are, upset because your dad sometimes wears chain mail. You'd never be able to handle it if you had a parent who was truly different."

"Actually," I said slowly, thinking about it, "I think I could handle it fine. Or, at least, a lot better than I used to." I remembered seeing Frankie's father in her mother's crystal ball. I thought maybe this was the reason it had happened. It was the final piece of a puzzle I had been working on for the past three thousand years.

"Hurry up, Mikey!" came a familiar voice. I turned to see our neighbor Mrs. Larrabee getting out of her minivan, pulling her two kids after her. "We have to show our support for Mr. Brody!" She tugged the twins toward the school. Mrs. Larrabee was a single parent, raising her kids all by herself, and she had only the one personality. I couldn't imagine how she did it.

"Holy cow!" I said. "It's Thursday night! They're going to decide whether or not to fire my dad at this meeting! We have to get in there!"

"That would explain why we arrived now, rather than yesterday," Frankie said breathlessly as she raced to keep up. "This must have been in the back of your mind all along! You affected our time trip!"

We reached the doors and I saw myself reflected in the glass. I skidded to a halt.

"Wait!" I said. "I can't go in there like this! This isn't how I want to look!"

"So? Take off the dress." Frankie sounded disappointed.

"That's not what I mean," I said, squaring my shoulders. I had made my decision, and I was sure it was the right one. "I've lost my bonnet. Can I borrow yours?"

Frankie's bedraggled bonnet hung from the tightly knotted string around her neck. She pulled it off, punched it back into shape, and fitted it to my head.

"How do I look?" I asked.

She pursed her lips and thought about it. "Like a hero," she said.

The auditorium was packed. It looked as though the entire town had gotten wind of the special meeting and had turned out in force.

The seven members of the school board sat on the stage, in the middle of the set for *The Crucible*. They had moved the Salem witch trial's judge's bench forward to the edge of the stage, and Principal McNamara occupied the center position. To his right sat the three board members we had overheard plotting with him the night before—Billy Osborn's father, Cynthia Moon, and Millicent Mordred. To his left were the other three board members. Their faces were familiar; I had seen them around town, but I wasn't sure who they were or how they would vote.

Quentin Garlock sat on the floor of the stage with his legs dangling over the edge, a little to one side of McNamara, like pictures I had seen of court jesters at the feet of their kings. My father occupied a folding chair stage left, picked out by a single spotlight that isolated him from the board members, who were sitting in a sea of red.

All the stage illumination came from the lighting designed

for *The Crucible*. Moments after Frankie and I entered, the spotlighted shadow of a dangling hangman's noose flickered and disappeared from the back wall as somebody in the control booth came to their senses and cut that particular switch.

My father was dressed as a Russian serf from the time of the czars. It was a good look for him. Wringing his peasant cap in his hands made him look humble, but the defiant set of his jaw suggested he might, at any moment, rise up and overthrow the government. I wondered if his decision not to dress as a samurai was because of me.

In the middle of the center aisle was a lectern with a microphone, and people were lined up behind it, awaiting their turn to speak. As we came in, the man at the mike was Bruno Killbreath, Lenny Killbreath's father, the man who, in the alternate reality we had prevented, had been president of the United States.

"...must be stopped," he was saying. "We can't let our kids be led astray! This whatchamacallit, this *trans-temple culture*—weasel words for *cross-time dressers!*—is flyin' in the face of our American way of life!" He waved a tablet over his head, displaying the home page of *Out of Time: A Journal for the Trans-Temporal Community*, as if this proved there *was* a trans-temporal community. He pointed the tablet at my father. "This son of a bickwidus—"

McNamara banged a gavel. "Language!" he said sternly, and I got a jolt, realizing our time trip had added a naughty word to the dictionary.

"Sorry," said Killbreath. "This *man's* behavior is NOT somethin' I want as an example to my kids. It's a...it's a—"

"Aberration?" suggested McNamara.

"Yeah! Right. A burration! Showing up in public wearin' the clothes of George Washington's day, or...or the woolly mammoth robes of a caveman—that's a crime against nature! For the sake of society, his suspension has to be permanent!"

"Thank you, Mr. Killbreath," said McNamara. Garlock nodded enthusiastically.

Killbreath shook his tablet one final time in my dad's direction and turned away. I cut ahead of the next person in line and grabbed the microphone. The man behind me *harrumphed*.

I popped the mike from its holder, stepped into the aisle, and froze. Everybody was staring at me. Out of the corner of my eye, I saw Frankie nodding encouragement. I took a deep breath, squared my shoulders, and said, "Hello! My name... is Ambrose Brody. Most of my friends call me Bro. A few call me Rose. I'm the son of Hannibal Brody—and I am a cross-time dresser!" I pulled the bonnet from my head and waved it in the air like a Fourth of July flag.

My father jumped to his feet the moment he heard my voice. He stood watching me with a look that I was pretty sure was pride. A woman sitting in the front row, in the seat closest to my dad, had also stood and looked my way.

My mom!

She was sitting with my aunt Maya.

"I don't dress this way often," I continued, "but over the past day or so I felt I needed to, just as my dad feels the need to, more often than that." I lifted one corner of my apron. "I think it's perfectly comfortable. I think it's perfectly all right! I didn't always think so, but now that I've swallowed an eraser, I know I can correct my mistakes!"

I ran down the aisle to where my mom was standing, turned my back to McNamara and the school board, gripped her hand briefly, and addressed the crowd.

"Yes! My father has a woolly mammoth caveman robe, but it's not *real* woolly mammoth fur. It's not animal fur at all. No woolly mammoths were hurt in the making of that robe. And that's the thing. What my father does doesn't hurt anybody, or anything. It just makes some of you uncomfortable. Because it's different. Because it's out of the ordinary. There was a time in this country when we *enslaved* people because they were different. Because they were extraordinary. That's all the justification we needed. We thought they were different. If we start thinking that way again, if we start fearing people who are different, where will it end? Mr. McNamara"—I spun and faced him—"what if you could be arrested for wearing a kilt?"

"That's different!" he sputtered. "I only wear it for parades and assemblies!"

"And Angus McOffal's birthday," I reminded him. "But if you start persecuting cross-time dressers, don't be surprised if you're next! Then it's anybody who isn't wearing the newest fashions, and then it's anybody who isn't wearing fashions approved by the state. There goes your turban, Mr. Singh; there goes your sari, Ms. Patil." I pointed out people I knew in the audience. "There goes whatever that is hanging off your earlobe, Mr. Curtis!"

"It's a small working glockenspiel," he called back, nodding his head and softly chiming. Mr. Curtis ran Freedom Falls' only coffeehouse. "My sister designs jewelry. I'm here tonight to support your dad, you know. I think quite a few of us are!"

A chorus of approval erupted, coming from about half the people there. I noticed the kids who were acting in *The Crucible* were scattered around the auditorium in their seventeenth-century costumes. Billy Osborn was there in his Becky Thatcher getup, the one he had gotten beaten up for wearing. He was sitting defiantly in the front row, his arms crossed, glaring up at his school board father. I found myself thinking his bonnet was nicer than mine.

The cheering gave way to booing from the other half of the crowd, and I realized the town was pretty evenly divided.

"My father has taught in this town for sixteen years," I reminded them. "He's a good teacher! There's no reason he shouldn't be allowed to keep doing it!"

The microphone cord had stretched as far as it would go. I dropped the mike in Billy Osborn's lap, jumped up on the stage, and hugged my dad. "He's my father, and I stand by him!" I shouted.

Half the audience applauded.

"I'm so glad I gave up my spot," said the man I had cut ahead of, who met Billy halfway to retrieve the mike. "I wasn't really sure what I was going to ask, but now I know."

"And you are, sir?" McNamara asked.

"A reporter for the Cleveland *Plain Dealer*. In town to

visit my daughter, who convinced me this meeting might be worth attending. I'm thinking a story about a school that fires a teacher for being a"—he looked at me—"what was it, Ambrose? A trans-time—?"

"A trans-temp," I answered. "Short for trans-temporal. A cross-time dresser."

"A story about a school that fires a teacher for being a cross-time dresser might be of interest to our readership."

McNamara digested this.

"And what about a story about a school that *doesn't* fire such a teacher?" he asked.

"Not so much. My question being, now that you've heard from both sides, and considering young Mr. Ambrose's quite eloquent plea—how do you expect the vote will go? I only ask now because I have someplace to be at eight thirty."

McNamara studied his hands, which were clenched together in front of him like he was praying, or strangling a rodent. He raised his head, grimaced, and said, "One way to find out. I declare the discussion part of this meeting at an end."

He patted the air to calm the angry murmur from those still waiting to speak. Then he banged his gavel again. "We have heard enough! Members of the board. All those in favor of dismissal of Mr. Hannibal Brody from his position with the English department of the Freedom Falls school district, by reason of said Mr. Brody being unfit to teach, please signify by raising your hands."

Millicent Mordred's hand shot up immediately, followed less quickly by Cynthia Moon's. Billy Osborn's father frowned down at his son. Mr. Osborn shook his head, then also lifted his hand.

"That's three in favor," acknowledged McNamara, to applause from a distressingly large part of the crowd. "All those against?"

The three board members to McNamara's left put up their hands. A different part of the crowd cheered.

"Three to three." McNamara sighed. "I get to cast the deciding vote."

"It would be a pity," said my father, "if we never got to see the heroic McNamara tartan again."

"That is not what is being decided here," McNamara shot back.

"It isn't?"

McNamara ignored him, or appeared to.

"After due consideration," he said, getting to his feet and glancing at the *Plain Dealer* reporter, "and as much to avoid some unpleasant publicity as to keep me in the good graces of a venerable clan, I vote against. Mr. Brody can keep his job and dress however he wants!"

Pandemonium broke out in the room, half the people cheering, half booing. My father clasped hands with my mother and hauled her up on the stage, where they hugged. I got the feeling she wouldn't be visiting her sister again anytime soon, not after a hug like that. I broke into a silly grin.

McNamara banged his gavel and restored something close to order. Quentin Garlock started to scramble to his feet, saying, "We had a deal—" and McNamara smacked him on the head with the gavel and he sat back down, much more quickly than he had gotten up.

"I trust," said McNamara, continuing to stare at the reporter, "very little of what just happened here was newsworthy."

"Not much," the reporter agreed. "Maybe a small article toward the back."

"Thank you. That is appreciated, Mr.—?"

"Whiffletree. Clarence Whiffletree. Don't mention it."

CHAPTER 26
Not Yet Completed

I t wasn't, of course, *our* Clarence Whiffletree, the one we had met in the engine room of the *Buckeye Beauty*. It was one of his descendants, from the family he began in 1853, the year after time travelers from the future had saved his life.

Frankie and I found a few minutes to discuss it after the meeting broke up, while my parents met with McNamara privately in his office. The two of us slipped into a room with a working computer, and I looked up information on the steamboat explosion. Frankie was still arguing that it had been irresponsible of me to scare everybody off the boat.

"Usually," she said, "when you mess with the past, more bad comes of it than good. You got lucky. Besides, the only reason the boiler exploded was because the boat got stuck on a sandbar, and it wouldn't have gotten stuck on a sandbar if it hadn't gone out of its way to rescue Killbreath, and Killbreath wouldn't have been floating around on a log if Mr. Ganto hadn't dragged him to the far side of the river. So *we* caused that boat to explode. If we hadn't been there, Clarence Whiffletree's life would never have been in danger!"

"But he was the engineer on a boat with faulty boiler-plates!" I argued. "Sooner or later, it would have blown, and he would have died. His life needed saving. We just did it sooner than later. Look!" I spun the monitor toward her and pointed to the article about the *Buckeye Beauty* that we had been trying to read when the tablet's battery had gone dead. It had taken some searching, but I had finally found it. I highlighted the important part.

> *... boiler exploded at ten min-*
> *utes to six on the evening of August*

*fourteenth, 1852, resulting in
no loss of life due to the earlier
abandonment of the boat because of
the alleged presence of an escaped circus monkey, thought to be rabid and
of a size some witnesses described as
'gargantuan.' The last overboard was
engineer Clarence Whiffletree, who,
upon reaching shore, announced his
decision to give up steam in favor of
employment in his brother's print-
ing office.*

"Amazing that the battery went dead only seconds before we read that," Frankie marveled.

"So, if Clarence had died, he never would have had a family, and that reporter from the *Plain Dealer* never would have been at the meeting, McNamara wouldn't have gotten embarrassed, and my father would have been fired."

"Actually," said Frankie, "I think your speech had a lot to do with saving your dad."

"You do?"

"It was a very good speech. Well delivered. I liked it."

I felt a warm glow all over. I decided it might be from lack of sleep.

• • •

At breakfast the next day I sat facing the fridge, where a smiley-face magnet held a photo of me and Tom with our arms around each other's shoulders, our grins both bigger than the smiley face's. I kept staring at it and forgetting to eat. I finally abandoned my English muffin and ran to my room. I had thought of something that might tell me what had happened to my friend.

I did an Internet search for *I-Ching* hexagrams and was surprised by how many sites had them. Some of the sites were totally loony, others were overly serious, but they all featured the hexagrams in the same order as the book.

Tom had consulted the *I-Ching* just as the soldiers came around the bend, only moments before he made the decision to cover his ears and remain in ancient China. I had no idea what question he had asked, but I knew the result had been the seventh hexagram. My own question, as I scrolled down to it, was simply—*what happened?*

The seventh hexagram was almost all broken *yin* lines, with only a single unbroken *yang*. It looked like this:

It was called *The Army*. Of the sixty-four hexagrams, it was definitely the one that best applied to the situation we'd been in at the time. Shang troops had been marching down on us.

But this didn't tell me what had happened to Tom.

I printed out the hexagram, then I printed a chart showing all the Morse code letters.

The hexagram started with eight dots, but no Morse code letter was made up of eight dots, so I started by assuming maybe the first three dots stood for the letter *S*, and then maybe the next dot was an *E*, and the next dot, maybe another *E*, followed by three dots that might have been another *S*. The single dash, I thought, could have been a *T*, and the final two dots together might have been the letter *I*. That gave me *seesti*, which, unfortunately, wasn't a word.

How had Tom been able to do it so quickly? I had a theory, but I couldn't believe it.

It took me half an hour to find a Morse code message in the lines of the hexagram known as *The Army*. And once I found it, I was pretty sure it was addressed to me.

The first broken line—two dots—was the letter *I*. It was followed by four dots—the letter *H*—and then another two dots, meaning another *I*, and then, finally, a dash and two dots, giving me the letter *D*.

Tom Xui, how did you escape the approaching army?

I hid.

He and Jiang must have made their way back to Jiang's hiding place before any of the soldiers noticed. Presumably, the army marched right past without seeing them.

And then what?

I flipped a coin. Six times. All the while talking to Tom directly, as if he were sitting there in the room with me.

"Tom Xui, what happened to you? Are you all right?"

The hexagram I got was this:

I looked it up and I was relieved to find it was called *Deliverance*, and it was all about past difficulties that had been successfully overcome. I worked out the Morse. It only took me twenty minutes this time. I was getting better. I would never be as good as Tom, but then, he had an advantage that I could never have.

The Morse was three dots followed by a dot and a dash, followed by two dots, a dash and a dot, ending with a final dot.

It spelled *safe*.

So Tom was safe, and he seemed happy to be where we had left him.

I did another six coin flips and got the very first hexagram. This, I could see, was a very special one.

It was called *Heaven*.

It was all solid *yang* lines, meaning the Morse would be nothing but dashes, with no dots. I looked at my Morse alphabet and discovered there were only three letters that used only dashes. When I saw what those letters were, I knew what the hexagram spelled.

I freaked.

I jumped up and hugged myself, I was shivering so badly.

Then I forced myself to calm down, and flipped my coin six more times.

It didn't surprise me when the hexagram it gave me was the very last one, hexagram sixty-four:

The last hexagram was just as special as the first. It had an equal number of *yin* lines and *yang* lines, and they alternated back and forth, sort of the way Frankie's mom and dad gave equal time to each other (I surprised myself, thinking of it that way). I was almost positive what the first Morse letter would be, and I wasn't wrong. And once I had the first letter, I knew the rest.

I couldn't believe it, but it made perfect sense.

The sixty-fourth hexagram was called *Not Yet Completed.* And it was right: Things were not yet completed.

I had to go see Mrs. Xui.

• • •

I pretended to head for the bus stop—Dad always left for school too early for me to ride with him—and after I passed the corner, I cut through a hedge, looped back, and made my way to the Xui residence.

Even though more than twenty-four hours had passed between the time my father dropped me off at Tom's on Wednesday and the Thursday night school board meeting when I returned with the others from our time-travel trip, nobody had missed me. My father had taken it for granted I would go to school with Tom on Thursday morning, and the school attendance office had left a message about my absence on voice mail that didn't get listened to until late Thursday night.

Tom, on the other hand, was missed at breakfast on Thursday morning. His mother, however, decided he had once again run away from home and this time taken his friend Ambrose with him. This meant he was most likely with me at my place. Mrs. Xui fully expected to see her son back by nightfall, or, at the very latest, sometime on Friday. Whenever he ran away, he never stayed gone for more than a day. She always made him make up the piano practice and studying he had missed, so staying away any longer only made his workload worse.

By the time I got to Tom's house, his sisters had left for school, and Mrs. Xui was off at the supermarket. It was Tom's great-grandfather—Gee Gee Pa—who opened the door when I knocked.

"Hello, Bro!" he said, giving me the very faintest of bows, to which I gave a much deeper one. "I am sorry. I do not know where Tom is."

"I do," I replied. "That's the reason I'm here. May I come in?"

He stepped aside, then ushered me into the living room. On the TV, a dark blue box was spinning through space. Gee Gee Pa switched it off.

"*Doctor Wu* marathon," he explained. "Most amusing."

"If you think that's amusing, wait'll you see this," I said, spreading my papers on the coffee table.

I explained to him what had happened to his great-grandson.

It went better than I expected. Possibly because his command of English was not as good as his Chinese, he sat quietly without interrupting me. I made the story simple. I skipped over the Time Trombone and everything that had happened to us in 1852 and mainly told him that his great-grandson had time-traveled to ancient China and decided to stay there, and I had messages from him to prove it.

Gee Gee Pa nodded and smiled, as if I were trying out a creative-writing assignment on him. But when he saw the *I-Ching* hexagrams on my computer printouts, and I showed him the chart I was using to decode the Morse, his smile vanished and he took me more seriously. He had heard of Morse code; he knew it involved a series of dots and dashes. When I showed him that the dots and the dashes contained in the fifty-sixth hexagram, *Travel*, spelled the English word *times*, he got up and left the room. He came back a few moments later with an old leather-bound book, which he opened on the table.

"*Book of Changes*," he said, and I saw that the book, written in Chinese, contained the familiar hexagrams. Gee Gee Pa had his own copy of the *I-Ching*, and I was sure it made more sense than the wacky version Tom had been using.

"Funny," said Gee Gee Pa, in the slow, halting, but very precise way he always spoke English, "hexagram fifty-six, about traveling, should contain code for *times*, and no one ever noticed. Traveling through times. Very clever."

I showed him more. I showed him how the hexagram called *Trouble* contained the code for *erase*; and *Decay*, *dead*; and *The Army*, *I hid*. I showed him every single hexagram that had guided us, and how each contained a Morse code message that had been important to us at the time.

Then I showed him the first hexagram and the last hexagram, and the Morse code they contained.

And he believed.

"Oh, my Tom Xui!" he said, clutching his leather book to his chest. "I knew you were born to do great things!"

"All he had with him," I said sadly, "was his *I-Ching* book and a gold coin with a nail hole through the middle."

"Ah," murmured Gee Gee Pa. "This would explain why early Chinese coins all had holes in the center. Inspired by my great-grandson's cash. More proof of what you say!"

He took it very well. It probably helped that he had been watching a *Doctor Wu* marathon.

I met Mrs. Xui at the door when she returned from shopping and helped her carry in her groceries.

"Ambrose! Good! The two of you are back! I wish Tom would outgrow this—he can't keep running away. His studies are important. I ride him for his own good! Where is he? Why aren't the two of you in school?"

Gee Gee Pa was waiting for us when I led Tom's mom into the living room.

"Granddaughter, you must listen," he said, and his presence was a help.

She threw me out of the house halfway through my explanation.

I waited patiently outside and listened to the voices

within. One murmured, while the other got louder and louder. Finally, the door flew open and Mrs. Xui dragged me back inside.

I finished explaining, and Gee Gee Pa showed her pages in his *I-Ching* book. She batted the book away and stomped angrily around the room.

Gee Gee Pa coaxed her back to the sofa with us, and I showed her the Morse code hidden in the first and final hexagrams. She swayed back and forth like she might fall, then she collapsed into her grandfather's arms and sobbed uncontrollably. Gee Gee Pa fluttered his hand at me behind her quaking back, suggesting I should leave, and I did. I let myself out.

On the doorstep, I cried, too. I never expected to see my friend again. He had obviously grown to manhood and become a very respected figure in the China of long ago.

I don't think Mrs. Xui would have believed it if it hadn't been for the Morse contained in the first and last hexagrams. Tom must have realized this.

The first hexagram was formed by a single dash, followed by three dashes, followed by a final two dashes.

The Morse code spelled *Tom*.

The last hexagram was formed by a dash, two dots and a dash, followed by two dots and a dash, followed by two dots.

The Morse code spelled *Xui*.

My best friend, Tom Xui, inventor of the three-thousand-year-old hexagrams of the *I-Ching*, had signed his work.

CHAPTER 27
Completed

Two days later, Sunday evening, as the sun was setting and Camlo's carnival was closing, Frankie and I sat swinging gently at the top of the Ferris wheel. Across the treetops we could just make out the sun's last rays glinting off the windows of the Dingleman Hole-Punch factory. It was the kind of view you never forget.

"Your school will be wondering where Tom went," said Frankie, sitting close to the center of the seat. I thought maybe there was gum or something on the far side of her that she didn't want to sit in.

"Gee Gee Pa is returning to China for a visit," I explained. "He leaves tomorrow. The Xui family has already gotten word out that Tom is going with him, and won't be back in school for a while. I'm guessing that, eventually, they'll say he decided to stay in China. That would be pretty much the truth. Tom's family seems okay with the idea of time travel. The rest of the world might have some trouble with it."

"And you explained it all to them without mentioning the Shagbolt. Thank you for that."

She patted my hand, then let her hand linger. I raised my hand and scratched the side of my nose.

"All I told them was, the time-travel thing seemed to involve some kind of psychic power that Tom possessed, and that he had only confided about it to me. They knew about Tom's ability to predict ringing telephones, and the evidence in the hexagrams was pretty convincing. I didn't have to tell them anything about Time Trombones or slave catchers or exploding steamboats."

"Well," said Frankie, drumming her fingers on the seat, "I guess this explains why your friend was able to decode the Morse code messages so quickly. He was the one who put them there!"

"Yeah," I agreed. "He was reading his own mind. I wish I had figured that out sooner."

A blue jay landed on the edge of the seat, hopped to the floor, and flew off with a piece of popcorn. Frankie and I were the only ones on the wheel. We had been at the top for a few minutes. I wondered if the ride's operator had fallen asleep.

"Speaking of the Time Trombone..." I said.

"My father put it someplace," Frankie said, clasping both hands in her lap and staring straight ahead. "I'm not sure if it's with the carnival, or if he's found a new place to hide it in your town. I can't believe he thinks it's more of a danger than a benefit to have around. When I'm officially the Shagbolt's Keeper, I will keep it with the carnival at all times. Just to be safe."

"Yeah. You never know when Nazis are going to come crashing through the trees."

"You joke. But it's truer than you think. My mother thinks I could be named Keeper as early as my fourteenth birthday."

"Does your father agree?"

"He's of two minds."

"You know," I said, "I thought about it, and that place

where the Shagbolt was hidden in the middle school—it's on the other side of the wall from the English department office, right near the desk where my father sits and grades papers."

"So?"

"So . . . is it possible being that close to a time machine somehow affected my dad? Maybe . . . made him need to dress in the clothing of other time periods?"

Frankie tapped her foot, as though she were irritated.

"Maybe," she conceded. "The Shagbolt gives off an energy we call the Aura of Inevitability. Long-term exposure to it can cause a variety of odd side effects."

"Does that mean that now that the Shagbolt's gone, my father will stop being a cross-time dresser?"

"No." Frankie shook her head emphatically. "I'm sorry, Rose. The aura's effects are permanent. Your father might as well have been born the way he is. He will always feel the need to put on homespun or togas or stovepipe hats. And, the way I see it, that's a good thing. Apparently, there are other people who feel the need to live the alternative lifestyle your father is living, even without any past exposure to a time machine. And your father seems willing to teach these people and reassure them that being different is perfectly all right. So it's really for the best."

"GOOD NIGHT, AND THANK YOU FOR ATTEND-ING!" a voice rang out from the carnival's public address system. "Camlo's Traveling Wonder Show is now closed. We will be breaking down our tents and moving on, with happy memories of all our delightful guests from *insert name of town here*—er—Freedom Falls—to warm us as we journey to our next destination. Good night! Good night! Lost children must be claimed within the next fifteen minutes, or they become property of the carnival. Good night!"

I had a final question, but I had been putting it off. I thought I might already know the answer.

"So why did your future self steal *Uncle Tom's Cabin*?"

"Because that was the book I happened to be reading just before we arrived in Freedom Falls." She shrugged. "It could just as easily have been *Ivanhoe*."

"Nobody reads *Ivanhoe*."

"Obviously, my future self knows me well enough to know my solution would be to find the Shagbolt and go back and try to replace the book. It was like she was deliberately telling me I had to go back to 1852."

"Why?"

"That, at first, was what I couldn't figure out. I thought maybe there was something I had to set right, or undo, or find. But it didn't matter, because I started out with all this confidence. I had *seen* my future self, so I knew I would survive whatever happened. But then I wound up traveling with you, and Tom, and Mr. Ganto, and I realized I had no idea if anything bad would happen to any of *you*, and I started to get worried, especially after we didn't go to New York, and we wound up in a much more dangerous place. And at first I thought you were such a goof, but then you rescued Dwina and figured out how to get the Shagbolt back, and saved us all when we were going over the falls. I'm not really sure when it was I knew."

I looked over the edge of the seat. I wondered how difficult it would be to climb to the ground. "Knew what?"

"I didn't fully understand at the time, but when my future self held her hand to her lips to keep me quiet, she wasn't just showing me my charm bracelet. She was showing me the ring on her finger. I think she stole the book to make sure you and I would have this adventure together!"

"Because," I said, gripping the handrail like we were spinning a mile a minute, "we've become good friends, and, and—I'll probably be the one who introduces you to your future husband! *Fiduciary!* It's probably somebody I already know! Maybe Mickey Steinmetz, he's really cool, he can burp the national anthem, or…or…Jamal Tremain, his family raises chinchillas, or Nooby Wilson, he's a little bit weird, he thinks inchworms should be converted to the metric system, or Sylvester Delgado—he broke the three middle teeth out of his comb so he can comb his hair without snagging the wart on the top of his head—"

"Are you aware that girls mature faster than boys?" Frankie swiveled her head and examined my expression.

"Uh, I had heard something like that—"

She leaned in close. The Ferris wheel lurched and threw us back in our seats. The wheel rolled forward and we swung down and around and halted with a bump at ground level.

The ride's operator turned out to be Orlando Tiresias Camlo.

"Dad!" cried Frankie.

He was wearing a T-shirt and jeans. At least, as far as I could tell.

"'The wheel is come full circle; I am here,' as Edmund said in *King Lear*. Our revels now are ended. Or, at least, they should be." He turned and shouted at a passing worker, "Adam! Give Dukker a hand with the game trailers! I want to be halfway to Louisville by midnight!" He looked back at us and added, "Time for you two to say good night."

"'A thousand times good night'?" Frankie asked in an impish tone, and I suspected she was quoting Shakespeare back at him. I decided I didn't want to know which play.

"Once will be quite sufficient. Parting may be sweet sorrow, but you'll get over it!" He hurried after one of his men. "Mander! Wait up!"

Frankie walked me to the exit, stopping at the ticket booths like they were a barrier she wasn't going to cross. The mood from the top of the Ferris wheel had been broken, and I certainly didn't want to pick up the conversation from where we had left off, but I wanted to talk to her some more, so I told her, "One of the boys in the school play—*The Crucible*— broke his leg skateboarding yesterday. They're holding emergency auditions tomorrow to find a replacement. I was thinking of trying out."

"I think you should! You have a great voice; it really carries. What part?"

"Giles Corey."

"He was a young black man?"

"He was an old white guy. But the part of the judge, Thomas Danforth, is being played by a girl, so I'm guessing casting is flexible."

"And who was Giles Corey?"

"He was one of the citizens of Salem who was accused of witchcraft."

"He was hanged?"

"They piled rocks on him until he died."

"Just because they thought he was different."

"Yeah. If I get the part, I'm going to ask the director if I can throw the rocks back at them. Make it a surprise ending."

"You can't rewrite history."

"Why not? I've done it before. And I get the impression *you* do it all the time."

She kissed me, a fast peck on the lips, and then she turned and disappeared into the growing chaos that was a carnival coming apart. I walked backward so I could see her until the last moment.

I collided with her father.

"Well met by moonlight," he said as I whirled to face him. He was dressed in the old-time suit and tie from our first meeting—or he appeared to be—only this time he was smoking a cigar, the way I had seen him in the crystal ball.

"Ambrose, is it?" he asked. "You and I won't be formally introduced for another year yet, but I feel compelled to thank you here and now for the way you protected my daughter during your recent excursion. Well done, sir!"

He took my hand and shook it firmly.

"She—she told you about it?" I stammered.

"Her future self did."

"Her future self?"

"Hard to believe a daughter of mine will ever wear that much eyeliner. I trust I did not keep you at the Ferris wheel's apex for a period beyond your own personal comfort. It was a tricky thing to judge."

"You wanted us up there?" I looked over my shoulder at the wheel. It was being disassembled. When I turned back, a woman in a kerchief and fancy robes stood where Frankie's dad had been standing. Instead of a cigar, she was chewing a strip of red licorice. She smiled and gave me an approving pat on the head. I blinked, and she was gone, replaced by Mr. Camlo.

"'We are such stuff as dreams are made on,'" he informed me.

"You don't smoke," I told him.

"Do you smell smoke?"

I sniffed. "No..."

"Then I'm not smoking. But I sometimes accessorize. The future Shofranka tells me that you, young Ambrose, will one day be important to her, and that in the protection of the Shagbolt, you will prove to be—if I may make a Bard-like pun—instrumental."

I didn't understand half the things he said. I had a feeling it was just as well.

"You . . . planned for us to time-travel?"

"Let's just say that when I leave a treasure map in a locked safe, I fully expect my daughter to get her hands on it. It was a small conspiracy between myself and the future Shofranka. I really *do* look forward to meeting you!"

He stepped around me and walked back to his carnival.

• • •

The next day, my father taught his classes dressed as Shoeless Joe Jackson, a baseball player from the early twentieth century. The uniform looked almost modern, but the cap looked more like a beanie.

"Shouldn't you be barefoot?" I asked him when we met in the parking lot at the end of the day. On the other side of the fence, the school's sports teams were starting to practice.

"What? Because they called him Shoeless?" My dad shook his head. "He only played barefoot once. It doesn't take much to get branded for life. Care to have a game of catch?" He nodded at an unused baseball field. "Or—" He hesitated. "Is it too public for you?"

I looked. Kids I knew were all over the place. But it didn't matter.

"Sure!" I said eagerly. "But on one condition!"

"What?"

"You let me wear that hat!"

He did, and we played, and the hat looked a little goofy—

—but I didn't mind a bit.

A FEW MORE LINES FROM THE AUTHOR

There has been positive proof of time travel ever since 1836, when Samuel Morse invented Morse code. Ever since then, had anybody bothered to look, they would have found Morse code messages in the three-thousand-year-old hexagrams contained in one of the world's oldest books, China's *I-Ching: The Book of Changes*.

Nobody bothered to look.

It doesn't surprise me that it was two middle-school kids who finally made the discovery. Middle schoolers are still intellectually curious, and they have not yet been taught that some things are impossible. (Or, if they have been taught this, they know enough not to believe it.) Finding Morse code in the *I-Ching* is the same as finding a cell phone in King Tut's mummy case, or a fossilized snow-blower in the La Brea Tar Pits, or a battery-powered nose-hair trimmer in the ruins of Machu Picchu. This is why the title is *The Book That Proves Time Travel Happens*. You can't argue with hard evidence.

A ·—	H ····	O ———	V ···—
B —···	I ··	P ·——·	W ·——
C —·—·	J ·———	Q ——·—	X —··—
D —··	K —·—	R ·—·	Y —·——
E ·	L ·—··	S ···	Z ——··
F ··—·	M ——	T —	
G ——·	N —·	U ··—	

What do we know about the time traveler who created the *I-Ching* hexagrams and their cleverly concealed Morse code messages?

We know a lot. For one thing, he made his base in the mountains. Hexagram fifty-two, called *Stillness of the Mountains*, contains the Morse code for *base*. He was also an avid follower of the weather—hexagram fifty-one, called *Thunder*, contains the Morse code for *sleet*. He liked to leave his dwelling for an occasional stroll—hexagram ten, *Walking*, contains the Morse for *out*. And his parents apparently came from two very different backgrounds—hexagram thirty-seven, *The Family*, contains the Morse for *mix*.

And, how appropriate is it, considering China's notorious rainy season, that hexagram fifty-seven, known as *Ground*, should be turned by its Morse into *mud*?

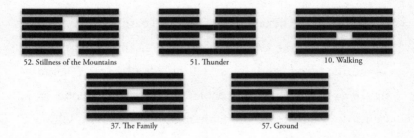

52. Stillness of the Mountains   51. Thunder   10. Walking

37. The Family   57. Ground

If you're thinking this is all just coincidence, our time traveler was sometimes exuberant—hexagram sixteen, *Enthusiasm*, is full of *sass*, as so many of the enthusiastic are, and when he was at peace, he hummed—hexagram eleven, *Peace*, contains *hum*—and he felt that change for the better almost always takes place in small increments, otherwise why would hexagram fifty-three, *Gradual Progress*, contain the tiny measurement of *mites*? He also, quite sensibly, preferred his seafood cooked, rather than raw, since hexagram thirty, *Fire*, is full of *tuna*.

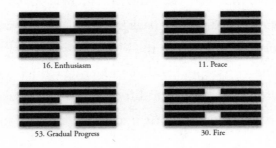

16. Enthusiasm   11. Peace

53. Gradual Progress   30. Fire

Added to the hexagrams mentioned earlier in the book—*Trouble* containing *erase*; *Observing* containing *miss*; *Decay* containing *dead*; and, most telling of all, *Travel* containing *times*—we have irrefutable proof that someone from the future visited, and probably made his home in, China at the time of the Zhou dynasty.

I am eagerly awaiting notification that I have won the Nobel Prize for time-travel research. To my mind, there are no other contenders.

Exactly half—thirty-two—of the *I-Ching*'s sixty-four hexagrams contain Morse code messages that relate to the topic of the hexagram they occur in. The *I-Ching* is all about opposites: *yin* versus *yang*, chaos versus order, hello versus goodbye. So, whoever created the *I-Ching* made a deliberate artistic choice to put messages in only half of the hexagrams: meaning vs. nonsense. Of the thirty-two nonsense hexagrams, most contain no messages whatsoever, while a few contain gibberish. (There is, for instance, no sensible reason why hexagram twenty-one, *Chewing Up and Spitting Out*, should contain the Morse code for *Tibet*, unless the *I-Ching*'s creator was making a veiled critique of modern-day China's internal policies.)

A few of the hexagrams contain more than one message, depending on how the dots and dashes are read. Here, for example, is hexagram eighteen, *Decay*:

It can be read from top to bottom in four different ways:

— • • = D	— • • • = B	— • • • = B	— • • = D
• = E	• — = A	• — = A	• • — = U
• — = A	— • • = D	— • = N	— • • = D
— • • = D		• = E	

393

All four words can relate to *Decay*, but *dead* is the most appropriate. The other three choices are just the *I-Ching*'s creator showing off, something he did fairly often. (For instance, hexagram fifteen, *Modesty*, contains either the Morse code for *hers*, or *seers*, and since it would be sexist to suppose that modesty is only appropriate to the female, he had to have meant that seers—fortune-tellers such as himself—should show a little more humility, which he easily could have done by being a little less clever.)

Do I believe all this?

Of course.

So should you.

It will make your world that much more intriguing.

The point here—or maybe it's a dot, possibly a dash, maybe even a dot *and* a dash—is that patterns are everywhere. Some patterns are easy to find; we're all aware of them. Other patterns are more complex, and we need artists, musicians, writers, and scientists to find them and point them out to us. Usually, once these people show us the patterns, the patterns make our lives a little richer: We say, cool, I like that song; this painting moves me; what you just said helps me understand the universe a little bit better, or it makes me laugh, or both.

When the scientist Sir William Ramsay first isolated the element helium in 1895, he did it by studying the patterns in something called a spectrogram. Spectrograms are a series of lines; they look like *I-Ching* hexagrams on steroids. Sir William's discovery of helium made modern MRI medical scanners possible, and has resulted in birthday balloons being 98 percent less droopy. (I like to think that Sir William ran out of his laboratory shouting, "I've discovered helium! I've discovered helium!" but that's just me.) His discovery would never have been made without his ability to recognize patterns.

The artist Pablo Picasso once removed the seat from a bicycle, welded a set of bicycle handlebars to the seat, hung it on a wall, and everybody who saw it said, "Ah! the head of a bull!" The handlebars became the horns, the seat became the bull's long face. The pattern was there; Picasso saw it first, and once he pointed it out, everybody could enjoy it, except possibly the guy who owned the bicycle. What Picasso did is called a visual pun. (People who hate puns call it found art.) It is very similar to seeing the dots and dashes of Morse code in the hexagrams of the *I-Ching*. (Am I comparing myself to Picasso? No, but I am saying my bull is every bit as good as Picasso's bull.)

Patterns are everywhere. In clouds, in junkyards, in

human behavior. We read to find patterns. If you've read this book, you're a pattern-seeker, and that's a very good thing to be. Some of the patterns in the book were deliberate—puns form a type of pattern; stories of prejudice through the ages form another—but I'm sure there are patterns within this book that the author was unaware of. Different readers will see different things. This is how books work.

Dear reader, new patterns are out there, waiting to be found, and waiting for their finders to show them to the rest of us.

Who will find them?

I'm betting it's you.

Acknowledgments

I would, first and foremost, like to thank history. History tells us that

- the pencil with attached eraser was first patented in 1858;

- *Moby-Dick*, a book with a narrator who wished to be called Ishmael, about the final voyage of a ship known as the *Pequod*, was published in 1851 to poor reviews that pretty much sank its author's career;

- the Fugitive Slave Act (referred to herein by Archie Killbreath and Frankie Camlo as the Fugitive Slave

Law) was enacted as a result of the Compromise of 1850 and required that all apprehended runaway slaves be returned to their original captors;

- *Uncle Tom's Cabin* was published in 1852 as a response to the Fugitive Slave Act and helped rally supporters to the antislavery cause;

- the steamboat *Buckeye Belle* exploded on the Muskingum River in November of 1852 with great loss of life;

- King Di Xin of China's Shang dynasty didn't—as far as we know—persecute people for wearing their clothes inside out, but he did persecute them for things just as trivial;

- in 1692, in Salem, Massachusetts, eighty-one-year-old Giles Corey was crushed to death because he refused to plead either guilty or not guilty to the charge of witchcraft;

- the writers Ambrose Bierce and Zane Grey were both born in Ohio;

- no one knows the actual date chopsticks premiered in America.

Without history, *The Book That Proves Time Travel Happens* would have been a very different book.

The book would have been even differenter (and included more words like *differenter*) without the patient, possibly bemused, editorial guidance of Andrea Spooner and Deirdre Jones. Copy editor Regina Castillo caught major goofs (Major Goofs will be a minor character in my next novel), and Ben Davidson offered helpful suggestions concerning nineteenth-century dialect and word usage.

My agent, Kate Epstein, would have been at the top of this list if I hadn't lowered myself to make the *different/differenter* joke, but then she understands I sometimes can't help myself.

Emma Joy Jampole made me start thinking along lines *yin* and *yang*, and Paul Feldman and Terry Hunt, along with the rest of the cast of the *Melvin Snodgrass Show* (improvised into a reel-to-reel tape recorder in my basement, circa 1964–1969) contributed to the genesis of the Time Trombone.

In my younger days, a number of teachers encouraged me to write, and they deserve special, reverent mention here, starting with Evadne Lovett in fourth grade, Leo Reardon in fifth, Egon Teichert in sixth, and, in high school, Eugene Murphy and especially Michael Stoller. (Mike also tried teaching me logic, and we can all see how well that turned out.) Judith Claire Mitchell was a fellow student in Mike's class, and she hints I'm in the acknowledgments of her *A Reunion of Ghosts*, so I'd better say hi here. She always said she'd publish her second novel three weeks before I published my second novel. (She also predicted the Internet.)

Last but not least, I am forever grateful to my wife, Kathy, and my daughter, Elyse, for giving me the time and space I needed to complete the book. (Love you guys!)

A major portion of this novel—all right, the limerick in chapter 15—first appeared in the October 1979 issue of *Isaac Asimov's Science Fiction Magazine*. I mention this only as a ploy to garner a possible review of *Time Travel Happens* from the current *Asimov's*, which was my long-range plan when I wrote the limerick and planted it in *Asimov's* to begin with.

I love it when a plan comes together.

Discussion Guide

1. Explain how the *I-Ching* contributes to the structure of the novel. How does Tom's T-shirt foreshadow the importance of the *I-Ching*?

2. Why might the Shagbolt be dangerous if in the possession of the wrong people? Explain what Frankie means when she calls the Shagbolt her family's "crown jewel."

3. Describe Ambrose and Tom's friendship. What special qualities does each boy bring to the relationship? Explain what Ambrose means when he says, "I lost my best friend, Tom Xui, twice. The first time, I simply wasn't paying attention." What happened the first time Ambrose lost Tom? Discuss the second time.

4. Contrast Ambrose's and Tom's families. Identify the major conflict in each family. Explain how these conflicts cause the boys to seek answers from a fortune-teller.

5. How might Frankie describe her father? What is Mr. Ganto's role in raising her? How does Frankie need the boys as much as they need a fortune-teller?

6. Ambrose says that his parents let him go to the carnival because he was showing more responsibility. Trace times in the novel when Ambrose, Tom, and Frankie show responsibility. When are they reckless and show poor judgment?

7. Explain the concept of glammering. Discuss how Tom, Ambrose, and Frankie would like others to see them. How do others see Hannibal Brody and Orlando Tiresias Camlo? How do they want others to see them?

8. What is symbolic about the Drama Club's production of *The Crucible*? What message is Mr. McNamara conveying by having the school board meet on the set of the play?

9. A reporter for the Cleveland *Plain Dealer* is visiting Freedom Falls and attends the school board meeting in search of a good story. Why is Mr. McNamara so concerned about publicity? Discuss the responsibility of the press to report things accurately. What would be an accurate portrayal of Mr. McNamara?

10. Identify the central themes of the novel. What does the reader learn about "differences" and "acceptance"?

11. Debate the surprise events at the end of the novel. At what point is it obvious that Tom will remain in ancient China? What clues lead to the revelation about Frankie's father? Which character grows the most throughout the novel?

12. In "A Few More Lines from the Author," Henry Clark says that readers will likely identify many patterns in the book. Besides the *I-Ching*, what other patterns are there? How does this contribute to the mystery and suspense of the novel?

GET READY FOR ONE WACKY ADVENTURE!

A 2013 American Booksellers Association New Voices Pick
A 2013 Association of Booksellers for Children Best Book
An Amazon Best Book of the Month
A Junior Library Guild Selection

"Clark's debut is **refreshingly bonkers**. It offers thinking kids humor that is neither afraid of the potty nor confined to it."
—*Kirkus Reviews*

"The kids' uncertainty about who to trust and the novel's swift pace create unyielding suspense....**For those destined to become Douglas Adams** fans it will be hilarious and gripping."
—*Publishers Weekly*

"**Fast paced and entertaining...an exciting, suspenseful adventure** with many unexpected twists....Those willing to take a chance on something odd will be rewarded."
—*School Library Journal*

"This **clever** story self-consciously and irreverently follows in the footsteps of **classic quest tales**....
[A] whirlwind adventure."
—*The Bulletin*

"Very funny...both **an intricate love letter to sussing out clues** and the realities that underpin kid-hood."
—*The Austin American-Statesman*

"**A hilarious tale** of attempted world domination."
—*Newsday*

"The **adventure and creativity** propel one to continue the story."
—*School Library Connection*

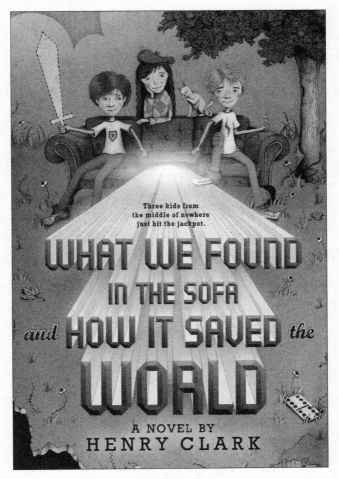

An Unexpected Sofa

The sofa wasn't there on Monday but it was there on Tuesday. It sat in the shade just down the road from the bus stop. A broken branch dangled from the tree above it, like maybe the sofa had fallen from the sky and damaged the tree as it fell. Then again, maybe the broken branch had been there the day before. I hadn't noticed.

When I got there, my friend Freak was sitting on the sofa, one arm on an armrest, eating taco chips out of a Ziploc bag. For him, it was a typical breakfast.

He raised his hand for a high five, shouted my name— "River!"—and slapped my palm.

"Where'd the sofa come from?" I asked.

"Brought it from home," he replied, as if I might believe it.

"Really," I said, looking down toward the bus stop, where the road curved to the right. When the bus got there, we would have to run to catch it. "You could have put it closer to the bus."

Freak shrugged and patted the cushion next to him. I noticed the fabric had a dark red stain on it, like dried blood, or maybe spaghetti sauce. I switched the cushion with the one next to it and sat.

"Chip?" Freak held the bag in my direction. With his blond hair and his pale blue T-shirt and jeans, he looked like a faded photograph. He did his own laundry and sometimes he used too much bleach.

"Thanks."

The sofa sat in the grass at the edge of Breeland Road. Behind it stretched the six-foot-high concrete wall surrounding the Underhill place.

"When's trash pickup?" I inquired.

"For big stuff? Friday."

"So this should still be here tomorrow."

"Provided Schimmelhorn doesn't get it."

Max Schimmelhorn runs a junk shop next to the Cheshire

hardware store. A lot of people think he and I are related because he's short and thin with a mop of red hair—but we're not.

"You want to get here early tomorrow?" asked Freak.

"And do what?"

"Sit."

I thought about it for a moment.

"Sure," I said. "What's the weather supposed to be?"

"No idea. Fiona can look it up on her phone."

It wasn't long before Fiona came into sight, crossing the field between Breeland Road and the houses off in the distance, where the three of us lived. Beyond our houses there was heat shimmer in the air. There usually was.

Fiona always looked like an explosion in a paint factory. Today she was wearing a red beret, a baggy green sweater, and orange-striped stockings that disappeared under the sweater, where they may or may not have clashed with her skirt, depending on whether or not she was wearing one.

"What's this?" she asked, coming up to the sofa.

"Hot-dog stand," said Freak.

Fiona examined the stained cushion. She flipped it over, decided the flip side was clean enough, and sat down next to me.

"This is nice," she announced.

"Freak and I are getting here early tomorrow," I told her.

"Why?"

"To sit. That is, if it's not going to rain."

"Could you check that?" inquired Freak.

Fiona pulled out her phone and poked it. She tickled it, massaged it, then tapped it three times. "Sunny tomorrow. Warmer than usual for October. You *do* realize it doesn't make sense for this sofa to be here."

"Old Man Underhill is throwing it out," I said.

"How do you know that?" she asked.

"It's in front of his place. It's near his gate. Where else would it have come from?"

"Who helped him bring it down from the house? Everybody says he lives alone. He's, like, a hundred years old. The driveway is really long. He couldn't have carried this thing all the way down by himself."

I turned and looked over my shoulder. Beyond the wall, one turret of the old house was visible above the trees at the top of the hill. The morning sun glinted off something in the uppermost window.

"Maybe it walked here," suggested Freak.

Fiona and I looked at him.

"Look at the feet."

The sofa had feet. Four of them, one at each corner, made of dark wood carved to resemble dragon claws. Each claw clutched a wooden ball.

"River's right," said Freak. "Who else would have furniture like this? It's old, it's clunky, it's creepy. It's gotta be Old Man Underhill's."

Fiona twirled a few strands of her long black hair around one of her fingers. "Have either of you ever seen a trash can out here?"

We discussed it and decided we hadn't.

"But I once saw a grocery delivery truck go in the gate," I said. "Maybe garbage trucks go in the same way."

"Either that," said Freak, "or that's one messy house."

A couple of bright yellow maple leaves chased each other down the road. I leaned back on the sofa, closed my eyes, and tilted my face toward the sun. After a minute or two, I felt Freak and Fiona relax into the cushions, too.

"Flash mob today?" asked Freak.

"I wouldn't know," said Fiona. "Never having seen a flash mob. Except on TV. I've certainly never been part of one. And I'm tired of you and your friend here"—I felt myself jabbed in the ribs with a bony elbow—"telling me I have. It doesn't even make sense as a joke."

"It said in the paper that all of you in the flash mobs have agreed to deny you were part of a flash mob," said Freak. "That's what I think is the really cool part. I haven't been able to shake anybody. Not even you. And you usually blab things like crazy."

"You're an idiot," Fiona stated. "How's that for blabbing?"

My eyes opened at the sound of an engine to our right, where the bus usually came from. When the red hood of a convertible came into view instead, Fiona sat straight up, like a gopher popping out of its hole. She scrambled over the back of the sofa and hid behind it.

"Forgot your bag," said Freak.

Fiona, moving faster than the speed of light, reached over the back of the sofa, snagged her paisley-print book bag, and disappeared again.

Travis Miller, whose name Fiona had written in flowery letters on the inside of her science notebook, went by, on his way to being dropped off at school by his older brother. His brother had a cell phone pressed against the side of his head and didn't notice us, but Travis looked quizzically at the sofa as the car went by.

"Are they gone?" came a quiet voice behind us.

"No," said Freak.

Fiona, who knew Freak almost as well as I did, left her hiding place and sat back down. "That was close," she said.

Fiona was willing to hang out with Freak and me until the bus arrived, because the bus was always empty when it picked us up. It was the first stop on the bus route. If the morning conversation interested her, she might even sit with us once we got on the bus, but when the second stop came into view, she would find a new seat, well away from us. For the rest of the day, she would pretend she had never seen us before. It was understood we should never approach her in school, even during the two classes the three of us shared.

"Don't take this personally," she'd explained once, "but girls mature faster than boys and I really need to be with people my own age."

"You're one year younger than we are," I'd pointed out.

"Yes," she'd admitted, "but, emotionally, you're both six."

"How can you say that?" Freak had asked, turning toward her with two drinking straws stuck up his nose so he looked like a walrus.

The sofa seemed to get more comfortable the longer we sat on it. I would have stretched out on it, if I'd been there by myself.

"Has anybody thought to look for loose change between the cushions?" Fiona asked.

Freak and I glanced at each other. He blinked. I blinked. Then we both jumped up and tossed aside the cushions we had been sitting on.

We found a flattened peanut shell, a chewing gum wrapper, and a plaid sock.

As I reached for the sock, Freak caught my hand.

"Touch nothing! This is all evidence! We must preserve it!"

He gingerly picked up the peanut shell, the gum wrapper, and the sock and placed them carefully in the Ziploc bag he had, moments earlier, been eating taco chips out of.

"You guys are so stupid," Fiona observed.

Freak pointed to the crease running beneath the sofa's back cushion. I stuck my fingers into the crease and searched along it.

"Bingo!" I said, and pulled out a coin.

It was about the size of a quarter, but the tarnished metal wasn't silver. One side had the head of a man with a goatee and the other side had a woman with a crown, both surrounded by words in an alphabet I didn't recognize. It was the sort of coin you did not want to bet "tails" on when it was flipped.

Freak held the plastic bag open for me and I dropped the coin in. Then he felt around in the crease at the base of the armrest and pulled out a small rectangular piece of wood. Grinning, he held it up to the light. It was a domino. Double-six. He deposited it in the evidence bag.

We both turned and faced Fiona.

"Your turn," announced Freak.

"What?" she said. "I'm not sticking my hand in this thing."

After a moment, though, she got up, handed me the cushion she had been sitting on, and cautiously felt around in the back crease.

"Nothing...nothing...wait. Something."

When she pulled out her hand, she was holding a dark green crayon. It looked as though it had never been used—fresh out of the box. The paper wrapper read ZUCCHINI.

"Zucchini?" said Freak. "What kind of color is that?"

"If you ever ate vegetables, you'd know," sniffed Fiona. "It's the rich, dark color of an early summer squash."

Freak looked at her. "And exactly what color is that?"

She held up the crayon and pointed at it. Freak took it from her and studied it. He frowned. "I don't remember ever seeing a zucchini crayon before." He looked at me as though I might be a crayon expert. I shook my head.

"Maybe it's from one of those really big sets you hear about," suggested Fiona. "I've seen a box with sixty-four crayons in it. They even sell a box with one hundred twenty." She blinked. "I can't imagine that many colors."

"I've got a shoe box full of my kid sister's old crayons," said Freak. "I know there aren't any zucchinis in it." He placed the crayon reverently into the bag.

I plunged my hand back into the crease where Fiona had left off, eager to find more stuff. I immediately yelped and yanked my hand back.

"Ow-ow-OW!"

I had a fishhook stuck in my palm, and blood was running down my fingers.

"Hold still!" ordered Fiona, whose favorite game was Operation. She held my arm steady by tucking it under her elbow and plucked the hook out. "Two hundred points!" I heard her mutter to herself, making the hook equal to the Funny Bone in the actual game. I jammed the wound in my mouth. Freak held out the evidence bag; Fiona gave him a scornful look and tossed the hook into a holly bush.

"Why would there be a fishhook in a sofa?" I demanded, feeling it was unfair that I was the one who found it.

"Why would there be a zucchini crayon?" Freak asked

with a shrug, taking things a little too lightly, I thought. I wanted to remind him that blood had just been spilled, but then the bus arrived, and the next thing I knew we were on it, discussing what time we planned to arrive the following morning.

As soon as the second stop came into view and Fiona deserted us, Freak started working on unfinished homework and I did something that people tell me I do too often.

I stared dreamily out the window and let my imagination run away with me.

I imagined the inside of the sofa being as deep as the sea, and then I imagined the zucchini crayon wiggling like a worm on a hook. I imagined a fishing line attached to the hook. I tried to see where the fishing line went. Every time I tried, the line went to the exact same place.

Over the wall and up the hill, into the forbidding mansion known as Underhill House.

About the Author

Henry Clark is the author of *What We Found in the Sofa and How It Saved the World*, an American Booksellers Association New Voices Pick, an Association of Booksellers for Children Best Book, an Amazon Best Book of the Month, and a Junior Library Guild selection. He has contributed articles to *MAD* magazine and published fiction in *Isaac Asimov's Science Fiction Magazine*, in addition to acting as the head phrenologist at Old Bethpage Village Restoration, a living-history museum in New York. He lives on Long Island, and he invites you to visit his website at indorsia.com.